Praise for #1 *New York Times* bestselling author

NORA
ROBERTS

"Her stories have fueled the dreams of twenty-five million readers."
—*Chicago Tribune*

"When Roberts puts her fingers on the pulse of romance, legions of fans feel the heartbeat."
—*Publishers Weekly*

"America's favorite writer."
—*The New Yorker*

"Roberts' bestselling novels are some of the best in the romance genre."
—*USA TODAY*

"Roberts is a storyteller of immeasurable diversity and talent."
—*Publishers Weekly*

"Roberts is indeed a word artist."
—*Los Angeles Daily News*

"Nora Roberts is among the best."
—*The Washington Post Book World*

Dear Reader,

With the holidays just around the corner, we're thrilled to present you with the perfect gift for the romance lover: two fan-favorite Nora Roberts holiday stories that wholly capture the spirit of the season.

All I Want for Christmas is the story of identical twins Zeke and Zach, who get their Christmas list to Santa early. The only things on it: new bicycles for them, and a new wife for their single dad, Mac. Now they just have to get him to cooperate, and to realize that their music teacher, Nell Davis, is perfect for him…

In *First Impressions*, Shane Abbott is determined to do a good deed for her standoffish neighbour, Vance Banning—only to have her kind offer of help thrown back in her face. Vance is determined to retreat from the world, but Shane, one of the most caring and beautiful women he's ever met, turns his plans upside down. First impressions, it seems, are not always reliable…

We hope you and your family have a wonderful holiday season and that you enjoy this very special volume of stories.

Happy Holidays!

The Editors
Silhouette Books

NORA ROBERTS

The Christmas Wish

Silhouette Books

Published by Silhouette Books

America's Publisher of Contemporary Romance

SILHOUETTE BOOKS

Recycling programs for this product may not exist in your area.

The Christmas Wish

ISBN-13: 978-0-373-28228-9

Copyright © 2016 by Harlequin Books S.A.

The publisher acknowledges the copyright holder of the individual works as follows:

All I Want for Christmas
Copyright © 1994 by Nora Roberts

First Impressions
Copyright © 1984 by Nora Roberts

Visit Silhouette Books at www.Harlequin.com

Printed in U.S.A.

CONTENTS

All I Want For Christmas

To Tom and Ky and Larry,
for having the good sense to marry well.

Prologue

Zeke and Zack huddled in the tree house. Important business, any plots or plans, and all punishments for infractions of the rules, were discussed in the sturdy wooden hideaway tucked in the branches of the dignified old sycamore.

Today, a light rain tapped on the tin roof and dampened the dark green leaves. It was still warm enough in the first days of September that the boys wore T-shirts. Red for Zeke, blue for Zack.

They were twins, as identical as the sides of a two-headed coin. Their father had used the color code since their birth to avoid confusion.

When they switched colors—as they often did—they could fool anyone in Taylor's Grove. Except their father.

He was on their minds at the moment. They had already

discussed, at length, the anticipated delights and terrors of their first day in real school. The first day in first grade.

They would ride the bus, as they had done the year before, in kindergarten. But this time they would stay in Taylor's Grove Elementary for a full day, just like the big kids. Their cousin Kim had told them that *real* school wasn't a playground.

Zack, the more introspective of the two, had thought over, worried about and dissected this problem for weeks. There were terrible, daunting terms like *homework* and *class participation,* that Kim tossed around. They knew that she, a sophomore in high school, was often loaded down with books. Big, thick books with no pictures.

And sometimes, when she was babysitting for them, she had her nose stuck in them for hours. For as long a time as she would have the telephone stuck to her ear, and that was long.

It was pretty scary stuff for Zack, the champion worrier.

Their father would help them, of course. This was something Zeke, the eternal optimist, had pointed out. Didn't they both know how to read stuff like *Green Eggs and Ham* and *The Cat in the Hat* because their dad helped them sound out the words? And they both knew how to write the whole alphabet, and their names and short things, because he showed them.

The trouble was, he had to work and take care of the house and them, as well as Commander Zark, the big yellow dog they'd saved from the animal shelter two years before. Their dad had, as Zack pointed out, an awful lot to do. And now that they were going to go to school, and have assignments and projects and real report cards, he was going to need help.

"He's got Mrs. Hollis to come in once a week and do stuff." Zeke ran his miniature Corvette around the imaginary racetrack on the tree-house floor.

"It's not enough." A frown puckered Zack's forehead and clouded his lake-blue eyes. He exhaled with a long-suffering sigh, ruffling the dark hair that fell over his forehead. "He needs the companionship of a good woman, and we need a mother's love. I heard Mrs. Hollis say so to Mr. Perkins at the post office."

"He hangs around with Aunt Mira sometimes. She's a good woman."

"But she doesn't live with us. And she doesn't have time to help us with science projects." Science projects were a particular terror for Zack. "We need to find a mom." When Zeke only snorted, Zack narrowed his eyes. "We're going to have to spell in first grade."

Zeke caught his lower lip between his teeth. Spelling was his personal nightmare. "How're we going to find one?"

Now Zack smiled. He had, in his slow, careful way, figured it all out. "We're going to ask Santa Claus."

"He doesn't bring moms," Zeke said with the deep disdain that can only be felt by one sibling for another. "He brings toys and stuff. And it's forever until Christmas, anyway."

"No, it's not. Mrs. Hollis was bragging to Mr. Perkins how she already had half her Christmas shopping done. She said how looking ahead meant you could enjoy the holiday."

"Everybody enjoys Christmas. It's the best."

"Uh-uh. Lots of people get mad. Remember how we went to the mall last year with Aunt Mira and she complained and complained about the crowds and the prices and how there weren't any parking spaces?"

Zeke merely shrugged. He didn't look back as often, or as clearly, as his twin, but he took Zack at his word. "I guess."

"So, if we ask now, Santa'll have plenty of time to find the right mom."

"I still say he doesn't bring moms."

"Why not? If we really need one, and we don't ask for too much else?"

"We were going to ask for two-wheelers," Zeke reminded him.

"We could still ask for them," Zack decided. "But not a bunch of other things. Just a mom and the bikes."

It was Zeke's turn to sigh. He didn't care for the idea of giving up his big, long list. But the idea of a mother was beginning to appeal. They'd never had one, and the mystery of it attracted. "So what kind do we ask for?"

"We got to write it down."

Zack took a notebook and a stubby pencil from the table pushed against the wall. They sat on the floor and, with much argument and discussion, composed.

Dear Santa,
We have been good.

Zeke wanted to put in *very good,* but Zack, the conscience, rejected the idea.

We feed Zark and help Dad. We want a mom for Crissmas. A nice one who smells good and is not meen. She can smile a lot and have yello hair. She has to like little boys and big dogs. She wont mind dirt and bakes cookys. We want a pretty one who is smart and helps us with homework. We will take good care of her. We want biks a red one and a bloo one. You have lots of time to find the mom and make the biks so you can enjoi the hollidays. Thank you. Love, Zeke and Zack.

One

Taylor's Grove, population two thousand three hundred and forty. No, forty-one, Nell thought smugly, as she strolled into the high school auditorium. She'd only been in town for two months, but already she was feeling territorial. She loved the slow pace, the tidy yards and little shops. She loved the easy gossip of neighbors, the front-porch swings, the frost-heaved sidewalks.

If anyone had told her, even a year before, that she would be trading in Manhattan for a dot on the map in western Maryland, she would have thought them mad. But here she was, Taylor's Grove High's new music teacher, as snug and settled in as an old hound in front of a fire.

She'd needed the change, that was certain. In the past year she'd lost her roommate to marriage and inherited a staggering rent she simply wasn't able to manage on her own. The replacement roommate, whom Nell had carefully interviewed, had moved out, as well. Taking everything of value out of the apartment. That nasty little adventure had led to the final, even nastier showdown with her almost-fiancé. When Bob berated her, called her stupid, naive and careless, Nell had decided it was time to cut her losses.

She'd hardly given Bob his walking papers when she received her own. The school where she had taught for three years was downsizing, as they had euphemistically put it. The position of music teacher had been eliminated, and so had Nell.

An apartment she could no longer afford, all but empty, a fiancé who had considered her optimistic nature a liability and the prospect of the unemployment line had taken the sheen off New York.

Once Nell decided to move, she'd decided to move big. The idea of teaching in a small town had sprung up fully rooted. An inspiration, she thought now, for she already felt as if she'd lived here for years.

Her rent was low enough that she could live alone and like it. Her apartment, the entire top floor of a remodeled old house, was a short, enjoyable walk from a campus that included elementary, middle and high schools.

Only two weeks after that first nervous day of school, she was feeling proprietary about her students and was looking forward to her first after-school session with her chorus.

She was determined to create a holiday program that would knock the town's socks off.

The battered piano was center stage. She walked to it and sat. Her students would be filing in shortly, but she had a moment.

She limbered up her mind and her fingers with the blues,

an old Muddy Waters tune. Old, scarred pianos were meant to play the blues, she thought, and enjoyed herself.

"Man, she's so cool," Holly Linstrom murmured to Kim as they slipped into the rear of the auditorium.

"Yeah." Kim had a hand on the shoulder of each of her twin cousins, a firm grip that ordered quiet and promised reprisals. "Old Mr. Striker never played anything like that."

"And her clothes are so, like, now." Admiration and envy mixed as Holly scanned the pipe-stem pants, long overshirt and short striped vest Nell wore. "I don't know why anybody from New York would come here. Did you see her earrings today? I bet she got them at some hot place on Fifth Avenue."

Nell's jewelry had already become legendary among the female students. She wore the unique and the unusual. Her taste in clothes, her dark gold hair, which fell just short of her shoulders and always seemed miraculously and expertly tousled, her quick, throaty laugh and her lack of formality had already gone a long way toward endearing her to her students.

"She's got style, all right." But, just then, Kim was more intrigued by the music than by the musician's wardrobe. "Man, I wish I could play like that."

"Man, I wish I could look like that," Holly returned, and giggled.

Sensing an audience, Nell glanced back and grinned. "Come on in, girls. Free concert."

"It sounds great, Miss Davis." With her grip firm on her two charges, Kim started down the sloping aisle toward the stage. "What is it?"

"Muddy Waters. We'll have to shoehorn a little blues ed-ucation into the curriculum." Sitting back, she studied the two sweet-faced boys on either side of Kim. There was a quick, odd surge of recognition that she didn't understand. "Well, hi, guys."

When they smiled back, identical dimples popped out on the left side of their mouths. "Can you play 'Chopsticks'?" Zeke wanted to know.

Before Kim could express her humiliation at the question, Nell spun into a rousing rendition.

"How's that?" she asked when she'd finished.

"That's neat."

"I'm sorry, Miss Davis. I'm kind of stuck with them for an hour. They're my cousins. Zeke and Zack Taylor."

"The Taylors of Taylor's Grove." Nell swiveled away from the piano. "I bet you're brothers. I see a slight family resemblance."

Both boys grinned and giggled. "We're twins," Zack informed her.

"Really? Now I bet I'm supposed to guess who's who." She came to the edge of the stage, sat and eyed the boys narrowly. They grinned back. Each had recently lost a left front tooth. "Zeke," she said, pointing a finger. "And Zack."

Pleased and impressed, they nodded. "How'd you know?"

It was pointless, and hardly fun, to mention that she'd had a fifty-fifty shot. "Magic. Do you guys like to sing?"

"Sort of. A little."

"Well, today you can listen. You can sit right in the front row and be our test audience."

"Thanks, Miss Davis," Kim murmured, and gave the boys a friendly shove toward the seats. "They're pretty good most of the time. Stay," she ordered, with an older cousin's absolute authority.

Nell winked at the boys as she stood, then gestured to the other students filing in. "Come on up. Let's get started."

A lot of the business onstage seemed boring to the twins. There was just talking at first, and confusion as sheet music was passed out and boys and girls were assigned positions.

But Zack was watching Nell. She had pretty hair and nice big brown eyes. Like Zark's, he thought with deep affection. Her voice was kind of funny, sort of scratchy and deep, but nice. Now and again she looked back toward him and smiled. When she did, his heart acted strange, kind of beating hard, like he'd been running.

She turned to a group of girls and sang. It was a Christmas song, which made Zack's eyes widen. He wasn't sure of the name, something about a midnight clear, but he recognized it from the records his dad played around the holiday.

A Christmas song. A Christmas wish.

"It's her." He hissed it to his brother, rapping Zeke hard in the ribs.

"Who?"

"It's the mom."

Zeke stopped playing with the action figure he'd had stuck in his pocket and looked up onstage, where Nell was now directing the alto section. "Kim's teacher is the mom?"

"She has to be." Deadly excited, Zeke kept his voice in a conspiratorial whisper. "Santa's had enough time to get the letter. She was singing a Christmas song, and she's got yellow hair and a nice smile. She likes little boys, too. I can tell."

"Maybe." Not quite convinced, Zeke studied Nell. She was pretty, he thought. And she laughed a lot, even when some of the big kids made mistakes. But that didn't mean she liked dogs or baked cookies. "We can't know for sure yet."

Zack huffed out an impatient breath. "She knew us. She knew which was which. Magic." His eyes were solemn as he looked at his brother. "It's the mom."

"Magic," Zeke repeated, and stared, goggle-eyed, at Nell. "Do we have to wait till Christmas to get her?"

"I guess so. Probably." That was a puzzle Zack would have to work on.

When Mac Taylor pulled his pickup truck in front of the high school, his mind was on a dozen varied problems. What to fix the kids for dinner. How to deal with the flooring on his Meadow Street project. When to find a couple hours to drive to the mall and pick up new underwear for the boys. The last time he folded laundry, he'd noticed that most of what they had was doomed for the rag pile. He had to deal with a lumber delivery first thing in the morning and a pile of paperwork that night.

And Zeke was nervous about his first spelling test, which was coming up in a few days.

Pocketing his keys, Mac rolled his shoulders. He'd been swinging a hammer for the better part of eight hours. He didn't mind the aches. It was a good kind of fatigue, a kind that meant he'd accomplished something. His renovation of the house on Meadow Street was on schedule and on budget. Once it was done, he would have to decide whether to put it on the market or rent it.

His accountant would try to decide for him, but Mac knew the final choice would remain in his own hands. That was the way he preferred it.

As he strode from the parking lot to the high school, he looked around. His great-great-grandfather had founded the town—hardly more than a village back then, settled along Taylor's Creek and stretching over the rolling hills to Taylor's Meadow.

There'd been no lack of ego in old Macauley Taylor.

But Mac had lived in D.C. for more than twelve years. It had been six years since he returned to Taylor's Grove, but he hadn't lost his pleasure or his pride in it, the simple appreciation for the hills and the trees and the shadows of mountains in the distance.

He didn't think he ever would.

There was the faintest of chills in the air now, and a good strong breeze from the west. But they had yet to have a frost, and the leaves were still a deep summer green. The good weather made his life easier on a couple of levels. As long as it held, he'd be able to finish the outside work on his project in comfort. And the boys could enjoy the afternoons and evenings in the yard.

There was a quick twinge of guilt as he pulled open the heavy doors and stepped into the school. His work had kept them stuck inside this afternoon. The coming of fall meant that his sister was diving headfirst into several of her community projects. He couldn't impose on her by asking her to watch the twins. Kim's after-school schedule was filling up, and he simply couldn't accept the idea of having his children becoming latchkey kids.

Still, the solution had suited everyone. Kim would take the kids to her rehearsals, and he would save his sister a trip to school by picking them all up and driving them home.

Kim would have a driver's license in a few more months.

A fact she was reminding everyone about constantly. But he doubted he'd plunk his boys down in the car with his sixteen-year-old niece at the wheel, no matter how much he loved and trusted her.

You coddle them. Mac rolled his eyes as his sister's voice played in his head. *You can't always be mother and father to them, Mac. If you're not interested in finding a wife, then you'll have to learn to let go a little.*

Like hell he would, Mac thought.

As he neared the auditorium, he heard the sound of young voices raised in song. Subtle harmony. A good, emotional sound that made him smile even before he recognized the tune. A Christmas hymn. It was odd to hear it now, with the sweat from his day just drying on his back.

He pulled open the auditorium doors, and was flooded with it. Charmed, he stood at the back and looked out on the singers. One of the students played the piano. A pretty little thing, Mac mused, who looked up now and then, gesturing, as if to urge her classmates to give more.

He wondered where the music teacher was, then spotted his boys sitting in the front row. He walked quietly down the aisle, raising a hand when he saw Kim's eyes shift to his. He settled behind the boys and leaned forward.

"Pretty good show, huh?"

"Dad!" Zack nearly squealed, then remembered just in time to speak in a hissing whisper. "It's Christmas."

"Sure sounds like it. How's Kim doing?"

"She's real good." Zeke now considered himself an expert on choral arrangements. "She's going to have a solo."

"No kidding?"

"She got red in the face when Miss Davis asked her to sing

by herself, but she did okay." Zeke was much more interested in Nell right then. "She's pretty, isn't she?"

A little amazed at this announcement—the twins were fond of Kim, but rarely complimentary—he nodded. "Yeah. The prettiest girl in school."

"We could have her over for dinner sometime," Zack said slyly. "Couldn't we?"

Baffled now, Mac ruffled his son's hair. "You know Kim can come over whenever she wants."

"Not her." In a gesture that mimicked his father, Zack rolled his eyes. "Jeez, Dad. Miss Davis."

"Who's Miss Davis?"

"The m—" Zeke's announcement was cut off by his twin's elbow.

"The teacher," Zack finished with a snarling look at his brother. "The pretty one." He pointed, and his father followed the direction to the piano.

"She's the teacher?" Before Mac could reevaluate, the music flowed to a stop and Nell rose.

"That was great, really. A very solid first run-through." She pushed her tousled hair back. "But we need a lot of work. I'd like to schedule the next rehearsal for Monday after school. Three forty-five."

There was already a great deal of movement and mumbling, so Nell pitched her voice to carry the rest of her instructions over the noise. Satisfied, she turned to smile at the twins and found herself grinning at an older, and much more disturbing version, of the Taylor twins.

No doubt he was the father, Nell thought. The same thick dark hair curled down over the collar of a grimy T-shirt. The same lake-water eyes framed in long, dark lashes stared back at her. His face might lack the soft, slightly rounded appeal of his sons', but the more rugged version was just as attractive. He was long, rangy, with the kind of arms that looked tough without being obviously muscled. He was tanned and more than a little dirty. She wondered if he had a dimple at the left corner of his mouth when he smiled.

"Mr. Taylor." Rather than bother with the stairs, she hopped off the stage, as agile as any of her students. She held out a hand decorated with rings.

"Miss Davis." He covered her hand with his callused one, remembering too late that it was far from clean. "I appreciate you letting the kids hang out while Kim rehearsed."

"No problem. I work better with an audience." Tilting her head, she looked down at the twins. "Well, guys, how'd we do?"

"It was really neat." This from Zeke. "We like Christmas songs the best."

"Me, too."

Still flustered and flattered by the idea of having a solo, Kim joined them. "Hi, Uncle Mac. I guess you met Miss Davis."

"Yeah." There wasn't much more to say. He still thought she looked too young to be a teacher. Not the teenager he'd taken her for, he realized. But that creamy, flawless skin and that tidy little frame were deceiving. And very attractive.

"Your niece is very talented." In a natural movement, Nell wrapped an arm around Kim's shoulders. "She has a wonderful voice and a quick understanding of what the music means. I'm delighted to have her."

"We like her, too," Mac said as Kim flushed.

Zack shifted from foot to foot. They weren't supposed to

be talking about dumb old Kim. "Maybe you could come visit us sometime, Miss Davis," he piped up. "We live in the big brown house out on Mountain View Road."

"That'd be nice." But Nell noted that Zack's father didn't second the invitation, or look particularly pleased by it. "And you guys are welcome to be our audience anytime. You work on that solo, Kim."

"I will, Miss Davis. Thanks."

"Nice to have met you, Mr. Taylor." As he mumbled a response, Nell hopped back onstage to gather her sheet music.

It was too bad, she thought, that the father lacked the outgoing charm and friendliness of his sons.

Two

It didn't get much better than a drive in the country on a balmy fall afternoon. Nell remembered how she used to spend a free Saturday in New York. A little shopping—she supposed if she missed anything about Manhattan, it was the shopping—maybe a walk in the park. Never a jog. Nell didn't believe in running if walking would get you to the same place.

And driving, well, that was even better. She hadn't realized what a pleasure it was to not only own a car but be able to zip it along winding country roads with the windows open and the radio blaring.

The leaves were beginning to turn now as September hit its stride. Blushes of color competed with the green. On one particular road that she turned down out of impulse, the big trees arched over the asphalt, a spectacular canopy that let light flicker and flit through as the road followed the snaking trail of a rushing creek.

It wasn't until she glanced up at a road sign that she realized she was on Mountain View.

The big brown house, Zack had said, she remembered. There weren't a lot of houses here, two miles outside of town, but she caught glimpses of some through the shading trees. Brown ones, white ones, blue ones—some close to the creek bed, others high atop narrow, pitted lanes that served as driveways.

A lovely place to live, she thought. And to raise children. However taciturn and stiff Mac Taylor might have been, he'd done a wonderful job with his sons.

She already knew he'd done the job alone. It hadn't taken long for Nell to understand the rhythm of small towns. A comment here, a casual question there, and she'd had what amounted to a full biography of the Taylor men.

Mac had lived in Washington, D.C., since his family moved out of town when he was a young teenager. Six years ago, twin infants in tow, he'd moved back. His older sister had gone to a local college and married a town boy and settled in Taylor's Grove years before. It was she, the consensus was, who had urged him to come back and raise his children there when his wife took off.

Left the poor little infants high and dry, Mrs. Hollis had told Nell over the bread rack at the general store. Run off with barely a word, and hadn't said a peep since. And young Macauley Taylor had been mother and father both to his twins ever since.

Maybe, Nell thought cynically, just maybe, if he'd actually talked to his wife now and again, she'd have stayed with him.

Not fair, she thought. There was no decent excuse she

could think of for a mother deserting her infant children, then not contacting them for six years. Whatever kind of husband Mac Taylor had been, the children deserved better.

She thought of them now, those impish mirror images. She'd always been fond of children, and the Taylor twins were a double dose of enjoyment. She'd gotten quite a kick out of having them in the audience once or twice a week during rehearsals. Zeke had even shown her his very first spelling test—with its big silver star. If he hadn't missed just one word, he'd told her, he'd have gotten a gold one.

Nor had she missed the shy looks Zack sent her, or the quick smiles before he flushed and lowered his eyes. It was very sweet to be responsible for his first case of puppy love.

She sighed with pleasure as the car burst out from under the canopy of trees and into the light. Here were the mountains that gave the road its name, streaking suddenly into the vivid blue sky. The road curved and snaked, but they were always there, dark, distant and dramatic.

The land rose on either side of the road, in rolling hills and rocky outcroppings. She slowed when she spotted a house on the crest of a hill. Brown. Probably cedar, she thought, with a stone foundation and what seemed like acres of sparkling glass. There was a deck stretched across the second story, and there were trees that shaded and sheltered. A tire swing hung from one.

She wondered if this was indeed the Taylor house. She hoped her new little friends lived in such a solid, well-planned home. Then she passed the mailbox planted at the side of the road just at the edge of the long lane.

M. Taylor and sons.

It made her smile. Pleased, she punched the gas pedal and was baffled when the car bucked and stuttered.

"What's the problem here?" she muttered, easing off on the pedal and punching it again. This time the car shuddered and stopped dead. "For heaven's sake." Only mildly annoyed, she started to turn the key to start it again, and glanced at the dash. The little gas pump beside the gauge was brightly lit.

"Stupid," she said aloud, berating herself. "Stupid, stupid. Weren't you supposed to get gas *before* you left town?" She sat back, sighed. She'd meant to, really. Just as she'd meant to stop and fill up the day before, right after class.

Now she was two miles out of town without even fumes to ride on. Blowing the hair out of her eyes, she looked out at the home of M. Taylor and sons. A quarter-mile hike, she estimated. Which made it a lot better than two miles. And she had, more or less, been invited.

She grabbed her keys and started up the lane.

She was no more than halfway when the boys spotted her. They came racing down the rocky, pitted lane at a speed that stopped her heart. Surefooted as young goats, they streaked toward her. Coming up behind was a huge yellow dog.

"Miss Davis! Hi, Miss Davis! Did you come to see us?"

"Sort of." Laughing, she crouched down to give them both a hug and caught the faint scent of chocolate. Before she could comment, the dog decided he wanted in on the action. He was restrained enough to plant his huge paws on her thighs, rather than her shoulders.

Zack held his breath, then let it out when she chuckled and bent down to rub Zark on head and shoulders. "You're a big one, aren't you? A big beauty."

Zark lapped her hand in perfect agreement. Nell caught a look exchanged quickly between the twins. One that seemed both smug and excited.

"You like dogs?" Zeke asked.

"Sure I do. Maybe I'll get one now. I never had the heart to lock one up in a New York apartment." She only laughed again when Zark sat and politely lifted a paw. "Too late for formalities now, buddy," she told him, but shook it anyway. "I was out driving, and I ran out of gas right smack at the bottom of your lane. Isn't that funny?"

Zack's grin nearly split his face. She liked dogs. She'd stopped right at their house. It was more magic, he was sure of it. "Dad'll fix it. He can fix anything." Confident now that he had her on his own ground, Zack took her hand. Not to be outdone, Zeke clasped the other.

"Dad's out back in the shop, building a 'rondak chair."

"A rocking chair?" Nell suggested.

"Nuh-uh. A 'rondak chair. Come see."

They hauled her around the house, passed a curving sun-room that caught the southern light. There was another deck in the back, with steps leading down to a flagstone patio. The shop in the backyard—the same cedar as the house—looked big enough to hold a family of four. Nell heard the thwack of a hammer on wood.

Bursting with excitement, Zeke raced through the shop door. "Dad! Dad! Guess what?"

"I guess you've taken another five years off my life."

Nell heard Mac's voice, deep and amused and tolerant, and found herself hesitating. "I hate to bother him when he's busy," she said to Zeke. "Maybe I can just call the station in town."

"It's okay, come on." Zack dragged her a few more feet into the doorway.

"See?" Zeke said importantly. "She came!"

"Yeah, I see." Caught off balance by the unexpected visit,

Mac set his hammer down on his workbench. He pushed up the brim of his cap and frowned without really meaning to. "Miss Davis."

"I'm sorry to bother you, Mr. Taylor," she began, then saw the project he was working on. "An Adirondack chair," she murmured, and grinned. "A 'rondak chair. It's nice."

"Will be." Was he supposed to offer her coffee? he wondered. A tour of the house? What? She shouldn't be pretty, he thought irrelevantly. There was nothing particularly striking about her. Well, maybe the eyes. They were so big and brown. But the rest really was ordinary. It must be the way it was put together, he decided, that made it extraordinary.

Not certain whether she was amused or uncomfortable at the way he was staring at her, Nell launched into her explanation. "I was out driving. Partly for the pleasure of it, and partly to try to familiarize myself with the area. I've only lived here a couple months."

"Is that right?"

"Miss Davis is from New York City, Dad," Zack reminded him. "Kim told you."

"Yeah, she did." He picked up his hammer again, set it down. "Nice day for a drive."

"I thought so. So nice I forgot to get gas before I left town. I ran out at the bottom of your lane."

A flicker of suspicion darkened his eyes. "That's handy."

"Not especially." Her voice, though still friendly, had cooled. "If I could use your phone to call the station in town, I'd appreciate it."

"I've got gas," he muttered.

"See, I told you Dad could fix it," Zack said proudly. "We've got brownies," he added, struggling madly for a way to get her to stay longer. "Dad made them. You can have one."

"I thought I smelled chocolate." She scooped Zack up and sniffed at his face. "I've got a real nose for it."

Moving on instinct, Mac plucked Zack out of her arms. "You guys go get some brownies. We'll get the gas."

"Okay!" They raced off together.

"I wasn't going to abduct him, Mr. Taylor."

"Didn't say you were." He walked to the doorway, glanced back. "The gas is in the shed."

Lips pursed, she followed him out. "Were you traumatized by a teacher at an impressionable age, Mr. Taylor?"

"Mac. Just Mac. No, why?"

"I wondered if we have a personal or a professional problem here."

"I don't have a problem." He stopped at the small shed where he kept his lawn mower and garden tools, then said, "Funny how the kids told you where we lived, and you ran out of gas right here."

She took a long breath, studying him as he bent over to pick up a can, straighten and turn. "Look, I'm no happier about it than you, and after this reception, probably a lot less happy. It happens that this is the first car I've ever owned, and I'm still a little rough on the finer points. I ran out of gas last month in front of the general store. You're welcome to check."

He shrugged, feeling stupid and unnecessarily prickly. "Sorry."

"Forget it. If you'll give me the can, I'll use what I need to get back to town, then I'll have it filled and returned."

"I'll take care of it," he muttered.

"I don't want to put you out." She reached for the can and

that started a quick tug-of-war. After a moment, the dimple at the corner of his mouth winked.

"I'm bigger than you."

She stepped back and blew the hair out of her eyes. "Fine. Go be a man, then." Scowling, she followed him around the house, then tried to fight off her foul mood as the twins came racing up. They each held a paper towel loaded with brownies.

"Dad makes the best brownies in the whole world," Zack told her, holding up his offering.

Nell took one and bit in. "You may be right," she was forced to admit, her mouth full. "And I know my brownies."

"Can you make cookies?" Zeke wanted to know.

"I happened to be known far and wide for my chocolate-chip." Her smile became puzzled as the boys eyed each other and nodded. "You come visit me sometime, and we'll whip some up."

"Where do you live?" Since his father wasn't paying close attention, Zeke stuffed an entire brownie in his mouth.

"On Market Street, right off the square. The old brick house with the three porches. I rent the top floor."

"Dad owns that," Zack told her. "He bought it and fixed it all up and now he rents it out. We're in real estate."

"Oh." She let out a long breath. "Really." Her rent checks were mailed to Taylor Management…on Mountain View Road.

"So you live in our house," Zack finished up.

"In a manner of speaking."

"The place okay with you?" Mac asked.

"Yes, it's fine. I'm very comfortable there. It's convenient to school."

"Dad buys houses and fixes them up all the time." Zeke

wondered if he could get away with another brownie. "He likes to fix stuff."

It was obvious from the tidy and thoughtful renovation of the old house she now lived in that their father fixed them very well. "You're a carpenter, then?" she asked, reluctantly addressing Mac.

"Sometimes." They'd reached her car. Mac merely jerked his thumb to signal the boys and dog to keep off the road. He unscrewed the gas cap and spoke without looking around. "If you eat another one of those, Zeke, I'm going to have to have your stomach pumped."

Sheepishly Zeke replaced the brownie on the paper towel.

"Excellent radar," Nell commented, leaning on the car as Mac added the gas.

"Goes with the territory." He looked at her then. Her hair was windblown and gilded by the sun. Her face was rosy from the walk and the breeze. He didn't like what looking at her did to his pulse rate. "Why Taylor's Grove? It's a long way from New York."

"That's why. I wanted a change." She breathed deep as she looked around, at rock and tree and hill. "I got one."

"Pretty slow, compared to what you'd be used to."

"Slow's something I do very well."

He only shrugged. He suspected she'd be bored senseless in six months and heading out. "Kim's pretty excited about your class. She talks about it almost as much as she does getting her driver's license."

"That's quite a compliment. It's a good school. Not all of my students are as cooperative as Kim, but I like a challenge. I'm going to recommend her for all-state."

Mac tipped the can farther up. "She's really that good?"

"You sound surprised."

He shrugged again. "She always sounded good to me, but the old music teacher never singled her out."

"Rumor is he never took much interest in any of his students individually, or in extra work."

"You got that right. Striker was an old—" He caught himself, glanced back at his kids, who were standing close by, all ears. "He was old," Mac repeated. "And set in his ways. Always the same Christmas program, the same spring program."

"Yes, I've looked over his class notes. I'd say everyone should be in for a surprise this year. I'm told no student from Taylor's Grove ever went to all-state."

"Not that I heard."

"Well, we're going to change that." Satisfied now that they had managed a reasonable conversation, she tossed back her hair. "Do you sing?"

"In the shower." His dimple flickered again as his sons giggled. "No comments from the brats."

"He sings really, really loud," Zeke said, without fear of reprisal. "And he gets Zark howling."

"I'm sure that would be quite a show." Nell scratched the grinning dog between the ears. He thumped his tail, and then some internal clock struck and had him pivoting and racing up the hill.

"Here you go, Miss Davis. Here." Both boys stuffed the loaded paper towels into her hands and barreled off after the dog.

"I guess they don't keep still very long," she murmured, watching them chase the dog up the rise.

"That was nearly a record. They like you."

"I'm a likable person." She smiled, glancing back at him, only to find him staring at her again with that not-quite-pleased look in his eyes. "At least in most cases. If you'd just put that on the backseat, I'll have it filled up for you."

"It's not a problem." Mac replaced her gas cap and kept the empty can. "We're friendly in Taylor's Grove. In most cases."

"Let me know when I'm off probation." She leaned into her car to set the brownies on the passenger seat. Mac had a tantalizing and uncomfortable view of her jean-clad bottom. He could smell her, too, something light and spicy that spun in his head a lot more potently than the gas fumes.

"I didn't mean it like that."

Her head popped back out of the car. She licked a smear of brownie from her finger as she straightened. "Maybe not. In any case, I appreciate the help." Her grin flashed as she opened the car door. "And the chocolate."

"Anytime," he heard himself say, and wanted to regret it.

She settled behind the steering wheel, tossed him a quick, saucy smile. "Like hell." Then she laughed and turned the ignition, revving the engine in a way that made Mac wince. "You should drop in on rehearsals now and again, Mac, instead of waiting out in the parking lot. You might learn something."

He wasn't certain he wanted to. "Put on your seat belt," he ordered.

"Oh, yeah." Obligingly, she buckled up. "Just not used to it yet. Say bye to the twins." She zoomed off at a speed just this side of reckless, waving a careless and glittering hand out the window.

Mac watched her until she rounded the bend, then slowly rubbed his stomach where the muscles were knotted. Something about that woman, he thought. Something about the way she was put together made him feel like he was defrosting after a very long freeze.

Three

Another half hour, Mac figured, and he could finish taping the drywall in the master bedroom. Maybe get the first coat of mud on. He glanced at his watch, calculated that the kids were home from school. But it was Mrs. Hollis's day, and she'd stay until five. That would give him plenty of time to hit the drywall, clean up and get home.

Maybe he'd give himself and the kids a treat and pick up pizza.

He'd learned not to mind cooking, but he still resented the time it took—the thinking, the preparation, the cleaning up afterward. Six years as a single parent had given him a whole new perspective on how hard his mother—that rare and old-fashioned homemaker—had worked.

Pausing a moment, he took a look around the master suite. He'd taken walls out, built others, replaced the old single-pane windows with double glazed. Twin skylights let in the fading sunlight of early October.

Now there were three spacious bedrooms on the second floor of the old house, rather than the four choppy rooms and oversize hallway he'd started with. The master suite would boast a bathroom large enough for tub and separate shower stall. He was toying with using glass block for that. He'd been wanting to work with it for some time.

If he stayed on schedule, the place would be put together by Christmas, and on the sale or rental market by the first of the year.

He really should sell it, Mac thought, running a hand over the drywall he'd nailed up that afternoon. He had to get over this sense of possession whenever he worked on a house.

In the blood, he supposed. His father had made a good living buying up damaged or depressed property, rehabing and renting. Mac had discovered just how satisfying it was to own something you'd made fine with your own hands.

Like the old brick house Nell lived in now. He wondered if she knew it was more than a hundred and fifty years old, that she was living in a piece of history.

He wondered if she'd run out of gas again.

He wondered quite a bit about Nell Davis.

And he shouldn't, Mac reminded himself, and turned away for his tools and tape. Women were trouble. One way or the other, they were trouble. One look at Nell and a smart man could see she was no exception.

He hadn't taken her up on her suggestion that he drop by the auditorium and catch part of a rehearsal. He'd started to a couple of times, but good sense had stopped him. She was the first woman in a very, very long time who had stirred him up. He didn't want to be stirred up, Mac thought with a scowl as he taped a seam. Couldn't afford to be, he reminded himself. He had too many obligations, too little free time, and, most important, two sons who were the focus of his life.

Daydreaming about a woman was bad enough. It made a man sloppy in his work, forgetful and…itchy. But doing something about it was worse. Doing something meant you had to find conversation and ways to entertain. A woman expected to be taken places, and pampered. And once you started to fall for her—really fall for her—she had the power to cut out your heart.

Mac wasn't willing to risk his heart again, and he certainly wasn't willing to risk his sons.

He didn't subscribe to that nonsense about children needing a woman's touch, a mother's love. The twins' mother had felt less connection with the children she'd borne than a cat felt toward a litter of kittens. Being female didn't give you a leg up on maternal feelings. It meant you were physically able to carry a child inside you, but it didn't mean that you'd care once that child was in your arms.

Mac stopped taping and swore. He hadn't thought about Angie in years. Not deeply. When he did, he realized the spot was still sore, like an old wound that had healed poorly. That was what he got, he supposed, for letting some little blonde stir him up.

Annoyed with himself, he stripped the last piece of tape off the roll. He needed to concentrate on his work, not on a woman. Determined to finish what he'd started, he marched down the stairs. He had more drywall tape in his truck.

The light outside was softening with the approach of dusk. Shorter days, he thought. Less time.

He was down the steps and onto the walk before he saw her. She was standing just at the edge of the yard, looking up at the house, smiling a little. She wore a suede jacket in a deep burnished orange over faded jeans. Some glittery stones dangled from her ears. Over her shoulder hung a soft-sided briefcase that looked well used.

"Oh. Hi." Surprise lit her eyes when she glanced over, and that immediately made him suspicious. "Is this one of your places?"

"That's right." He moved past her toward the truck and wished he'd held his breath. That scent she wore was subtle and sneaky.

"I was just admiring it. Beautiful stonework. It looks so sturdy and safe, tucked in with all the trees." She took a deep breath. There was the slap of fall in the air. "It's going to be a beautiful night."

"I guess." He found his tape, then stood, running the roll around in his hands. "Did you run out of gas again?"

"No." She laughed, obviously amused at herself. "I like walking around town this time of day. As a matter of fact, I was heading down to your sister's. She's a few doors down, right?"

His eyes narrowed. He didn't like the idea of the woman he was spending too much time thinking about hanging out with his sister. "Yeah, that's right. Why?"

"Why?" Her attention had been focused on his hands. There was something about them. Hard, callused. Big. She felt a quick and very pleasant flutter in the pit of her stomach. "Why what?"

"Why are you going to Mira's?"

"Oh. I have some sheet music I thought Kim would like."

"Is that right?" He leaned on the truck, measuring her. Her smile was entirely too friendly, he decided. Entirely too attractive. "Is it part of your job description to make house calls with sheet music?"

"It's part of the fun." Her hair ruffled in the light breeze. She scooped it back. "No job's worth the effort or the head-aches if you don't have some fun." She looked back at the house. "You have fun, don't you? Taking something and making it yours?"

He started to say something snide, then realized she'd put her finger right on the heart of it. "Yeah. It doesn't always seem like fun when you're tearing out ceilings and having insulation raining down on your head." He smiled a little. "But it is."

"Are you going to let me see?" She tilted her head. "Or are you like a temperamental artist, not willing to show his work until the final brushstroke?"

"There's not much to see." Then he shrugged. "Sure, you can come in if you want."

"Thanks." She started up the walk, glanced over her shoul-der when he stayed by the truck. "Aren't you going to give me a tour?"

He moved his shoulders again, and joined her.

"Did you do the trim on my apartment?"

"Yeah."

"It's beautiful work. Looks like cherry."

He frowned, surprised. "It is cherry."

"I like the rounded edges. They soften everything. Do you get a decorator in for the colors or pick them out yourself?"

"I pick them." He opened the door for her. "Is there a problem?"

"No. I really love the color scheme in the kitchen, the slate blue counters, the mauve floor. Oh, what fabulous stairs." She hurried across the unfinished living area to the staircase.

Mac had worked hard and long on it, tearing out the old and replacing it with dark chestnut, curving and widening the landing at the bottom so that it flowed out into the living space.

It was, undeniably, his current pride and joy.

"Did you build these?" she murmured, running a hand over the curve of the railing.

"The old ones were broken, dry-rotted. Had to go."

"I have to try them." She dashed up, turning back at the top to grin at him. "No creaks. Good workmanship, but not very sentimental."

"Sentimental?"

"You know, the way you look back on home, how you snuck downstairs as a kid and knew just which steps to avoid because they'd creak and wake up Mom."

All at once he was having trouble with his breathing. "They're chestnut," he said, because he could think of nothing else.

"Whatever, they're beautiful. Whoever lives here has to have kids."

His mouth was dry, unbearably. "Why?"

"Because." On impulse, she planted her butt on the railing and pushed off. Mac's arms came out of their own volition to catch her as she flew off the end. "It was made for sliding," she said breathlessly. She was laughing as she tilted her head up to his.

Something clicked inside her when their eyes met. And the fluttering, not so pleasant this time, came again. Disconcerted, she cleared her throat and searched for something to say.

"You keep popping up," Mac muttered. He had yet to release her, couldn't seem to make his hands obey his head.

"It's a small town."

He only shook his head. His hands were at her waist now, and they seemed determined to slide around and stroke up her back. He thought he felt her tremble—but it might have been him.

"I don't have time for women," he told her, trying to convince himself.

"Well." She tried to swallow, but there was something hard and hot lodged in her throat. "I'm pretty busy myself." She let out a slow breath. Those hands stroking up and down her back were making her weak. "And I'm not really interested. I had a really bad year, as far as relationships go. I think…"

It was very hard to think. His eyes were such a beautiful shade of blue, and so intensely focused on hers. She wasn't sure what he saw, or what he was looking for, but she knew her knees were about to give out.

"I think," she began again, "we'd both be better off if you decide fairly quickly if you're going to kiss me or not. I can't handle this much longer."

Neither could he. Still, he took his time. He was, in all things, a thorough and thoughtful man. His eyes were open and on hers as he lowered his head, as his mouth hovered a breath from hers, as a small, whimpering moan sounded in her throat.

Her vision dimmed as his lips brushed hers. His were soft, firm, terrifyingly patient. The whisper of contact slammed a punch into her stomach. He lingered over her like a gourmet sampling delicacies, deepening the kiss degree by staggering degree until she was clinging to him.

No one had ever kissed her like this. She hadn't known anyone could. Slow and deep and dreamy. The floor seemed to tilt under her feet as he gently sucked her lower lip into his mouth.

She shuddered, groaned, and let herself drown.

She was very potent. The scent and feel and taste of her was overwhelming. He knew he could lose himself here, for a moment, for a lifetime. Her small, tight body was all but plastered to his. Her hands clutched his hair. In contrast to that aggressive gesture, her head fell limply back in a kind of sighing surrender that had his blood bubbling.

He wanted to touch her. His hands were aching with the need to peel off layer after layer and find the pale, smooth skin beneath. To test himself, and her, he slipped his fingers under her sweater, along the soft, hot flesh of her back, while his mouth continued its long, lazy assault on hers.

He imagined laying her down on the floor, on a tarp, on the grass. He imagined watching her face as he pleasured them both, of feeling her arch toward him, open, accepting.

It had been too long, he told himself as his muscles began to coil and his lungs to labor. It had just been too long.

But he didn't believe it. And it frightened him.

Unsteady, he lifted his head, drew back. Even as he began the retreat, she leaned against him, letting her head fall onto his chest. Unable to resist, he combed his fingers through her hair and cradled her there.

"My head's spinning," she murmured. "What was that?"

"It was a kiss, that's all." He needed to believe that. It would help to ease the tightness around his heart and his loins.

"I think I saw stars." Still staggered, she shifted so that she could look up at him. Her lips curved, but her eyes didn't echo the smile. "That's a first for me."

If he didn't do something fast, he was going to kiss her again. He set her firmly on her feet. "It doesn't change anything."

"Was there something to change?"

The light was nearly gone now. It helped that he couldn't see her clearly in the gloom. "I don't have time for women. And I'm just not interested in starting anything."

"Oh." Where had that pain come from? she wondered, and had to fight to keep from rubbing a hand over her heart. "That was quite a kiss, for a disinterested man." Reaching down, she scooped up the briefcase she'd dropped before she'd run up the stairs. "I'll get out of your way. I wouldn't want to waste any more of your valuable time."

"You don't have to get huffy about it."

"Huffy." Her teeth snapped together. She jabbed a finger into his chest. "I'm well beyond huffy, pal, and working my way past steamed. You've got some ego, Mac. What, do you think I came around here to seduce you?"

"I don't know why you came around."

"Well, I won't be around again." She settled her briefcase strap on her shoulder, jerked her chin up. "Nobody twisted your arm."

He was dealing with an uncomfortable combination of desire and guilt. "Yours, either."

"I'm not the one making excuses. You know, I can't figure out how such an insensitive clod could raise two charming and adorable kids."

"Leave my boys out of this."

The edge to the order had her eyes narrowing to slits. "Oh, so I have designs on them now, too? You idiot!" She stormed for the door, whirling at the last moment for a parting shot. "I hope they don't inherit your warped view of the female species!"

She slammed the door hard enough to have the bad-tempered sound echoing through the house. Mac scowled and jammed his hands in his pockets. He didn't have a warped view, damn it. And his kids were his business.

Four

Nell stood center stage and lifted her hands. She waited until she was sure every student's eyes were on her, then let it rip.

There was very little that delighted her more than the sound of young voices raised in song. She let the sound fill her, keeping her ears and eyes sharp as she moved around the stage directing. She couldn't hold back the grin. The kids were into this one. Doing Bruce Springsteen and the E Street Band's version of "Santa Claus is Coming to Town" was a departure from the standard carols and hymns their former choral director had arranged year after year.

She could see their eyes light up as they got into the rhythm. *Now punch it,* she thought, pulling more from the bass section as they hit the chorus. *Have fun with it.* Now the soprano section, high and bright… And the altos… Tenors… Bass…

She flashed a smile to signal her approval as the chorus flowered again.

"Good job," she announced. "Tenors, a little more next time. You guys don't want the bass section drowning you out. Holly, you're dropping your chin again. Now we have time for one more run-through of 'I'll Be Home for Christmas.' Kim?"

Kim tried to ignore the little flutter around her heart and the elbow nudge from Holly. She stepped down from her position in the second row and stood in front of the solo mike as though she were facing a firing squad.

"It's okay to smile, you know," Nell told her gently. "And remember your breathing. Sing to the last row, and don't forget to feel the words. Tracy." She held out a finger toward the pianist she'd dragooned from her second-period music class.

The intro started quietly. Using her hands, her face, her eyes, Nell signaled the beginning of the soft, harmonious, background humming. Then Kim began to sing. Too tentatively at first. Nell knew they would have to work on those initial nerves.

But the girl had talent, and emotion. Three bars in, Kim was too caught up in the song to be nervous. She was pacing it well, Nell thought, pleased. Kim had learned quite a bit in the past few weeks about style. The sentimental song suited her, her range, her looks.

Nell brought the chorus in, holding them back. They were background now for Kim's rich, romantic voice. Feeling her own eyes stinging, Nell thought that if they did it this well on the night of the concert, there wouldn't be a dry eye in the house.

"Lovely," Nell said when the last notes had died away.

"Really lovely. You guys have come a long way in a very short time. I'm awfully proud of you. Now scram, and have a great weekend."

While Nell moved to the piano to gather up music, the chatter began behind her.

"You sounded really good," Holly told Kim.

"Honest?"

"Honest. Brad thought so, too." Holly shifted her eyes cagily to the school heartthrob, who was shrugging into his school jacket.

"He doesn't even know I'm alive."

"He does now. He was watching you the whole time. I know, because I was watching him." Holly sighed. "If I looked like Miss Davis, *he'd* be watching *me*."

Kim laughed, but shot a quick glance toward Brad under her lashes. "She's really fabulous. Just the way she talks to us and stuff. Mr. Striker always crabbed."

"Mr. Striker *was* a crab. See you later, huh?"

"Yeah." It was all Kim could manage, because it looked, it really looked, as though Brad were coming toward her. And he *was* looking at her.

"Hi." He flashed a grin, all white teeth, with a crooked incisor that made her heart flop around in her chest. "You did real good."

"Thanks." Her tongue tied itself into knots. This was Brad, she kept thinking. A senior. Captain of the football team. Student council president. All blond hair and green eyes.

"Miss Davis sure is cool, isn't she?"

"Yeah." *Say something,* she ordered herself. "She's coming to a party at my house tonight. My mom's having some people over."

"Adults only, huh?"

"No, Holly's coming by and a couple other people." Her heart thundered in her ears as she screwed up her courage. "You could drop by if you wanted."

"That'd be cool. What time?"

She managed to close her mouth and swallow. "Oh, about eight," she said, struggling for the casual touch. "I live on—"

"I know where you live." He grinned at her again, and all but stopped her thundering heart. "Hey, you're not going with Chuck anymore, are you?"

"Chuck?" Who was Chuck? "Oh, no. We hung out for a while, but we sort of broke up over the summer."

"Great. See you later."

He strolled off to join a group of boys who were trooping offstage.

"That's a very cute guy," Nell commented from behind Kim.

"Yeah." The word was a sigh. Kim had stars in her eyes.

"Kimmy has a boyfriend," Zeke sang, in the high-pitched, annoying voice that was reserved for addressing younger siblings—or female cousins.

"Shut up, brat."

He only giggled and began to dance around the stage, singsonging the refrain. Nell saw murder shoot into Kim's eyes and created a diversion.

"Well, I guess you guys don't want to practice 'Jingle Bells' today."

"Yes, we do." Zack stopped twirling around the stage with his brother and dashed to the piano. "I know which one it is," he said, attacking Nell's neat pile of sheet music. "I can find it."

"I'll find it," Zeke said, but his brother was already holding the music up triumphantly.

"Good going." Nell settled on the bench with a boy on either side of her. She played a dramatic opening chord that made them both giggle. "Please, music is a serious business. And one, and two, and..."

They actually sang it now, instead of screaming it, as they had the first time she invited them to try. What they lacked in style, they made up for in enthusiasm. In spades.

Even Kim was grinning by the time they'd finished.

"Now you do one, Miss Davis." Zack gave her his soulful look. "Please."

"Your dad's probably waiting."

"Just one."

"Just one," Zeke echoed.

In a few short weeks, it had become impossible for her to resist them. "Just one," Nell agreed, and reached into the now-messy pile of music. "I picked up something you might like at the mall. I bet you've seen *The Little Mermaid*."

"Lots of times," Zeke boasted. "We've got the tape and everything."

"Then you'll recognize this." She played the opening of "Part of Your World."

Mac hunched his shoulders against the wind as he headed into the school. He was damn sick and tired of waiting out in the parking lot. He'd seen the other kids filing out more than ten minutes before.

He had things to do, damn it. Especially since he was stuck going over to Mira's for a party.

He hated parties.

He stomped down the hall. And he heard her. Not the words. He couldn't make out the words, because they were muffled by the auditorium doors. But the sound of her voice, rich and deep. A Scotch-and-soda voice, he'd thought more than once. Sensual, seductive. Sexy.

He opened the door. He had to. And the lush flow of it rolled over him.

A kid's song. He recognized it now from the mermaid movie the boys were still crazy about. He told himself no sane man would get tied up in knots when a woman sang a kid's song.

But he wasn't feeling very sane. Hadn't been since he made the enormous mistake of kissing her.

And he knew that if she'd been alone he would have marched right over to the piano and kissed her again.

But she wasn't alone. Kim was standing behind her, and his children flanked her. Now and again she glanced down at them as she sang, and smiled. Zack was leaning toward her, his head tilting in the way it did just before he climbed into your lap.

Something shifted inside him as he watched. Something painful and frightening. And very, very sweet.

Shaken, Mac stuffed his hands into his pockets, curled those hands into fists. It had to stop. Whatever was happening to him had to stop.

He took a long breath when the music ended. He thought—foolishly, he was sure—that there was something magical humming in the instant of silence that followed.

"We're running late," he called out, determined to break the spell.

Four heads turned his way. The twins began to bounce on the bench.

"Dad! Hey, Dad! We can sing 'Jingle Bells' really good! Want to hear us?"

"I can't." He tried to smile, softening the blow, when Zack's lip poked out. "I'm really running late, kids."

"Sorry, Uncle Mac." Kim scooped up her coat. "We kind of lost track."

While Mac shifted uncomfortably, Nell leaned over and murmured something to his sons. Something, Mac noted, that put a smile back on Zack's face and took the mutinous look off Zeke's. Then both of them threw arms around her and kissed her before they raced offstage for their coats.

"Bye, Miss Davis! Bye!"

"Thanks, Miss Davis," Kim added. "See you later."

Nell made a humming sound and rose to straighten her music.

Mac felt the punch of her cold shoulder all the way in the back of the auditorium. "Ah, thanks for entertaining them," he called out.

Nell lifted her head. He could see her clearly in the stage lights. Clearly enough that he caught the lift of her brow, the coolness of her unsmiling mouth, before she lowered her head again.

Fine, he told himself as he caught both boys on the fly. He didn't want to talk to her anyway.

Five

She didn't have to ignore him so completely. Mac sipped the cup of hard cider his brother-in-law had pressed on him and resentfully studied Nell's back.

She'd had it turned in his direction for an hour.

A hell of a back, too, he thought, half listening as the mayor rattled on in his ear. Smooth and straight, topped off by the fluid curve of her shoulders. It looked very seductive in the thin plum-colored jacket she wore over a short matching dress.

She had terrific legs. He didn't think he'd ever actually seen them before. He would have remembered. Every other time he'd run into her she'd had them covered up.

She'd probably worn a dress tonight to torment him.

Mac cut the mayor off in midstream and strode over to her. "Look, this is stupid."

Nell glanced up. She'd been having a pleasant conversa-

tion with a group of Mira's friends—and thoroughly enjoying the simple act of ignoring Mira's brother.

"Excuse me?"

"It's just stupid," he repeated.

"The need to raise more money for the arts in public
school is stupid?" she asked, well aware he wasn't referring
to the topic she'd been discussing.

"What? No. Damn it, you know what I mean."

"I'm sorry." She started to turn back to the circle of very
interested faces, but he took her arm and pulled her aside.
"Do you want me to cause a scene in your sister's house?"
Nell said between her teeth.

"No." He weaved his way through the minglers, around
the dining room table and through the kitchen door. His
sister was busy replenishing a tray of canapés. "Give us a
minute," he ordered Mira.

"Mac, I'm busy here." Distracted, Mira smoothed a hand
over her short brunette hair. "Would you find Dave and tell
him we're running low on cider?" She sent Nell a frazzled
smile. "I thought I was organized."

"Give us a minute," Mac repeated.

Mira let out an impatient breath, but then her eyebrows
shot up, drew in. "Well, well," she murmured, amused and
clearly delighted. "I'll just get out of your way. I want a closer
look at that boy Kim's so excited about." She picked up the
tray of finger food and swung through the kitchen door.

Silence fell like a hammer.

"So." Casually, Nell plucked a carrot stick from a bowl.
"Something on your mind, Macauley?"

"I don't see why you have to be so…"

"So?" She crunched into the carrot. "What?"

"You're making a point of not talking to me."

She smiled. "Yes, I am."

"It's stupid."

She located an open bottle of white wine, poured some into a glass. After a sip, she smiled again. "I don't think so. It seems to me that, for no discernible reason, I annoy you. Since I'm quite fond of your family, it seems logical and courteous to stay as far out of your way as I possibly can." She sipped again. "Now, is that all? I've been enjoying myself so far this evening."

"You don't annoy me. Exactly." He couldn't find anything to do with his hands, so he settled on taking a carrot stick and breaking it in half. "I'm sorry…for before."

"You're sorry for kissing me, or for behaving like a jerk afterward?"

He tossed the pieces of carrot down. "You're a hard one, Nell."

"Wait." Eyes wide, she pressed a hand to her ear. "I think something's wrong with my hearing. I thought, for just a minute, you actually said my name."

"Cut it out," he said. Then, deliberately: "Nell."

"This is a moment," she declared, and toasted him. "Macauley Taylor has actually initiated a conversation with me, *and* used my name. I'm all aflutter."

"Look." Temper had him rounding the counter. He'd nearly grabbed her before he pushed his anger back. "I just want to clear the air."

Fascinated, she studied his now-impassive face. "That's quite a control button you've got there, Mac. It's admirable. Still, I wonder what would happen if you didn't push it so often."

"A man raising two kids on his own needs control."

"I suppose," she murmured. "Now, if that's all—"

"I'm sorry," he said again.

This time she softened. She was simply no good at holding a grudge. "Okay. Let's just forget it. Friends," she offered, and held out a hand.

He took it. It was so soft, so small, he couldn't make himself give it up again. Her eyes were soft, too, just now. Big, liquid eyes you'd have expected to see on a fawn. "You… look nice."

"Thanks. You, too."

"You like the party?"

"I like the people." Her pulse was starting to jump. Damn him. "Your sister's wonderful. So full of energy and ideas."

"You have to watch her." His lips curved slowly. "She'll rope you into one of her projects."

"Too late. She's got me on the arts committee already. And I've been volunteered to help with the recycling campaign."

"The trick is to duck."

"I don't mind, really. I think I'm going to enjoy it." His thumb was brushing over her wrist now, lightly. "Mac, don't start something you don't intend to finish."

Brow creased, he looked down at their joined hands. "I think about you. I don't have time to think about you. I don't want to have time."

It was happening again. The flutters and quivers she seemed to have no control over. "What do you want?"

His gaze lifted, locked with hers. "I'm having some trouble with that."

The kitchen door burst open, and a horde of teenagers

piled in, only to be brought up short as Kim, in the lead, stopped on a dime.

Her eyes widened as she watched her uncle drop her teacher's hand, and the two of them jumped apart like a couple of teenagers caught necking on the living room sofa.

"Sorry. Ah, sorry," she repeated, goggling. "We were just…" She turned on her heel and shoved back at her friends. They scooted out, chuckling.

"That ought to add some juice to the grapevine," Nell said wryly. She'd been in town long enough to know that everyone would be speculating about Mac Taylor and Nell Davis by morning. Steadier now, she turned back to him. "Listen, why don't we try this in nice easy stages? You want to go out to dinner tomorrow? See a movie or something?"

Now it was his turn to stare. "A date? Are you asking me out on a date?"

Impatience flickered back. "Yes, a date. It doesn't mean I'm asking to bear you more children. On second thought, let's just quit while we're ahead."

"I want to get my hands on you." Mac heard himself say the words, knew it was too late to take them back.

Nell reached for her wine in self-defense. "Well, that's simple."

"No, it's not."

She braced herself and looked up at him again. "No," she agreed quietly. Just how many times, she wondered, had his face popped into her mind in the past few weeks? She couldn't count them. "It's not simple."

But something had to be done, he decided. A move forward, a move back. Take a step, he ordered himself. See what happens. "I haven't been to a movie without the kids… I can't remember. I could probably line up a sitter."

"All right." She was watching him now almost as carefully as he watched her. "Give me a call if it works out. I'll be home most of tomorrow, correcting papers."

It wasn't the easiest thing, stepping back into the dating pool—however small the pool and however warm the water. It irritated him that he was nervous, almost as much as his niece's grins and questions had irritated when she agreed to babysit.

Now, as he climbed the sturdy outside steps to Nell's third-floor apartment, Mac wondered if it would be better all around if they forgot the whole thing.

As he stepped onto her deck, he noted that she'd flanked the door with pots of mums. It was a nice touch, he thought. He always appreciated it when someone who rented one of his homes cared enough to bother with those nice touches.

It was just a movie, he reminded himself, and rapped on the door. When she opened it, he was relieved that she'd dressed casually—a hip-grazing sweater over a pair of those snug leggings Kim liked so much.

Then she smiled and had his mouth going dry.

"Hi. You're right on time. Do you want to come in and see what I've done to your place?"

"It's your place—as long as you pay the rent," he told her, but she was reaching out, taking his hand, drawing him in.

Mac had dispensed with the walls that had made stingy little rooms and had created one flowing space of living, dining and kitchen area. And she'd known what to do with it.

There was a huge L-shaped couch in a bold floral print that

should have been shocking, but was, instead, perfect. A small table under the window held a pot of dried autumn leaves. Shelves along one wall held books, a stereo and a small TV, and the sort of knickknacks he knew women liked.

She'd turned the dining area into a combination music room and office, with her desk and a small spinet. A flute lay on a music stand.

"I didn't bring a lot with me from New York," she said as she shrugged into her jacket. "Only what I really cared about. I'm filling in with things from antique shops and flea markets."

"We got a million of them," he murmured. "It looks good." And it did—the old, faded rug on the floor, the fussy priscillas at the windows. "Comfortable."

"Comfortable's very important to me. Ready?"

"Sure."

And it wasn't so hard after all.

He'd asked her to pick the movie, and she'd gone for comedy. It was surprisingly relaxing to sit in the darkened theater and share popcorn and laughter.

He only thought about her as a woman, a very attractive woman, a couple of dozen times.

Going for pizza afterward seemed such a natural progression, he suggested it himself. They competed for a table in the crowded pizzeria with teenagers out on date night.

"So..." Nell stretched out in the booth. "How's Zeke's career in spelling coming along?"

"It's a struggle. He really works at it. It's funny, Zack can spell almost anything you toss at him first time around, but Zeke has to study the word like a scholar with the Dead Sea Scrolls."

"He's good at his arithmetic."

"Yeah." Mac wasn't sure how he felt about her knowing so much about his kids. "They're both taken with you."

"It's mutual." She skimmed a hand through her hair. "It's going to sound odd, but…" She hesitated, not quite sure how to word it. "But that first day at rehearsal, when I looked around and saw them? I had this feeling, this— I don't know, it was like, 'Oh, there you are. I was wondering when you'd show up.' It sounds strange, but it was as if I was expecting them. Now, when Kim comes without them, I feel let down."

"I guess they kind of grow on you."

It was more than that, but she didn't know how to explain. And she wasn't entirely sure Mac would accept the fact that she'd very simply fallen for them. "I get a kick out of them telling me about their school day, showing me their papers."

"First report cards are almost here." His grin flashed. "I'm more nervous than they are."

"People put too much emphasis on grades."

His brows shot up at the comment. "This from a teacher?"

"Individual ability, application, effort, retention. Those things are a lot more important than *A, B* or *C*. But I can tell you, in confidence, that Kim's aceing advanced chorus and music history."

"No kidding?" He felt a quick surge of pride. "She never did that well before. *B*s mostly."

"Mr. Striker and I have markedly different approaches."

"You're telling me. Word around town is that the chorus is dynamite this year. How'd you pull it off?"

"The kids pull it off," she told him, sitting up when their pizza was served. "My job is to make them think and sing like a team. Not to slam Mr. Striker," she added, taking a generous bite. "But I get the impression he was just putting in time, counting the days until he could retire. If you're going to teach kids, you have to like them, and respect them. There's a lot of talent there, some of it extremely rough." When she laughed, the roses in her cheek bloomed deeper. "And some of those kids will do nothing more than sing in the shower for the rest of their lives—for which the world can be grateful."

"Got some clinkers, huh?"

"Well…" She laughed again. "Yes, I have a few. But they're enjoying themselves. That's what counts. And there are a few, like Kim, who are really something special. I'm sending her and two others for auditions to all-state next week. And after the holiday concert I'm going to hold auditions for the spring musical."

"We haven't had a musical at the high school in three years."

"We're going to have one this year, Buster. And it's going to be terrific."

"It's a lot of work for you."

"I like it. And it's what I'm paid for."

Mac toyed with a second slice. "You really do like it, don't you? The school, the town, the whole bit?"

"Why shouldn't I? It's a fine school, a fine town."

"It ain't Manhattan."

"Exactly."

"Why'd you leave?" He winced. "Sorry, none of my business."

"It's all right. I had a bad year. I guess I was getting restless before that, but the last year was just the pits. They eliminated my job at the school. Economic cutbacks. Downsizing. The arts are always the first to suffer." She shrugged. "Anyway, my roommate got married. I couldn't afford the rent on my own—not if I wanted to eat with any regularity—so I advertised for another one. Took references, gauged personalities." With a sigh, she propped her chin on her elbow. "I thought I was careful. But about three weeks after she moved in, I came home and found that she'd cleaned me out."

Mac stopped eating. "She robbed you?"

"She skinned me. TV, stereo, whatever good jewelry I had, cash, the collection of Limoges boxes I'd started in college. I was really steamed, and then I was shaken. I just wasn't comfortable living there after it happened. Then the guy I'd been seeing for about a year started giving me lectures on my stupidity, my naïveté. As far as he was concerned, I'd gotten exactly what I'd deserved."

"Nice guy," Mac muttered. "Very supportive."

"You bet. In any case, I took a good look at him and our relationship and figured he was right on one level. As long as I was in that rut, with him, I was getting what I deserved. So I decided to climb out of the rut, and leave him in it."

"Good choice."

"I thought so." And so was he, she thought, studying Mac's face. A very good choice. "Why don't you tell me what your plans are with the house you're renovating."

"I don't guess you'd know a lot about plumbing."

She only smiled. "I'm a quick learner."

It was nearly midnight when he pulled up in front of her apartment. He hadn't intended to stay out so late. He certainly hadn't expected to spend more than an hour talking to her about wiring and plumbing and load-bearing walls. Or drawing little blueprints on napkins.

But somehow he'd managed to get through the evening without feeling foolish, or pinned down or out of step. Only one thing worried him. He wanted to see her again.

"I think this was a good first step." She laid a hand over his, kissed his cheek. "Thanks."

"I'll walk you up."

Her hand was already on the door handle. Safer, she'd decided for both of them, if she just hurried along. "You don't have to. I know the way."

"I'll walk you up," he repeated. He stepped out, rounded the hood. They started up the stairs together. The tenant on the first floor was still awake. The mutter of a television, and its ghost gray light, filtered through the window.

Since the breeze had died, it was the only sound. And overhead countless stars wheeled in a clear black sky.

"If we do this again," Mac began, "people in town are going to start talking about us, making out that we're…" He wasn't quite sure of the right phrase.

"An item?" Nell supplied. "That bothers you."

"I don't want the kids to get any ideas, or worry, or… whatever." As they reached the landing, he looked down at her and was caught again. "It must be the way you look," he murmured.

"What must?"

"That makes me think about you." It was a reasonable explanation, he decided. Physical attraction. After all, he wasn't a dead man. He was just a careful one. "That makes me think about doing this."

He cupped her face in his hands—a gesture so sweet, so tender, it had every muscle in her body going lax. It was just as slow, as stunning, as sumptuous, as the first time. The touch of his mouth on hers, the shuddering patience, the simple wonder of it.

Could it be this? she wondered. Could it be this that she'd been waiting for? Could it be him?

He heard her soft, breathy sigh as he eased his mouth from hers. Lingering, he knew, would be a mistake, and he let his hands fall away before they could reach for more.

As if to capture one final taste, Nell ran her tongue over her lips. "You're awfully good at that, Macauley. Awfully good."

"You could say I've been saving up." But he didn't think it was that at all. He was very much worried it wasn't that. "I'll see you."

She nodded weakly as he headed down the steps. She was still leaning dreamily against the door when she heard his car start and drive away.

For a moment, she would have sworn the air rang with the distant music of sleigh bells.

Six

The end of October meant parent-teacher confer-
ences, and a much-anticipated holiday for students.
It also meant a headache for Mac. He had to juggle
the twins from his sister to Kim to Mrs. Hollis, fitting in a
trip to order materials and an electrical inspection.

When he turned his truck into the educational complex,
he was jumpy with nerves. Lord knew what he was about to
be told about his children, how they behaved when they were
out of his sight and his control. He worried that he hadn't
made enough time to help them with their schoolwork and
somehow missed a parental step in preparing them for the
social, educational and emotional demands of first grade.

Because of his failure, his boys would become antisocial,
illiterate neurotics.

He knew he was being ridiculous, but he couldn't stop

his fears from playing over and over like an endless loop in his brain.

"Mac!" The car horn and the sound of his name had him turning and focusing, finally, on his sister's car. She leaned out the window, shaking her head at him. "Where were you? I called you three times."

"Bailing my kids out of jail," he muttered, and changed course to walk to her car. "I've got a conference in a minute."

"I know. I've just come from a meeting at the high school. Remember, we compared schedules."

"Right. I shouldn't be late."

"You don't get demerits. My meeting was about raising funds for new chorus uniforms. Those kids have been wearing the same old choir robes for twelve years. We're hoping to raise enough to put them in something a little snazzier."

"Fine, I'll give you a donation, but I shouldn't be late." Already he was imagining the young, fresh-faced first grade teacher marking him tardy, just another item on a growing list of negatives about Taylor males.

"I just wanted to say that Nell seemed upset about something."

"What?"

"Upset," Mira repeated, pleased that she finally had his full attention. "She came up with a couple of nice ideas for fund-raisers, but she was obviously distracted." Mira lifted a brow, eyeing her brother slyly. "You haven't done anything to annoy her, have you?"

"No." Mac caught himself before he shifted guiltily from foot to foot. "Why should I?"

"Couldn't say. But since you've been seeing her—"

"We went to the movies."

"And for pizza," Mira added. "A couple of Kim's friends spotted you."

The curse of small towns, Mac thought, and stuffed his hands in his pockets. "So?"

"So nothing. Good for you. I like her a lot. Kim's crazy about her. I suppose I'm feeling a bit protective. She was definitely upset, Mac, and trying not to show it. Maybe she'd talk to you about it."

"I'm not going to go poking around in her personal life."

"The way I see it, you're part of her personal life. See you later." She pulled off without giving him a chance for a parting shot.

Muttering to himself, Mac marched up to the elementary school. When he marched out twenty minutes later, he was in a much lighter mood. His children had not been declared social misfits with homicidal tendencies after all. In fact, their teacher had praised them.

Of course, he'd known all along.

Maybe Zeke forgot the rules now and then and talked to his neighbor. And maybe Zack was a little shy about raising his hand when he knew an answer. But they were settling in.

With the weight of first grade off his shoulders, Mac headed out. Impulse had him swinging toward the high school. He knew his conference had been one of the last of the day. He wasn't sure how teachers' meetings worked at the high school, but the lot was nearly empty. He spotted Nell's car, however, and decided it wouldn't hurt just to drop in.

It wasn't until he was inside that he realized he didn't have a clue as to where to find her.

Mac poked his head into the auditorium, but it was empty. Since he'd come that far, he backtracked to the main office and caught one of the secretaries as she was leaving for the day. Following her directions, he turned down a corridor, headed up a ramp and turned right.

Nell's classroom door was open. Not like any classroom he'd done time in, he thought. This one had a piano, music stands, instruments, a tape recorder. There was the usual blackboard, wiped clean, and a desk where Nell was currently working.

He watched her for a long moment, the way her hair fell, the way her fingers held the pen, the way her sweater draped at the neck. It occurred to him that if he'd ever had a teacher who looked like that, he would have been a great deal more interested in music.

"Hi."

Her head snapped up. There was a martial light in her eyes that surprised him, a stubborn set to her jaw. Even as he watched, she took a long breath and worked up a smile.

"Hello, Mac. Welcome to bedlam."

"Looks like a lot of work." He stepped inside, up to the desk. It was covered with papers, books, computer printouts and sheet music, all in what appeared to be ordered piles.

"Finishing up the first marking period, grades, class planning, fund-raising strategy, fine-tuning the holiday concert—and trying to make the budget stretch to producing the spring musical." Trying to keep her foul mood to herself, she sat back. "So, how was your day?"

"Pretty good. I just had a conference with the twins' teacher. They're doing fine. I can stop sweating report cards."

"They're great kids. You've got nothing to worry about."

"Worry comes with the territory. What are you worried

about?" he asked before he could remind himself he wasn't going to pry.

"How much time have you got?" she shot back.

"Enough." Curious, he eased a hip onto the edge of her desk. He wanted to soothe, he discovered, to stroke away that faint line between her brows. "Rough day?"

She jerked her shoulders, then pushed away from her desk. Temper always forced her to move. "I've had better. Do you know how much school and community support the football team gets? All the sports teams." She began to slap cassette tapes into a box—anything to keep her hands busy. "Even the band. But the chorus, we have to go begging for every dollar."

"You're ticked off about the budget?"

"Why shouldn't I be?" She whirled back, eyes hot. "No problem getting equipment for the football team so a bunch of boys can go out on the field and tackle each other, but I have to spend an hour on my knees if I want eighty bucks to get a piano tuned." She caught herself, sighed. "I don't have anything against football. I like it. High school sports are important."

"I know a guy who tunes pianos," Mac said. "He'd probably donate his time."

Nell rubbed a hand over her face, slid it around to soothe the tension at the back of her neck. *Dad can fix anything,* she thought, just as the twins had claimed. Have a problem? Call Mac.

"That would be great," she said, and managed a real smile. "If I can beat my way through the paperwork and get approval. You can't even take freebies without going through the board." It irritated her, as always. "One of the worst aspects of teaching is the bureaucracy. Maybe I should have stuck with performing in clubs."

"You performed in clubs?"

"In another life," she muttered, waving it away. "A little singing to pay my way through college. It was better than waiting tables. Anyway, it's not the budget, not really. Or even the lack of interest from the community. I'm used to that."

"Do you want to tell me what it is, or do you want to stew about it?"

"I was having a pretty good time stewing about it." She sighed again, and looked up at him. He seemed so solid, so dependable. "Maybe I'm too much of an urbanite after all. I've had my first run-in with old-fashioned rural attitude, and I'm stumped. Do you know Hank Rohrer?"

"Sure. He has a dairy farm out on Old Oak Road. I think his oldest kid is in the same class as Kim."

"Hank, Jr. Yes. Junior's one of my students—a very strong baritone. He has a real interest in music. He even writes it."

"No kidding? That's great."

"You'd think so, wouldn't you?" Nell tossed her hair back and went to her desk again to tidy her already tidy papers. "Well, I asked Mr. and Mrs. Rohrer to come in this morning because Junior backed out of going to all-state auditions this weekend. I knew he had a very good chance of making it, and I wanted to discuss the possibility with his parents of a music scholarship. When I told them how talented Junior was and how I hoped they'd encourage him to change his mind about the auditions, Hank Senior acted as though I'd just insulted him. He was appalled." There was bitterness in her voice now, as well as anger. "'No son of his was going to waste his time on singing and writing music like some...'"

She trailed off, too furious to repeat the man's opinion of musicians. "They didn't even know Junior was in my class. Thought he was taking shop as his elective this year. I tried to smooth it over, said that Junior needed a fine-art credit to graduate. I didn't do much good. Mr. Rohrer could barely swallow the idea of Junior staying in my class. He went on about how Junior didn't need singing lessons to run a farm. And he certainly wasn't going to allow him to take a Saturday and go audition when the boy had chores. And I'm to stop putting any fancy ideas about college in the boy's head."

"They've got four kids," Mac said slowly. "Tuition might be a problem."

"If that were the only obstacle, they should be grateful for the possibility of scholarship." She slapped her grade book closed. "What we have is a bright, talented boy who has dreams, dreams he'll never be able to explore because his parents won't permit it. Or his father won't," she added. "His mother didn't say two words the entire time they were here."

"Could be she'll work on Hank once she has him alone."

"Could be he'll take out his annoyance with me on both of them."

"Hank's not like that. He's set in his ways and thinks he knows all the answers, but he isn't mean."

"It's a little tough for me to see his virtues after he called me—" she had to take a deep breath "—a slick-handed flat-lander who's wasting his hard-earned tax dollars. I could have made a difference with that boy," Nell murmured as she sat again. "I know it."

"So maybe you won't be able to make a difference with

Junior. You'll make a difference with someone else. You've already made one with Kim."

"Thanks." Nell's smile was brief. "That helps a little."

"I mean it." He hated to see her this way, all that brilliant energy and optimism dimmed. "She's gained a lot of confidence in herself. She's always been shy about her singing, about a lot of things. Now she's really opening up."

It did help to hear it. This time Nell's smile came easier. "So I should stop brooding."

"It doesn't suit you." He surprised himself, and her, by reaching down to run his knuckles over her cheek. "Smiling does."

"I've never been able to hold on to temperament for long. Bob used to say it was because I was shallow."

"Who the hell's Bob?"

"The one who's still in the rut."

"Clearly where he belongs."

She laughed. "I'm glad you dropped by. I'd have probably sat here for another hour clenching my jaw."

"It's a pretty jaw," Mac murmured, then shifted away. "I've got to get going. I've got Halloween costumes to put together."

"Need any help?"

"I…" It was tempting, too tempting, and far too dangerous, he thought, to start sharing family traditions with her. "No, I've got it covered."

Nell accepted the disappointment, nearly masked it. "You'll bring them by Saturday night, won't you? To trick-or-treat?"

"Sure. I'll see you." He started out but stopped at the doorway and turned back. "Nell?"

"Yes?"

"Some things take a while to change. Change makes some people nervous."

She tilted her head. "Are you talking about the Rohrers, Mac?"

"Among others. I'll see you Saturday night."

Nell studied the empty doorway as his footsteps echoed away. Did he think she was trying to change him? Was she? She sat back, pushing away from the paperwork. She'd never be able to concentrate on it now.

Whenever she was around Macauley Taylor, it was hard to concentrate. When had she become so susceptible to the slow, thorough, quiet type? From the moment he'd walked into the auditorium to pick up Kim and the twins, she admitted.

Love at first sight? Surely she was too sophisticated, too smart, to believe in such a thing. And surely, she added, she was too smart to put herself in the vulnerable position of falling in love with a man who didn't return her feelings.

Or didn't want to, she thought. And that was even worse.

It couldn't matter that he was sweet and kind and devoted to his children. It shouldn't matter that he was handsome and strong and sexy. She wouldn't let it matter that being with him, thinking of him, had her longing for things. For home, for family, for laughter in the kitchen and passion in bed.

She let out a long breath, because it did matter. It mattered very much when a woman was teetering right on the edge of falling in love.

Seven

Mid-November had stripped the leaves from the trees. There was a beauty even in this, Nell had decided. Beauty in the dark, denuded branches, in the papery rustle of dried leaves along the curbs, in the frost that shimmered like diamond dust on the grass in the mornings.

She caught herself staring out of the window too often, wishing for snow like a child hoping for a school holiday.

It felt wonderful. Wonderful to anticipate the winter, to remember the fall. She often thought about Halloween night, and all the children who had come knocking on her door dressed as pirates and princesses. She remembered the way Zeke and Zack had giggled when she pretended not to recognize them in the elaborate astronaut costumes Mac had fashioned for them.

She found herself reminiscing about the bluegrass concert

Mac had taken her to. Or the fun they'd had when she ran into him and the boys at the mall just last week, all of them on a mission to complete their Christmas lists early.

Now, strolling past the house Mac was remodeling, she thought of him again. It had been so sweet, the way he'd struggled over choosing just the right outfit for Kim's present. No thoughtless gifts from Macauley Taylor for those he cared about. It had to be the right color, the right style.

She'd come to believe everything about him was right.

She passed the house, drawing in the chilly air of evening, her mood buoyant. That afternoon she'd been proud to announce that two of her students would participate in all-state chorus.

She had made a difference, Nell thought, shutting her eyes on the pleasure of it. Not just the prestige, certainly not simply the delight of having the principal congratulate her. The difference, the important one, had been the look on her students' faces. The pride, not just on Kim's face and that of the tenor who would go to all-state with her. But on the faces of the entire chorus. They all shared in the triumph, because over the past few weeks they had become a team.

Her team. Her kids.

"It's cold for walking."

Nell jolted, tensed, then laughed at herself when she saw Mac step away from the shadow of a tree in his sister's yard. "Lord, you gave me a start. I nearly went into my repel-the-mugger stance."

"Taylor's Grove's a little sparse when it comes to muggers. Are you going to see Mira?"

"No, actually, I was just out walking. Too much energy

to stay in." The smile lit her face. "You've heard the good news?"

"Congratulations."

"It's not me——"

"Yeah, it is. A lot of it." It was the only way he knew to tell her how proud he was of what she'd done. He glanced back toward the house, where lights gleamed. "Mira and Kim are in there crying."

"Crying? But——"

"Not that kind of crying." Female tears always embarrassed him. He shrugged. "You know, the other kind."

"Oh." In response, Nell felt her own eyes sting. "That's nice."

"Dave's going around with a big fat grin on his face. He was talking to his parents when I ducked out. Mira's already called ours, as well as every other friend and relative in the country."

"Well, it's a big deal."

"I know it is." His teeth flashed. "I've made a few calls myself. You must be feeling pretty pleased with yourself."

"You bet I am. Seeing the kids today when I made the announcement...well, it was the best. And it's a hell of a kick-off for our fund-raiser." She shivered as the wind shuddered through the trees.

"You're getting cold. I'll drive you home."

"That'd be nice. I keep waiting for snow."

In the way of every countryman since Adam, he sniffed the air, checked out the sky. "You won't have to wait much longer." He opened the truck door for her. "The kids have already gotten their sleds out."

"I might buy one for myself." She settled back, relaxed. "Where are the boys?"

"There's a sleepover at one of their friends'." He gestured toward the house across the street from Mira's. "I just dropped them off."

"They must be thinking a lot about Christmas now, with snow in the air."

"It's funny. Usually right after Halloween they start barraging me with lists and pictures of toys from catalogs, stuff they see on TV." He turned the truck and headed for the square. "This year they told me Santa's taking care of it. I know they want bikes." His brow creased. "That's all I've heard. They've been whispering together about something else, but they clam up when I come around."

"That's Christmas," Nell said easily. "It's the best time for whispers and secrets. What about you?" She turned to smile at him. "What do you want for Christmas?"

"More than the two hours' sleep I usually get."

"You can do better than that."

"When the kids come downstairs in the morning, and their faces light up, I've got all I want." He stopped in front of her apartment. "Are you going back to New York for the holiday?"

"No, there's nothing there."

"Your family?"

"I'm an only child. My parents usually spend the holiday in the Caribbean. Do you want to come in, have some coffee?"

It was a much more appealing idea than going home to an empty house. "Yeah, thanks." When they started up the stairs, he tried to swing tactfully back to the holidays and her family. "Is that where you spent Christmas as a kid? In the Caribbean?"

"No. We had a fairly traditional setting in Philadelphia. Then I went to school in New York, and they moved to Florida." She opened the door and took off her coat. "We aren't very close, really. They weren't terribly happy with my decision to study music."

"Oh." He tossed his jacket over hers while she moved into the kitchen to put on the coffee. "I guess that's why you got so steamed about Junior."

"Maybe. They didn't really disapprove so much as they were baffled. We get along much better long-distance." She glanced over her shoulder. "I think that's why I admire you."

He stopped studying the rosewood music box on a table and stared at her. "Me?"

"Your interest and involvement with your children, your whole family. It's so solid, so natural." Tossing back her hair, she reached into the cookie jar and began to spread cookies on a plate. "Not everyone is as willing, or as able, to put in so much time and attention. Not everyone loves as well, or as thoroughly." She smiled. "Now I've embarrassed you."

"No. Yes," he admitted, and took one of the cookies. "You haven't asked about their mother." When she said nothing, Mac found himself talking. "I was just out of college when I met her. She was a secretary in my father's real estate office. She was beautiful. I mean eye-popping beautiful, the kind that bowls you over. We went out a couple of times, we went to bed, she got pregnant."

The flat-voiced recitation had Nell looking up. Mac bit into the cookie, tasting bitterness. "I know that sounds like

she did it on her own. I was young, but I was old enough
to know what I was doing, old enough to be responsible."

He had always taken his responsibilities seriously, Nell
thought, and he always would. You only had to look at him
to see the dependability.

"You didn't say anything about love."

"No, I didn't." It was something he didn't take lightly. "I
was attracted, so was she. Or I thought she was. What I didn't
know was that she'd lied about using birth control. It wasn't
until after I'd married her that I found out she'd set out to
'snag the boss's son.' Her words," he added. "Angie saw an
opportunity to improve her standard of living."

It surprised him that even now, after all this time, it hurt
both pride and heart to know he'd been so carelessly used.

"To make a long story short," he continued, in that same
expressionless tone, "she hadn't counted on twins, or the
hassle of motherhood. So, about a month after the boys were
born, she cleaned out my bank account and split."

"I'm so sorry, Mac," Nell murmured. She wished she knew
the words, the gesture, that would erase that cool dispassion
from his eyes. "It must have been horrible for you."

"It could have been worse." His eyes met Nell's briefly
before he shrugged it off. "I could have loved her. She con-
tacted me once, telling me she wanted me to foot the bill
for the divorce. In exchange for that, I could have the kids
free and clear. Free and clear," he repeated. "As if they were
stocks and bonds instead of children. I took her up on it.
End of story."

"Is it?" Nell moved to him, took his hands in hers. "Even
if you didn't love her, she hurt you."

She rose on her toes to kiss his cheek, to soothe, to comfort. She saw the change in his eyes—and, yes, the hurt in them. It explained a great deal, she thought, to hear him tell the story. To see his face as he did. He'd been disillusioned, devastated. Instead of giving in to it, or leaning on his parents for help with the burden, he'd taken his sons and started a life with them. A life for them.

"She didn't deserve you, or the boys."

"It wasn't a hardship." He couldn't take his eyes off hers now. It wasn't the sympathy so much as the simple, unquestioning understanding that pulled at him. "They're the best part of me. I didn't mean it to sound like it was a sacrifice."

"You didn't. You don't." Her heart melted as she slid her arms around him. She'd meant that, too, as a comfort. But something more, something deeper, was stirring inside her. "You made it sound as if you love them. It's very appealing to hear a man say that he thinks of his children as a gift. And to know he means it."

He was holding her, and he wasn't quite sure how it had happened. It seemed so easy, so natural, to have her settled in his arms. "When you're given a gift, an important one, you have to be careful with it." His voice thickened with a mix of emotions. His children. Her. Something about the way she was looking up at him, the way her lips curved. He lifted a hand to stroke her hair, lingered over it a moment before he remembered to back away. "I should go."

"Stay." It was so easy, she discovered, to ask him. So easy, after all, to need him. "You know I want you to stay. You know I want you."

He couldn't take his eyes off her face, and the need was so much bigger, so much sweeter, than he'd ever imagined.

"It could complicate things, Nell. I've got a lot of baggage. Most of it's in storage, but—"

"I don't care." Her breath trembled out. "I don't even have any pride at the moment. Make love with me, Mac." On a sigh, she pulled his head down and pressed her lips to his. "Just love me tonight."

He couldn't resist. It was a fantasy that had begun to wind through him, body and mind, the moment he first met her. She was all softness, all warmth. He'd done without both of those miraculous female gifts for so long.

Now, with her mouth on his and her arms twined around him, she was all he could want.

He'd never considered himself romantic. He wondered if a woman like Nell would prefer candlelight, soft music, perfumed air. But the scene was already set. He could do nothing more than lift her into his arms and carry her to the bedroom.

He turned on a lamp, surprised at how suddenly his nerves vanished when he saw hers reflected in her eyes.

"I've thought about this a long time," he told her. "I want to see you, every minute I'm touching you. I want to see you."

"Good." She looked up at him and his smile soothed away some of her tension. "I want to see you."

He carried her to the bed and lay down beside her, stroking a hand through her hair, over her shoulders. Then he dipped his head to kiss her.

It was so easy, as if they had shared nights and intimacy for years. It was so thrilling, as if each of them had come to the bed as innocent as a babe.

A touch, a taste, patient and lingering. A murmur, a sigh,

soft and quiet. His hands never rushed, only pleasured, stroking over her, unfastening buttons, pausing to explore.

Her skin quivered under his caress even as it heated. A hundred pulse points thrummed, speeding at the brush of a fingertip, the flick of a tongue. Her own hands trembled, pulling a laughing groan from her that ended on a broken whimper when she at last found flesh.

Making love. The phrase had never been truer to her. For here was an exquisite tenderness mixed with a lustful curiosity that overpowered the senses, tangled in the system like silken knots. Each time his mouth returned to hers, it went deeper, wider, higher, so that he was all that existed for her. All that needed to.

She gave with a depthless generosity that staggered him. She fit, body to body, with him, with a perfection that thrilled. Each time he thought his control would slip, he found himself sliding easily back into the rhythm they set.

Slow, subtle, savoring.

She was small, delicately built. The fragility he sensed made his hands all the more tender. Even as she arched and cried out the first time, he didn't hurry. It was gloriously arousing for him simply to watch her face, that incredibly expressive face, as every emotion played over it.

He fought back the need to bury himself inside her, clung to control long enough to protect them both. Their eyes locked when at last he slipped into her. Her breath caught and released, and then her lips curved.

Outside, the wind played against the windows, making a music like sleigh bells. And the first snow of the season began to fall as quietly as a wish.

Eight

He couldn't get enough of her. Mac figured at worst it was a kind of insanity, at best a temporary obsession. No matter how many demands there were on his time, his brain, his emotions, he still found odd moments, day and night, to think about Nell.

Though he knew it was cynical, he wished it could have been just sex. If it was only sex, he could put it down to hormones and get back to business. But he didn't just imagine her in bed, or fantasize about finding an hour to lose himself in that trim little body.

Sometimes, when she slipped into his head, she was standing in front of a group of children, directing their voices with her hands, her arms, her whole self. Or she'd be seated at the piano, with his boys on either side of her, laughing with them. Or she'd just be walking through town, with her hands in her pockets and her face lifted toward the sky.

She scared him right down to the bone.

And she, he thought as he measured his baseboard trim, she was so easy about the whole thing. That was a woman for you, he decided. They didn't have to worry about making the right moves, saying the right thing. They just had to... to be, he thought. That was enough to drive a man crazy.

He couldn't afford to be crazy. He had kids to raise, a business to run. Hell, he had laundry to do if he ever got home. And damn it, he'd forgotten to take the chicken out of the freezer again.

They'd catch burgers on the way to the concert, he told himself. He had enough on his mind without having to fix dinner. Christmas was barreling toward him, and the kids were acting strange.

Just the bikes, Dad, they told him. *Santa's making them, and he's taking care of the big present.*

What big present? Mac wondered. No interrogation, no tricks, had pulled out that particular answer. For once his kids were closed up tight. That was an idea that disturbed him. He knew that in another year, two if he was lucky, they'd begin to question and doubt the existence of Santa and magic. The end of innocence. Whatever it was they were counting on for Christmas morning, he wanted to see that they found it under the tree.

But they just grinned at him when he prodded and told him it was a surprise for all three of them.

He'd have to work on it. Mac hammered the trim into place. At least they'd gotten the tree up and baked some cookies, strung the popcorn. He felt a little twinge of guilt over the fact that he'd evaded Nell's offer to help with the decorating. And ignored the kids when they asked if she could come over and trim the tree with them.

Was he the only one who could see what a mistake it would be to have his children become too attached? She'd only been in town for a few months. She could leave at any time. Nell might find them cute, attractive kids, but she didn't have any investment in them.

Damn it, now *he* was making them sound like stocks and bonds.

It wasn't what he meant, Mac assured himself. He simply wasn't going to allow anyone to walk out on his sons again.

He wouldn't risk it, not for anything in heaven or on earth.

After nailing the last piece of baseboard in place, he nodded in approval. The house was coming together just fine. He knew what he was doing there. Just as he knew what he was doing with the boys.

He only wished he had a better idea of what to do with Nell.

"Maybe it'll happen tonight." Zeke watched his breath puff out like smoke as he and his twin sat in the tree house, wrapped against the December chill in coats and scarves.

"It's not Christmas yet."

"But it's the Christmas concert," Zeke said stubbornly. He was tired of waiting for the mom. "That's where we saw her first. And they'll have the music and the tree and stuff, so it'll be like Christmas."

"I don't know." Zack liked the idea, a lot, but was more cautious. "Maybe, but we don't get any presents until Christmas."

"We do, too. When Mr. Perkins pretends to be Santa at the party at the firehouse. That's whole weeks before Christmas, and he gives all the kids presents."

"Not *real* presents. Not stuff you ask for." But Zack set his mind to it. "Maybe if we wish real hard. Dad likes her a lot. Aunt Mira was telling Uncle Dave that Dad's found the right woman even if he doesn't know it." Zack's brow creased. "How could he not know it if he found her?"

"Aunt Mira's always saying stuff that doesn't make sense," Zeke said, with the easy disdain of the young. "Dad's going to marry her, and she's going to come live with us and be the mom. She has to be. We've been good, haven't we?"

"Uh-huh." Zack played with the toe of his boot. "Do you think she'll love us and all that?"

"Probably." Zeke shot his twin a look. "I love her already."

"Me, too." Zack smiled in relief. Everything was going to be okay after all.

"All right, people." Nell pitched her voice above the din in the chorus room. It doubled as backstage on concert nights, and students were swarming around, checking clothes, makeup and hair and working off preperformance jitters by talking at the top of their lungs. "Settle down."

One of her students had his head between his knees, fighting off acute stage fright. Nell sent him a sympathetic smile as her group began to quiet.

"You've all worked really hard for tonight. I know a lot of you are jumpy because you have friends and family out in the audience. Use the nerves to sharpen your performance. Please try to remember to go out onstage in the organized, dignified manner we've practiced."

There were some snickers at that. Nell merely lifted a brow. "I should have said remember to be more dignified and more orderly than you've managed at practice. Diaphragms," she said. "Projection. Posture. Smiles." She paused, lifted a hand. "And above all, I expect you to remember the most vital ingredient in tonight's performance. Enjoy it," she said, and grinned. "It's Christmas. Now let's go knock 'em dead."

Her heart was doing some pretty fancy pumping of its own as she directed the children onstage, watched them take their positions on the risers as the murmurs from the audience rose and ebbed. For many, Nell knew, this concert would be her first test. Decisions from the community would be made tonight as to whether the school board had made a good or a bad choice in their new music teacher.

She took a deep breath, tugged at the hem of her velvet jacket and stepped onstage.

There was polite applause as she approached the solo mike.

"Welcome to Taylor's Grove High School's holiday concert," she began.

"Gosh, Dad, doesn't Miss Davis look pretty?"

"Yeah, Zack, she does." *Lovely* was more the word, he thought, in that soft-looking deep forest-green suit, with holly berries in her hair and a quick, nervous smile on her face.

She looked terrific in the spotlight. He wondered if she knew it.

At the moment, all Nell knew was nerves. She wished she could see faces clearly. She'd always preferred seeing her audience when she was performing. It made it more intimate, more fun. After her announcement, she turned, saw every student's eyes on hers, then smiled in reassurance.

"Okay, kids," she murmured, in an undertone only they could hear. "Let's rock."

She started them off with a bang, the Springsteen number,

and it had eyes popping wide in the audience. This was not the usual yawn-inspiring program most had been expecting.

When the applause hit, Nell felt the tension dissolve. They'd crossed the first hurdle. She segued from the fun to the traditional, thrilled when the auditorium filled with the harmony on "Cantate Domine," delighted when her sopranos soared on "Adeste Fideles," grinning when they bounced into "Jingle Bell Rock," complete with the little stage business of swaying and hand clapping they'd worked on.

And her heart swelled when Kim approached the mike and the first pure notes of her solo flowed into the air.

"Oh, Dave." Sniffling, Mira clutched her husband's hand, then Mac's. "Our baby."

Nell's prediction had been on target. When Kim stepped back in position, there were damp eyes in every row. They closed the concert with "Silent Night," only voices, no piano. The way it was meant to be sung, Nell had told her students. The way it was written to be sung.

When the last note died and she turned to gesture to her chorus, the audience was already on its feet. The kick of it jolted through her as she turned her head, saw the slack jaws, wide eyes and foolish grins of her students.

Nell swallowed tears, waiting until the noise abated slightly before crossing to the mike again. She knew how to play it.

"They were terrific, weren't they?"

As she'd hoped, that started the cheers and applause all over again. She waited it out.

"I'd like to thank you all for coming, for supporting the chorus. I owe a special thanks to the parents of the singers onstage tonight for their patience, their understanding and their willingness to let me share their children for a few hours every day. Every student onstage has worked tremendously hard for tonight, and I'm delighted that you appreciate their talent, and their effort. I'd like to add that the poinsettias you see onstage were donated by Hill Florists and are for sale at three dollars a pot. Proceeds to go to the fund for new choir uniforms. Merry Christmas, and come back."

Before she could step away from the mike, Kim and Brad were standing on either side of her.

"There's just one more thing." Brad cleared his throat until the rustling in the audience died down. "The chorus would like to present a token of appreciation to Miss Davis for all her work and encouragement. Ah…" Kim had written the speech out, but Brad had been designated to say it. He fumbled a little, grinned self-consciously at Kim. "This is Miss Davis's first concert at Taylor High. Ah…" He just couldn't remember all the nice words Kim had written, so he said what he felt. "She's the best. Thanks, Miss Davis."

"We hope you like it," Kim murmured under the applause as she handed Nell a brightly wrapped box. "All the kids chipped in."

"I'm…" She didn't know what to say, was afraid to try. When she opened the box, she stared, misty-eyed, down at a pin shaped like a treble clef.

"We know you like jewelry," Kim began. "So we thought—"

"It's beautiful. It's perfect." Taking a steadying breath, she turned to the chorus. "Thanks. It means almost as much to me as you do. Merry Christmas."

"She got a present," Zack pointed out. They were waiting in the crowded corridor outside the auditorium to congratulate Kim. "That means we could get one tonight. We could get her."

"Not if she goes home right after." Zack had already worked this out. He was waiting for his moment. When he saw her, he pounced. "Miss Davis! Over here, Miss Davis!"

Mac didn't move. Couldn't. Something had happened while he sat three rows back, watching her on the stage. Seeing her smile, seeing tears in her eyes. Just seeing her.

He was in love with her. It was nothing he'd ever experienced. Nothing he knew how to handle. Running seemed the smartest solution, but he didn't think he could move.

"Hi!" She crouched down for hugs, squeezing the boys tight, kissing each cheek. "Did you like the concert?"

"It was real good. Kim was the best."

Nell leaned close to Zeke's ear. "I think so, too, but it has to be a secret."

"We're good at keeping secrets." He smiled smugly at his brother. "We've had one for weeks and weeks."

"Can you come to our house now, Miss Davis?" Zack clung to her hand and put all his charm into his eyes. "Please? Come see our tree and the lights. We put lights everywhere so you can see them from all the way down on the road."

"I'd like that." Testing the water, she glanced up at Mac. "But your dad might be tired."

He wasn't tired, he was flattened. Her lashes were still damp, and the little pin the kids had given her glinted against her velvet jacket. "You're welcome to come out, if you don't mind the drive."

"I'd like it. I'm still wired up." She straightened, searching for some sign of welcome or rebuff in Mac's face. "If you're sure it isn't a bad time."

"No." His tongue was thick, he realized. As if he'd been drinking. "I want to talk to you."

"I'll head out as soon as I'm finished here, then." She winked at the boys and melted back into the crowd.

"She's done wonders with those kids." Mrs. Hollis nodded to Mac. "It'll be a shame to lose her."

"Lose her?" Mac glanced down at his boys, but they were already in a huddle, exchanging whispers. "What do you mean?"

"I heard from Mr. Perkins, who got it from Addie McVie at the high school office, that Nell Davis was offered her old position back at that New York school starting next fall. Nell and the principal had themselves a conference just this morning." Mrs. Hollis babbled on as Mac stared blankly over her head. "Hate to think about her leaving us. Made a difference with these kids." She spied one of her gossip buddies and elbowed her way through the crowd.

Nine

Control came easily to Mac—or at least it had for the past seven years. He used all the control at his disposal to keep his foul mood and bubbling temper from the boys.

They were so excited about her coming, he thought bitterly. Wanted to make certain all the lights were lit, the cookies were out, the decorative bell was hung on Zark's collar.

They were in love with her, too, he realized. And that made it a hell of a mess.

He should have known better. He *had* known better. Somehow he'd let it happen anyway. Let himself slip, let himself fall. And he'd dragged his kids along with him.

Well, he'd have to fix it, wouldn't he? Mac got himself a beer, tipped the bottle back. He was good at fixing things.

"Ladies like wine," Zack informed him. "Like Aunt Mira does."

He remembered Nell had sipped white wine at Mira's party. "I don't have any," he muttered.

Because his father looked unhappy, Zack hugged Mac's leg. "You can buy some before she comes over next time."

Reaching down, Mac cupped his son's upturned face. The love was so strong, so vital, Mac could all but feel it grip him by the throat. "Always got an answer, don't you, pal?"

"You like her, don't you, Dad?"

"Yeah, she's nice."

"And she likes us, too, right?"

"Hey, who wouldn't like the Taylor guys?" He sat at the kitchen table, pulled Zack into his lap. He'd discovered when his sons were infants that there was nothing more magical than holding your own child. "Most of the time *I* even like you."

That made Zack giggle and cuddle closer. "She has to live all by herself, though." Zack began to play with the buttons of his father's shirt. A sure sign, Mac knew, that he was leading up to something.

"Lots of people live alone."

"We've got a big house, and two whole rooms nobody sleeps in except when Grandma and Pop come to visit."

His radar was humming. Mac tugged on his son's ear. "Zack, what are you getting at?"

"Nothing." Lip poked out, Zack toyed with another button. "I was just wondering what it would be like if she came and lived here." He peeked up under his lashes. "So she wouldn't be lonely."

"Nobody said she was lonely," Mac pointed out. "And I think you should—"

The doorbell rang, sending the dog into a fit of excited

barking and jingling. Zeke flew into the kitchen, dancing from foot to foot. "She's here! She's here!"

"I got the picture." Mac ruffled Zack's hair, set him on his feet. "Well, let her in. It's cold out."

"I'll do it!"

"*I'll* do it!"

The twins had a fierce race through the house to the front door. They hit it together, fought over the knob, then all but dragged Nell over the threshold once they'd yanked the door open.

"You took so long," Zeke complained. "We've been waiting forever. I put on Christmas music. Hear? And we've got the tree lit and everything."

"So I see." It was a lovely room, one she tried not to resent having only now been invited into.

She knew Mac had built most of the house himself. He'd told her that much. He'd created an open, homey space, with lots of wood, a glass-fronted fireplace where stockings were already hung. The tree, a six-foot blue spruce, was wildly decorated and placed with pride in front of the wide front window.

"It's terrific." Letting the boys pull her along, Nell crossed over to give the tree a closer look. "Really wonderful. It makes the little one in my apartment look scrawny."

"You can share ours." Zack looked up at her, his heart in his eyes. "We can get you a stocking and everything, and have your name put on it."

"They do it at the mall," Zeke told her. "We'll get you a big one."

Now they were pulling at her heart, as well as her hands. Filled with the emotion of the moment, she crouched down to hug them to her. "You guys are the best." She laughed as

Zark pushed in for attention. "You, too." Her arms full of kids and dog, she looked up to smile at Mac as he stepped in from the kitchen. "Hi. Sorry I took so long. Some of the kids hung around, wanting to go over every mistake and triumph of the concert."

She shouldn't look so right, so perfect, snuggling his boys under the tree. "I didn't hear any mistakes."

"They were there. But we'll work on them."

She scooted back, sitting on a hassock and taking both boys with her. As if, Mac thought, she meant to keep them.

"We don't have any wine," Zack informed her solemnly. "But we have milk and juice and sodas and beer. Lots of other things. Or…" He cast a crafty look in his father's direction. "Somebody could make hot cocoa."

"One of my specialties." Nell stood to shrug out of her coat. "Where's the kitchen?"

"I'll make it," Mac muttered.

"I'll help." Baffled by his sudden distance, she walked to him. "Or don't you like women in your kitchen?"

"We don't get many around here. You looked good up onstage."

"Thanks. It felt good being there."

He looked past her, into the wide, anticipation-filled eyes of his children. "Why don't you two go change into your pajamas? The cocoa'll be finished by the time you are."

"We'll be faster," Zeke vowed, and shot toward the stairs.

"Only if you throw your clothes on the floor. And don't." He turned back into the kitchen.

"Will they hang them up, or push them under the bed?" Nell asked.

"Zack'll hang them up and they'll fall on the floor. Zeke'll push them under the bed."

She laughed, watching him get out milk and cocoa. "I meant to tell you, a few days ago they came in with Kim to rehearsal. They'd switched sweaters—you know, the color code. I really impressed them when I knew who was who anyway."

He paused in the act of measuring cocoa into a pan. "How did you?"

"I guess I didn't think about it. They're each their own person. Facial expressions. You know how Zeke's eyes narrow and Zack looks under his lashes when they're pleased about something. Inflections in the voice." She opened a cupboard at random, looking for mugs. "Posture. There are all sorts of little clues if you pay attention and look closely enough. Ah, found them." Pleased with herself, she took out four mugs and set them on the counter. She tilted her head when she saw him studying her. Analytically, she thought. As if she were something to be measured and fit into place. "Is something wrong?"

"I wanted to talk to you." He busied himself with heating the cocoa.

"So you said." She found she needed to steady herself with a hand on the counter. "Mac, am I misreading something, or are you pulling back?"

"I don't know that I'd call it that."

Something was going to hurt. Nell braced for it. "What would you call it?" she said, as calmly as she could.

"I'm a little concerned about the boys. About the fallout when you move on. They're getting too involved." Why did that sound so stupid? he wondered. Why did he feel so stupid?

"*They* are?"

"I think we've been sending the wrong signals, and it would be best for them if we backed off." He concentrated on the cocoa as if it were a nuclear experiment. "We've gone out a few times, and we've…"

"Slept together," she finished, cool now. It was the last defense.

He looked around, sharply. But he could still hear the stomping of little feet in the room overhead. "Yeah. We've slept together, and it was great. The thing is, kids pick up on more things than most people think. And they get ideas. They get attached."

"And you don't want them to get attached to me." Yes, she realized. It was going to hurt. "You don't want to get attached."

"I just think it would be a mistake to take it any further."

"Clear enough. The No Trespassing signs are back up, and I'm out."

"It's not like that, Nell." He set the spoon down, took a step toward her. But there was a line he couldn't quite cross. A line he'd created himself. If he didn't make certain they both stayed on their own sides of it, the life he'd so carefully built could crumble. "I've got things under control here, and I need to keep them that way. I'm all they've got. They're all I've got. I can't mess that up."

"No explanations necessary." Her voice had thickened. In a moment, she knew, it would begin to shake. "You made it clear from the beginning. Crystal clear. Funny, the first time you invite me into your home, it's to toss me out."

"I'm not tossing you out, I'm trying to realign things."

"Oh, go to hell, and keep your realignments for your houses." She sprinted out of the kitchen.

"Nell, don't go like this." But by the time he reached the living room, she was grabbing her coat, and his boys were racing down the stairs.

"Where are you going, Miss Davis? You haven't—" Both boys stopped, shocked by the tears streaming down her face.

"I'm sorry." It was too late to hide them, so she kept heading for the door. "I have to do something. I'm sorry."

And she was gone, with Mac standing impotently in the living room and both boys staring at him. A dozen excuses spun around in his head. Even as he tried to grab one, Zack burst into tears.

"She went away. You made her cry, and she went away."

"I didn't mean to. She—" He moved to gather his sons up and was met with a solid wall of resistance.

"You ruined everything." A tear spilled out of Zeke's eyes, heated by temper. "We did everything we were supposed to, and you ruined it."

"She'll never come back." Zack sat on the bottom step and sobbed. "She'll never be the mom now."

"What?" At his wit's end, Mac dragged his hand through his hair. "What are you two talking about?"

"You ruined it," Zeke said again.

"Look, Miss Davis and I had a…disagreement. People have disagreements. It's not the end of the world." He wished it didn't feel like the end of his world.

"Santa sent her." Zack rubbed his eyes with his fists. "He sent her, just like we asked him. And now she's gone."

"What do you mean, Santa sent her?" Determined, Mac sat on the steps. He pulled a reluctant Zack into his lap and tugged Zeke down to join them. "Miss Davis came from New York to teach music, not from the North Pole."

"We know that." Temper set aside, Zeke sought comfort, turning his face into his father's chest. "She came because we sent Santa a letter, months and months ago, so we'd be early and he'd have time."

"Have time for what?"

"To pick out the mom." On a shuddering sigh, Zack sniffed and looked up at his father. "We wanted someone nice, who smelled good and liked dogs and had yellow hair. And we asked, and she came. And you were supposed to marry her and make her the mom."

Mac let out a long breath and prayed for wisdom. "Why didn't you tell me you were thinking about having a mother?"

"Not *a* mom," Zeke told him. "*The* mom. Miss Davis is the mom, but she's gone now. We love her, and she won't like us anymore because you made her cry."

"Of course she'll still like you." She'd hate him, but she wouldn't take it out on the boys. "But you two are old enough to know you don't get moms from Santa."

"He sent her, just like we asked him. We didn't ask for anything else but the bikes." Zack burrowed into his lap. "We didn't ask for any toys or any games. Just the mom. Make her come back, Dad. Fix it. You always fix it."

"It doesn't work like that, pal. People aren't broken toys or old houses. Santa didn't send her, she moved here for a job."

"He did, too, send her." With surprising dignity, Zack pushed off his father's lap. "Maybe you don't want her, but we do."

His sons walked up the stairs, a united front that closed him out. Mac was left with emptiness in the pit of his stomach and the smell of burned cocoa.

Ten

She should get out of town for a few days, Nell thought. Go somewhere. Go anywhere. There was nothing more pathetic than sitting alone on Christmas Eve and watching other people bustle along the street outside your window.

She'd turned down every holiday party invitation, made excuses that sounded hollow even to her. She was brooding, she admitted, and it was entirely unlike her. But then again, she'd never had a broken heart to nurse before.

With Bob it had been wounded pride. And that had healed itself with embarrassing speed.

Now she was left with bleeding emotions at the time of year when love was most important.

She missed him. Oh, she hated to know that she missed him. That slow, hesitant smile, the quiet voice, the gentleness of him. In New York, at least, she could have lost herself in the crowds, in the rush. But here, everywhere she looked was another reminder.

Go somewhere, Nell. Just get in the car and drive.

She ached to see the children. Wondered if they'd taken their sleds out in the fresh snow that had fallen yesterday. Were they counting the hours until Christmas, plotting to stay awake until they heard reindeer on the roof?

She had presents for them, wrapped and under her tree. She'd send them via Kim or Mira, she thought, and was miserable all over again because she wouldn't see their faces as they tore off the wrappings.

They're not your children, she reminded herself. On that point Mac had always been clear. Sharing himself had been difficult enough. Sharing his children had stopped him dead.

She would go away, she decided, and forced herself to move. She would pack a bag, toss it in the car and drive until she felt like stopping. She'd take a couple of days. Hell, she'd take a week. She couldn't bear to stay here alone through the holidays.

For the next ten minutes, she tossed things into a suitcase without any plan or sense of order. Now that the decision was made, she only wanted to move quickly. She closed the lid on the suitcase, carried it into the living room and started for her coat.

The knock on her door had her clenching her teeth. If one more well-meaning neighbor stopped by to wish her Merry Christmas and invite her to dinner, she was going to scream.

She opened the door and felt the fresh wound stab through her. "Well, Macauley… Out wishing your tenants happy holidays?"

"Can I come in?"

"Why?"

"Nell." There was a wealth of patience in the word. "Please, let me come in."

"Fine, you own the place." She turned her back on him. "Sorry, I haven't any wassail, and I'm very low on good cheer."

"I need to talk to you." He'd been trying to find the right way and the right words for days.

"Really? Excuse me if I don't welcome it. The last time you needed to talk to me is still firmly etched in my mind."

"I didn't mean to make you cry."

"I cry easily. You should see me after a greeting-card commercial on TV." She couldn't keep up the snide comments, and she gave in, asking the question that was uppermost in her mind. "How are the kids?"

"Barely speaking to me." At her blank look, he gestured toward the couch. "Will you sit down? This is kind of a complicated story."

"I'll stand. I don't have a lot of time, actually. I was just leaving."

His gaze followed hers and landed on the suitcase. His mouth tightened. "Well, it didn't take long."

"What didn't?"

"I guess you took them up on that offer to teach back in New York."

"Word does travel. No, I didn't take them up. I like my job here, I like the people here, and I intend to stay. I'm just going on a holiday."

"You're going on a holiday at five o'clock on Christmas Eve?"

"I can come and go as I please. No, don't take off your coat," she snapped. Tears were threatening. "Just say your piece and get out. I still pay the rent here. On second thought, just leave now. Damn it, you're not going to make me cry again."

"The boys think Santa sent you."

"Excuse me?"

As the first tear spilled over, he moved to her, brushed it away with his thumb. "Don't cry, Nell. I hate knowing I made you cry."

"Don't touch me." She whirled away and fumbled a tissue out of the box.

He was discovering exactly how it felt to be sliced in two. "I'm sorry." Slowly he lowered his hand to his side. "I know how you must feel about me now."

"You don't know the half of it." She blew her nose, struggled for control. "What's this about the boys and Santa?"

"They wrote a letter back in the fall, not long before they met you. They decided they wanted a mom for Christmas. Not *a* mom," Mac explained as she turned back to stare at him. "*The* mom. They keep correcting me on that one. They had pretty specific ideas about what they wanted. She was supposed to have yellow hair and smile a lot, like kids and dogs and bake cookies. They wanted bikes, too, but that was sort of an afterthought. All they really wanted was the mom."

"Oh." She did sit now, lowering herself onto the arm of the sofa. "That explains a couple of things." Steadying herself, she looked back at him. "Put you in quite a spot, didn't it? I know you love them, Mac, but starting a relationship with me to try to please your children takes things beyond parental devotion."

"I didn't know. Damn it, do you think I'd play with their feelings, or yours, that way?"

"Not theirs," she said hollowly. "Certainly not theirs."

He remembered how delicate she had seemed when they made love. There was more fragility now. No roses in her cheeks, he saw with a pang of distress. No light in her eyes. "I know what it's like to be hurt, Nell. I never would have hurt you deliberately. They didn't tell me about the letter until the night... You weren't the only one I made cry that night. I tried to explain that Santa doesn't work that way, but they've got it fixed in their heads that he sent you."

"I'll talk to them if you want me to."

"I don't deserve—"

"Not for you," she said. "For them."

He nodded, accepting. "I wondered how it would make you feel to know they wished for you."

"Don't push me, Mac."

He couldn't help it, and he kept his eyes on hers as he moved closer. "They wished for you for me, too. That's why they didn't tell me. You were our Christmas present." He reached down, touched her hair. "How does that make you feel?"

"How do you think I feel?" She batted his hand away and rose to face the window. "It hurts. I fell in love with the three of you almost from the first glance, and it hurts. Go away, leave me alone."

Somehow a fist had crept into his chest and was squeezing at his heart. "I thought you'd go away. I thought you'd leave us alone. I wouldn't let myself believe you cared enough to stay."

"Then you were an idiot," she mumbled.

"I was clumsy." He watched the tiny lights on her tree shining in her hair and gave up any thought of saving himself. "All right, I was an idiot. The worst kind, because I kept hiding from what you might feel, from what I felt. I didn't fall in love with you right away. At least I didn't know it. Not until the night of the concert. I wanted to tell you. I didn't know how to tell you. Then I heard something about the New York offer and it was the perfect excuse to push you out. I thought I was protecting the kids from getting hurt." No, he wouldn't use them, he thought in disgust. Not even to get her back. "That was only part of it. I was protecting myself. I couldn't control the way I felt about you. It scared me."

"Now's no different from then, Mac."

"It could be different." He took a chance and laid his hands on her shoulders, turned her to face him. "It took my own sons to show me that sometimes you've just got to wish. Don't leave me, Nell. Don't leave us."

"I was never going anywhere."

"Forgive me." She started to turn her head away, but he cupped her cheek, held it gently. "Please. Maybe I can't fix this, but give me a chance to try. I need you in my life. We need you."

There was such patience in his voice, such quiet strength in the hand on her face. Even as she looked at him, her heart began to heal. "I love you. All of you. I can't help it."

Relief and gratitude flavored the kiss as he touched his lips to hers. "I love you. I don't want to help it." Drawing her close, he cradled her head on his shoulder. "It's just been the three of us for so long, I didn't know how to make room. I think I'm figuring it out." He eased her away again and reached into his coat pocket. "I bought you a present."

"Mac." Still staggered from the roller-coaster emotions, she rubbed her hands over her damp cheeks. "It isn't Christmas yet."

"Close enough. I think if you'd open it now, I'd stop having all this tightness in my chest."

"All right." She dashed another tear aside. "We'll consider it a peace offering, then. I may even decide to…" She trailed off when the box was open in her hand. A ring, the traditional single diamond crowning a gold band.

"Marry me, Nell," he said quietly. "Be the mom."

She raised dazzled eyes to his. "You move awfully quickly for someone who always seems to take his time."

"Christmas Eve." He watched her face as he took the ring out of the box. "It seemed like the night to push my luck."

"It was a good choice." Smiling, she held out her hand. "A very good choice." When the ring was on her finger, she lifted her hand to his cheek. "When?"

He should have known it would be simple. With her, it would always be simple. "New Year's Eve's only a week away. It would be a good start to a new year. A new life."

"Yes."

"Will you come home with me tonight? I left the kids at Mira's. We could pick them up, and you'd spend Christmas where you belong." Before she could answer, he smiled and kissed her hand. "You're already packed."

"So I am. It must be magic."

"I'm beginning to believe it." He framed her face with his hands, lowered his mouth for a long, lingering kiss. "Maybe I didn't wish for you, but you're all I want for Christmas, Nell."

He rubbed his cheek over her hair, looked out at the colored lights gleaming on the houses below. "Did you hear something?" he murmured.

"Mmm…" She held him close, smiled. "Sleigh bells."

★ ★ ★ ★ ★

First Impressions

To Georgeann, neighbor and friend

One

The morning sun shot shafts of light over the mountains. It picked up the hints of red and gold among the deep green leaves and had them glowing. From somewhere in the woods came a rustling as a rabbit darted back to its burrow, while overhead a bird chirped with an insistent cheerfulness. Clinging to the line of fences along the road were clumps of honeysuckle. The light scent from the few lingering blossoms wafted in the air. In a distant field a farmer and his son harvested the last of the summer hay. The rumble of the baler was steady and distinct.

Over the mile trek to town only one car passed. Its driver lifted his hand in a salute. Shane waved back. It was good to be home.

Walking on the grassy shoulder of the road, she plucked a blossom of honeysuckle and, as she had as a child, drew in the fleetingly sweet aroma. When she crushed the flower between her fingers, its fragrance briefly intensified. It was a scent she associated with summer, like barbecue smoke and new grass. But this was summer's end.

Shane looked forward to fall eagerly, when the mountains would be at their best. Then the colors were breathtaking and the air was clean and crisp. When the wind came, the world would be full of sound and flying leaves. It was the time of woodsmoke and fallen acorns.

Curiously, she felt as though she'd never been away. She might still have been twenty-one, walking from her grandmother's to Sharpsburg to buy a gallon of milk or a loaf of bread. The busy Baltimore streets, the sidewalks and crowds of the last four years might have been a dream. She might never have spent those four years teaching in an inner-city school, correcting exams and attending faculty meetings.

Yet four years had passed. Her grandmother's narrow two-story house was now Shane's. The uneven, wooded three acres of land were hers as well. And while the mountains and woods were the same, Shane was not.

Physically, she looked almost as she had when she had left western Maryland for the job in a Baltimore high school. She was small in height and frame, with a slender figure that had never developed the curves and roundness she'd hoped for. Her face was subtly triangular with its creamy skin touched with warm color. It had been called peaches and cream often enough to make Shane wince. There were dimples that flashed when she smiled, rather than the elegant cheekbones she had wished for. Her nose was small, dusted with freckles, tilted up at the end. Pert. Shane had suffered the word throughout her life.

Under thin arched brows, her eyes were large and dark.

Whatever emotion she felt was mirrored in them. They were rarely cool. Habitually, she wore her hair short, and it curled naturally to frame her face in a deep honey blond. As her temperament was almost invariably happy, her face was usually animated, her small, sculpted mouth tilted up. The adjective used most to describe her was *cute*. Shane had grown to detest the word, but lived with it. Nothing could be done to alter sharp, vital attractiveness into sultry beauty.

As she rounded the last curve in the road before coming into town, she had a sudden flash of having done so before—as a child, as a teenager, as a girl on the brink of womanhood. It gave her a sense of security and belonging. Nothing in the city had ever given her the simple pleasure of being part of the whole.

Laughing, she took the final yards at a run, then burst through the door of the general store. The bells jingled fiercely before it slammed shut.

"Hi!"

"Hi, yourself." The woman behind the counter grinned at her. "You're out early this morning."

"When I woke up, I discovered I was out of coffee." Spotting the box of fresh doughnuts on the counter, Shane rolled her eyes and headed for them. "Oh, Donna, cream filled?"

"Yeah." Donna watched with an envious sigh as Shane chose one and bit into it. For the better part of twenty years, she'd seen Shane eat like a linebacker without gaining an ounce of fat.

Though they had grown up together, they were as different as night and day. Where Shane was fair, Donna was dark. Shane was small; Donna was tall and well rounded. For most of their lives, Donna had been content to play follower to

Shane's leader. Shane was the adventurer. Donna had liked nothing better than to point out all the flaws in whatever plans she was hatching, then wholeheartedly fall in with it.

"So, how are you settling in?"

"Pretty well," Shane answered with her mouth full.

"You've hardly been in since you got back in town."

"There's been so much to do. Gran couldn't keep the place up the last few years." Both affection and grief came through in her voice. "She was always more interested in her garden-ing than a leaky roof. Maybe if I had stayed—"

"Oh, now don't start blaming yourself again." Donna cut her off, drawing her straight dark brows together. "You know she wanted you to take that teaching job. Faye Abbott lived to be ninety-four. That's more than a lot of people can hope for. And she was a feisty old devil right to the end."

Shane laughed. "You're absolutely right. Sometimes I'm sure she's sitting in her kitchen rocker making certain I wash up my dishes at night." The thought made her want to sigh for the childhood that was gone, but she pushed the mood away. "I saw Amos Messner out in the field with his son haying." After finishing off the doughnut, Shane dusted her hands on the seat of her pants. "I thought Bob was in the army."

"Got discharged last week. He's going to marry a girl he met in North Carolina."

"No kidding?"

Donna smiled smugly. It always pleased her, as proprietor of the general store, to be the ears and eyes of the town. "She's coming to visit next month. She's a legal secretary."

"How old is she?" Shane demanded, testing.

"Twenty-two."

Throwing back her head, Shane laughed in delight. "Oh, Donna, you're terrific. I feel as though I've never been away."

The familiar unrestricted laugh made Donna grin. "I'm glad you're back. We missed you."

Shane settled a hip against the counter. "Where's Benji?"

"Dave's got him upstairs." Donna preened a bit, thinking of her husband and son. "Letting that little devil loose down here's only asking for trouble. We'll switch off after lunch."

"That's the beauty of living on top of your business."

Finding the opening she had hoped for, Donna pounced on it. "Shane, are you still thinking about converting the house?"

"Not thinking," Shane corrected. "I'm going to do it." She hurried on, knowing what was about to follow. "There's always room for another small antique shop, and with the museum attached, it'll be distinctive."

"But it's such a risk," Donna pointed out. The excited gleam in Shane's eyes had her worrying all the more. She'd seen the same gleam before the beginning of any number of outrageous and wonderful plots. "The expense—"

"I have enough to set things up." Shane shrugged off the pessimism. "And most of my stock can come straight out of the house for now. I want to do it, Donna," she went on as her friend frowned at her. "My own place, my own business." She glanced around the compact, well-stocked store. "You should know what I mean."

"Yes, but I have Dave to help out, to lean on. I don't think I could face starting or managing a business all on my own."

"It's going to work." Her eyes drifted beyond Donna, fixed on their own vision. "I can already see how it's going to look when I'm finished."

"All the remodeling."

"The basic structure of the house will stay the same," Shane countered. "Modifications, repairs." She brushed them away with the back of her hand. "A great deal of it would have to be done if I were simply going to live there."

"Licenses, permits."

"I've applied for everything."

"Taxes."

"I've already seen an accountant." She grinned as Donna sighed. "I have a good location, a solid knowledge of antiques, and I can re-create every battle of the Civil War."

"And do at the least provocation."

"Be careful," Shane warned her, "or I'll give you another rundown on the Battle of Antietam."

When the bells on the door jingled again, Donna heaved an exaggerated sigh of relief. "Hi, Stu."

The next ten minutes were spent in light gossiping as Donna rang up and bagged dry goods. It would take little time to catch up on the news Shane had missed over the last four years.

Shane was accepted as an oddity—the hometown girl who had gone to the city and come back with big ideas. She knew that to the older residents of the town and countryside she would always be Faye Abbott's granddaughter. They were a proprietary people, and she was one of their own. She hadn't settled down and married Cy Trainer's boy as predicted, but she was back now.

"Stu never changes," Donna said when she was alone with Shane again. "Remember in high school when we were sophomores and he was a senior, captain of the football team and the best-looking hunk in a sweaty jersey?"

"And nothing much upstairs," Shane added dryly.

"You always did go for the intellectual type. Hey," she continued before Shane could retort, "I might just have one for you."

"Have one what?"

"An intellectual. At least that's how he strikes me. He's your neighbor too," she added with a growing smile.

"*My* neighbor?"

"He bought the old Farley place. Moved in early last week."

"The Farley place?" Shane's brows arched, giving Donna the satisfaction of knowing she was announcing fresh news. "The house was all but gutted by the fire. Who'd be fool enough to buy that ramshackle barn of a place?"

"Vance Banning," Donna told her. "He's from Washington, D.C."

After considering the implications of this, Shane shrugged. "Well, I suppose it's a choice piece of land even if the house should be condemned." Wandering to a shelf, she selected a pound can of coffee then set it on the counter without checking the price. "I guess he bought it for a tax shelter or something."

"I don't think so." Donna rang up the coffee and waited while Shane dug bills out of her back pocket. "He's fixing it up."

"The courageous type." Absently, she pocketed the loose change.

"All by himself too," Donna added, fussing with the display of candy bars on the counter. "I don't think he has a lot of money to spare. No job."

"Oh." Shane's sympathies were immediately aroused. The

spreading problem of unemployment could hit anyone, she knew. Just the year before, the teaching staff at her school had been cut by three percent.

"I heard he's pretty handy though," Donna went on. "Archie Moler went by there a few days ago to take him some lumber. He said he's already replaced the old porch. But the guy's got practically no furniture. Boxes of books, but not much else." Shane was already wondering what she could spare from her own collection. She had a few extra chairs... "And," Donna added warmly, "he's wonderful to look at."

"You're a married woman," Shane reminded her, clucking her tongue.

"I still like to look. He's tall." Donna sighed. At five foot eight, she appreciated tall men. "And dark with a sort of lived-in face. You know, creases, lots of bone. And shoulders."

"You always did go for shoulders."

Donna only grinned. "He's a little lean for my taste, but the face makes up for it. He keeps to himself, hardly says a word."

"It's hard being a stranger." She spoke from her own experience. "And being out of work too. What do you think—"

Her question was cut off by the jingle of bells. Glancing over, Shane forgot what she had been about to ask.

He was tall, as Donna had said. In the few seconds they stared at each other, Shane absorbed every aspect of his physical appearance. Lean, yes, but his shoulders were broad, and the arms exposed by the rolled-up shirtsleeves were corded with muscle. His face was tanned, and it narrowed down to a trim, clipped jaw. Thick and straight, his black hair fell carelessly over a high forehead.

His mouth was beautiful. It was full and sharply sculpted, but she knew instinctively it could be cruel. And his eyes, a clear deep blue, were cool. She was certain they could turn to ice. She wouldn't have called it a lived-in face, but a remote one. There was an air of arrogant distance about him. Aloofness seemed to vie with an inner charge of energy.

The spontaneous physical pull was unexpected. In the past, Shane had been attracted to easygoing, good-natured men. This man was neither, she knew, but what she felt was undeniable. For a flash, all that was inside her leaned toward him in a knowledge that was as basic as chemistry and as insubstantial as dreams. Five seconds, it could have been no longer. It didn't need to be.

Shane smiled. He gave her the briefest of acknowledging nods, then walked to the back of the store.

"So, how soon do you think you'll have the place ready to open?" Donna asked Shane brightly with one eye trained toward the rear of the store.

"What?" Shane's mind was still on the man.

"Your place," Donna said meaningfully.

"Oh, three months, I suppose." She glanced blankly around the store as if she had just come in. "There's a lot of work to do."

He came back with a quart of milk and set it on the counter, then reached for his wallet. Donna rang it up, shooting Shane a look from under her lashes before she gave him his change. He left the store without having spoken a word.

"That," Donna announced grandly, "was Vance Banning."

"Yes." Shane exhaled. "So I gathered."

"You see what I mean. Great to look at, but not exactly the friendly sort."

"No." Shane walked toward the door. "I'll see you later, Donna."

"Shane!" With a half laugh, Donna called after her. "You forgot your coffee."

"Hmm? Oh, no thanks," she murmured absently. "I'll have a cup later."

When the door swung shut, Donna stared at it, then at the can of coffee in her hand. "Now what got into her?" she wondered aloud.

As she walked home, Shane felt confused. Though emotional by nature, she could, when necessary, be very analytical. At the moment, she was dealing with the shock of what had happened to her in a few fleeting seconds. It had been much more than a feminine response to an attractive man.

She had felt, inexplicably, as though her whole life had been a waiting period for that quick, silent meeting. Recognition. The word came to her out of nowhere. She had recognized him, not from Donna's description, but from some deep inner knowledge of her own needs. *This was the man.*

Ridiculous, she told herself. Idiotic. She didn't know him, hadn't even heard him speak. No sensible person felt so strongly about a total stranger. More likely, her response had stemmed from the fact that she and Donna had been speaking of him as he had walked in.

Turning off the main road, she began to climb the steep lane that led to her house. He certainly hadn't been friendly, she thought. He hadn't answered her smile or made the slightest attempt at common courtesy. Something in the cool blue eyes had demanded distance. Shane didn't think he was the kind of man she usually liked. Then again, her reaction had been far removed from the calm emotion of liking.

As always when she saw the house, Shane felt a rush of pleasure. This was hers. The woods, thick and touched with the first breath of autumn; the narrow struggling creek; the rocks that worked their way through the ground every-where—they were all hers.

Shane stood on the wooden bridge over the creek and looked at the house. It did need work. Some of the boards on the porch needed replacing, and the roof was a big problem. Still, it was a lovely little place, nestled comfortably before woods, rolling hills and distant blue mountains. It was more than a century old, fashioned from local stone. In the rain, the colors would burst out of the old rock and gleam like new. Now, in the sunlight, it was comfortably gray.

The architecture was simple—straight lines for durability rather than style. The walkway ran to the porch, where the first step sagged a bit. Shane's problem wouldn't be with the stone but with the wood. She overlooked the rough edges to take in the beauty of the familiar.

The last of the summer flowers were fading. The roses were brown and withered, while the first fall blooms were coming to life. Shane could hear the hiss of water traveling over rocks, the faint whisper of wind through leaves, and the lazy drone of bees.

Her grandmother had guarded her privacy. Shane could turn a full circle without seeing a sign of another house. She had only to walk a quarter mile if she wanted company, or stay at home if she didn't. After four years of crowded class-rooms and daily confinement, Shane was ready for solitude.

And with luck, she thought as she continued walking, she could have her shop open and ready for business before Christmas. Antietam Antiques and Museum. Very dignified and to the point, she decided. Once the outside repairs were accomplished, work could start on the interior. The picture was clear in her mind.

The first floor would be structured in two informal sections. The museum would be free, an inducement to lure people into the antique shop. Shane had enough from her family collection to begin stocking the museum, and six rooms of antique furniture to sort and list. She would have to go to a few auctions and estate sales to increase her inventory, but she felt her inheritance and savings would hold her for a while.

The house and land were hers free and clear, with only the yearly taxes to pay. Her car, for what it was worth, was paid for. Every spare penny could go into her projected business. She was going to be successful and independent—and the last was more important than the first.

As she walked toward the house, Shane paused and glanced down the overgrown logging trail, which led to the Farley property. She was curious to see what this Vance Banning was doing with the old place. And, she admitted, she wanted to see him again when she was prepared.

After all, they were going to be neighbors, she told herself as she hesitated. The least she could do was to introduce herself and start things off on the right foot. Shane set off into the woods.

She knew the trees intimately. Since childhood she had raced or walked among them. Some had fallen and lay aging and rotting on the ground among layers of old leaves. Overhead, branches arched together to form an intermittent roof pierced by streams of morning sunlight. Confidently she followed the narrow, winding path. She was still yards from the house when she heard the muffled echo of hammering.

Though it disturbed the stillness of the woods, Shane liked the sound. It meant work and progress. Quickening her pace, she headed toward it.

She was still in the cover of the trees when she saw him. He stood on the newly built porch of the old Farley place, hammering the supports for the railing. He'd stripped off his shirt, and his brown skin glistened with a light film of sweat. The dark hair on his chest tapered down, then disappeared into the waistband of worn, snug jeans.

As he lifted the heavy top rail into place, the muscles of his back and shoulders rippled. Totally intent on his work, Vance was unaware of the woman who stood at the edge of the woods and watched. For all his physical exertion, he was relaxed. There was no hardness around his mouth now or frost in his eyes.

When she stepped into the clearing, Vance's head shot up. His eyes instantly filled with annoyance and suspicion. Overlooking it, Shane went to him.

"Hi." Her quick friendly smile had her dimples flashing. "I'm Shane Abbott. I own the house at the other end of the path."

His brow lifted in acknowledgment as he watched her. What the hell does she want? he wondered, and set his hammer on the rail.

Shane smiled again, then took a long, thorough look at the house. "You've got your work cut out for you," she commented amiably, sticking her hands into the back pockets of her jeans. "Such a big place. They say it was beautiful once. I think there used to be a balcony around the second story."

She glanced up. "It's a shame the fire did so much damage to the inside—and then all the years of neglect." She looked at him then with dark, interested eyes. "Are you a carpenter?"

Vance hesitated briefly, then shrugged. It was close to the truth. "Yes."

"That's handy then." Shane accepted the answer, attributing his hesitation to embarrassment at being out of work. "After D.C. you must find the mountains a change." His mobile brow lifted again and Shane grinned. "I'm sorry. It's the curse of small towns. Word gets around quickly, especially when a flatlander moves in."

"Flatlander?" Vance leaned against the post of the railing.

"You're from the city, so that's what you are." She laughed, a quick bubbling sound. "If you stay for twenty years, you'll still be a flatlander, and this will always be the old Farley place."

"It hardly matters what it's called," he said coldly.

The faintest of frowns shadowed her eyes at his response. Looking at the proud, set face, Shane decided he would never accept open charity. "I'm doing some work on my place too," she began. "My grandmother loved clutter. I don't suppose you could use a couple of chairs? I'm going to have to haul them up to the attic unless someone takes them off my hands."

His eyes stayed level on hers with no change of expression. "I have all I need for now."

Because it was the answer she had expected, Shane treated it lightly. "If you change your mind, they'll be gathering dust in the attic. You've got a good piece of land," she commented, gazing over at the section of pasture in the distance. There were several outbuildings, though most were in desperate need of repair. She wondered if he would see to them before winter set in. "Are you going to have livestock?"

Vance frowned, watching her eyes roam over his property. "Why?"

The question was cold and unfriendly. Shane tried to overlook that. "I can remember when I was a kid, before the fire. I used to lie in bed at night in the summer with the windows open. I could hear the Farley cows as clearly as if they were in my grandmother's garden. It was nice."

"I don't have any plans for livestock," he told her shortly, and picked up his hammer again. The gesture of dismissal was crystal clear.

Puzzled, Shane studied him. Not shy, she concluded. Rude. He was plainly and simply rude. "I'm sorry I disturbed your work," she said coolly. "Since you're a flatlander, I'll give you some advice. You should post your property lines if you don't want trespassers."

Indignantly, Shane strode back to the path to disappear among the trees.

Two

Little twit, Vance thought as he gently tapped the hammer against his palm. He knew he'd been rude, but felt no particular regret. He hadn't bought an isolated plot of land on the outskirts of a dot on the map because he wanted to entertain. Company he could do without, particularly the blond cheerleader type with big brown eyes and dimples.

What the hell had she been after? he wondered as he drew a nail from the pouch on his hip. A cozy chat? A tour of the house? He gave a quick, mirthless laugh. Very neighborly. Vance pounded the nail through the wood in three sure strokes. He didn't want neighbors. What he wanted, what he intended to have, was time to himself. It had been too many years since he had taken that luxury.

Drawing another nail out of the pouch, he moved down the rail. He set it, then hammered it swiftly into place. In particular, he hadn't cared for the one moment of attraction he had felt when he had seen her in the general store. Women, he thought grimly, had an uncanny habit of taking advantage of a weakness like that. He didn't intend for it to happen to him again. He had plenty of scars to remind him what went on behind big, guileless eyes.

So now I'm a carpenter, he mused. With a sardonic grin, Vance turned his hands palms up and examined them. They were hard and calloused. For too many years, he mused, they had been smooth, used to signing contracts or writing checks. Now for a time, he was back where he had started—with wood. Yes, until he was ready to sit behind a desk again, he was a carpenter.

The house, and the very fact that it was falling to pieces, gave him the sense of purpose that had slipped from him over the last couple of years. He understood pressure, success, duty, but the meaning of simple enjoyment had become lost somewhere beneath the rest.

Let the vice-president of Riverton Construction, Inc., run the show for a few months, he mused. He was on vacation. And let the little blonde with her puppy-dog eyes keep on her own land, he added, pounding in another nail. He didn't want any part of the good-neighbor policy.

When he heard leaves rustling underfoot, Vance turned. Seeing Shane striding back up the path, he muttered a long stream of curses in a low voice. With the exaggerated care of a man greatly aggravated, he set down his hammer.

"Well?" He aimed cold blue eyes and waited.

Shane didn't pause until she had reached the foot of the steps. She was through being intimidated. "I realize you're *extremely* busy," she began, matching his coolness ice for ice, "but I thought you might be interested in knowing there's a nest of copperheads very close to the footpath. On *your* edge of the property," she added.

Vance gave her a narrowed glance, weighing the possibility of her fabricating the snakes to annoy him. She didn't budge under the scrutiny, but paused just long enough to let the silence hang before she turned. She'd gone no more than two more yards when Vance let out an impatient breath and called her back.

"Just a minute. You'll have to show me."

"I don't *have* to do anything," Shane began, but found herself impotently talking to the swinging screen door. Briefly, she wished that she'd never seen the nest, or had simply ignored it and continued down the path to her own home. Then, of course, if he'd been bitten, she would have blamed herself.

Well, you'll do your good deed, she told herself, and that will be that. She kicked a rock with the toe of her shoe and thought how simple it would have been if she'd stayed home that morning.

The screen door shut with a bang. Looking up, Shane watched Vance come down the steps with a well-oiled rifle in his hands. The sleek, elegant weapon suited him. "Let's go," he said shortly, starting off without her. Gritting her teeth, Shane followed.

The light dappled over them once they moved under the cover of trees. The scent of earth and sun-warmed leaves warred with the gun oil. Without a word, Shane skirted around him to take the lead. Pausing, she pointed to a pile of rocks and brown, dried leaves.

"There."

After taking a step closer, Vance spotted the hourglass-shaped crossbands on the snakes. If she hadn't shown him the exact spot, he never would have noticed the nest...unless, of course, he'd stepped right on it. An unpleasant thought, he mused, calculating its proximity to the footpath. Shane said nothing, watching as he found a thick stick and overturned the rocks. Immediately the hissing sounded.

With her eyes trained on the angry snakes, she didn't see Vance heft the rifle to his shoulder. The first shot jolted her. Her heart hammered during the ensuing four, her eyes riveted to the scene.

"That should do it," Vance muttered, lowering the gun. After switching on the safety, he turned to Shane. She'd turned a light shade of green. "What's the matter?"

"You might have warned me," she said shakily. "I wish I'd looked away."

Vance glanced back to the gruesome mess on the side of the path. That, he told himself grimly, had been incredibly stupid. Silently, he cursed her, then himself, before he took her arm.

"Come back and sit down."

"I'll be all right in a minute." Embarrassed and annoyed, Shane tried to pull away. "I don't want your gracious hospitality."

"I don't want you fainting on my land," he returned, drawing her into the clearing. "You didn't have to stay once you'd shown me the nest."

"Oh, you're very welcome," she managed as she placed a hand on her rolling stomach. "You are the most ill-mannered, unfriendly man I've ever met."

"And I thought I was on my best behavior," he murmured,

opening the screen door. After pulling Shane inside, Vance led her through the huge empty room toward the kitchen.

After a glance at the dingy walls and uncovered floor, Shane sent him what passed as a smile. "You must give me the name of your decorator."

She thought he laughed, but could have been mistaken.

The kitchen, in direct contrast to the rest of the house, was bright and clean. The walls had been papered, the counters and cabinets refinished.

"Well, this is nice," she said as he nudged her into a chair. "You do good work."

Without responding, Vance set a kettle on the stove. "I'll fix you some coffee."

"Thank you."

Shane concentrated on the kitchen, determined to forget what she'd just seen. The windows had been reframed, the wood stained and lacquered to match the grooved trim along the floor and ceiling. He had left the beams exposed and polished the wood to a dull gleam. The original oak floor had been sanded and sealed and waxed. Vance Banning knew how to use wood, Shane decided. The porch was basic mechanics, but the kitchen showed a sense of style and an appreciation for fine detail.

It seemed unfair to her that a man with such talent should be out of work. Shane concluded that he had used his savings to put a down payment on the property. Even if the house had sold cheaply, the land was prime. Remembering the barrenness of the rest of the first floor, she couldn't prevent her sympathies from being aroused again. Her eyes wandered to his.

"This really is a lovely room," she said, smiling. The faintest hint of color had seeped back into her cheeks. Vance turned his back to her to take a mug from a hook.

"You'll have to settle for instant," he told her.

Shane sighed. "Mr. Banning... Vance," she decided, and waited for him to turn. "Maybe we got off on the wrong foot. I'm not a nosy, prying neighbor—at least not obnoxiously so. I was curious to see what you were doing to the house and what you were like. I know everyone within three miles of here." With a shrug, she rose. "I didn't mean to bother you."

As she started to brush by him, Vance took her arm. Her skin was still chilled. "Sit down... Shane," he said.

For a moment, she studied his face. It was cool and unyielding, but she sensed some glimmer of suppressed kindness. In response to it, her eyes warmed. "I disguise my coffee with milk and sugar," she warned. "Three spoonsful."

A reluctant smile tugged at his mouth. "That's disgusting."

"Yes, I know. Do you have any?"

"On the counter."

Vance poured the boiling water, and after a moment's hesitation, took down a second mug for himself. Carrying them both, he joined Shane at the drop-leaf table.

"This really is a lovely piece." Before reaching for the milk, she ran her fingers over the table's surface. "Once it's refinished, you'll have a real gem." Shane added three generous spoons of sugar to her mug. Wincing a little, Vance sipped his own black coffee. "Do you know anything about antiques?"

"Not really."

"They're a passion of mine. In fact, I'm planning on opening a shop." Shane brushed absently at the hair that fell over her forehead, then leaned back. "As it turns out, we're both settling in at the same time. I've been living in Baltimore for the last four years, teaching U.S. history."

"You're giving up teaching?" Her hands, Vance noted, were small like the rest of her. The light trail of blue veins under the pale skin made her seem very delicate. Her wrists were narrow, her fingers slender.

"Too many rules and regulations," Shane claimed, gesturing with the hands that had captured his attention.

"You don't like rules and regulations?"

"Only when they're mine." Laughing, she shook her head. "I was a pretty good teacher, really. My problem was discipline." She gave him a rueful grin as she reached for her coffee. "I'm the worst disciplinarian on record."

"And your students took advantage of that?"

Shane rolled her eyes. "Whenever possible."

"But you stuck with it for four years?"

"I had to give it my best shot." Leaning her elbow on the table, Shane rested her chin on her palm. "Like a lot of people who grow up in a small, rural town, I thought the city was my pot of gold. Bright lights, crowds, hustle-bustle. I wanted excitement with a capital *E*. I had four years of it. That was enough." She picked up her coffee again. "Then there are people from the city who think their answer is to move to the country and raise a few goats and can some tomatoes." She laughed into her cup. "The grass is always greener."

"I've heard it said," he murmured, watching her. There were tiny gold flecks in her eyes. How had he missed them before?

"Why did you choose Sharpsburg?"

Vance shrugged negligently. Questions about himself were

to be evaded. "I've done some work in Hagerstown. I like the area."

"Living this far back from the main road can be inconvenient, especially in the winter, but I've never minded being snowed in. We lost power once for thirty-two hours. Gran and I kept the woodstove going, taking shifts, and we cooked soup on top of it. The phone lines were down too. We might have been the only two people in the world."

"You enjoyed that?"

"For thirty-two hours," she told him with a friendly grin. "I'm not a hermit. Some people are city people, some are beach people."

"And you're a mountain person."

Shane brought her eyes back to him. "Yes."

The smile she had started to give him never formed. Something in the meeting of their eyes was reminiscent of the moment in the store. It was only an echo, but somehow more disturbing. Shane understood it was bound to happen again and again. She needed time to decide just what she was going to do about it. Rising, she walked to the sink to rinse out her mug.

Intrigued by her reaction, Vance decided to test her. "You're a very attractive woman." He knew how to make his voice softly flattering.

Laughing, Shane turned back to him. "The perfect face for advertising granola bars, right?" Her smile was devilish and appealing. "I'd rather be sexy, but I settled for wholesome." She gave the word a pained emphasis as she came back to the table.

There was no guile in her manner or her expression. What, Vance wondered again, was her angle? Shane was involved in studying the details of the kitchen and didn't see him frown at her.

"I do admire your work." Inspired, she turned back to him. "Hey listen, I've got a lot of remodeling and renovating to do before I can open. I can paint and do some of the minor stuff myself, but there's a lot of carpentry work."

Here it is, Vance reflected coolly. What she wanted was some free labor. She would pull the helpless-female routine and count on his ego to take over.

"I have my own house to renovate," he reminded her coolly as he stood and turned toward the sink.

"Oh, I know you wouldn't be able to give me a lot of time, but we might be able to work something out." Excited by the idea, she followed him. Her thoughts were already racing ahead. "I wouldn't be able to pay what you could make in the city," she continued. "Maybe five dollars an hour. If you could manage ten or fifteen hours a week..." She chewed on her bottom lip. It seemed a paltry amount to offer, but it was all she could spare at the moment.

Incredulous, Vance turned off the water he had been running, then faced her. "Are you offering me a job?"

Shane flushed a bit, afraid she'd embarrassed him. "Well, only part-time, if you're interested. I know you can make more somewhere else, and if you find something, I wouldn't expect you to keep on, but in the meantime..." She trailed off, not certain how he would react to her knowing he was out of work.

"You're serious?" Vance demanded after a moment.

"Well...yes."

"Why?"

"I need a carpenter. You're a carpenter. There's a lot of

work. You might decide you don't want any part of it. But why don't you think about it, drop by tomorrow and take a look?" She turned to leave, but paused for an instant with her hand on the knob. "Thanks for the coffee."

For several minutes, Vance stared at the door she had closed behind her. Abruptly, he burst into deep, appreciative laughter. This, he thought, was one for the books.

Shane rose early the next morning. She had plans and was determined to begin systematically. Organization didn't come naturally to her. It was one more reason why teaching hadn't suited her. If she was to plan a business, however, Shane knew an inventory was a primary factor—what she had, what she could bear to sell, what she should pack away for the museum.

Having decided to start downstairs and work her way up, Shane stood in the center of the living room and took stock of the situation. There was a good Chippendale fireplace seat in mahogany and a gateleg table that needed no refinishing, a ladderback chair that needed new caning in the seat, a pair of Aladdin lamps, and a tufted sofa that would require upholstering. On a Sheridan coffee table was a porcelain pitcher, circa 1830, that held a spray of flowers Shane's grandmother had dried. She touched them once briefly before she picked up her clipboard. There was too much of her childhood there to allow herself the luxury of thinking of any of it. If her grandmother had been alive, she would have told Shane to be certain what she did was right, then do it. Shane was certain she was right.

Systematically, she listed items in two columns: one for items that would need repairs; one for stock she could sell as it was. Everything would have to be priced, which would be a huge job in itself. Already she was spending her evenings poring through catalogs and making notations. There wasn't an antique shop within a radius of thirty miles she hadn't visited. Shane had taken careful account of pricing and procedure. She would incorporate what appealed to her and disregard what didn't. Whatever else her shop would be, she was determined it would be her own.

On one wall of the living room was a catchall shelf that had been built before she'd been born. Moving to it, Shane began a fresh sheet of items she designated for the museum.

An ancestor's Civil War cap and belt buckle, a glass jar filled with spent shells, a dented bugle, a cavalry officer's sabre, a canteen with the initials JDA scratched into the metal—these were only a few pieces of the memorabilia that had been passed down to her. Shane knew there was a trunk in the attic filled with uniforms and old dresses. There was a scrawled journal that had been kept by one of her great-great-uncles during the three years he fought for the South, and letters written to an ancestral aunt by her father, who had served the North. Every item would be listed, dated, then put behind glass.

Shane might have inherited her grandmother's fascination for the relics of history, but not her casualness. It was time the old photos and objects came down from the shelf. But as always when she examined or handled the pieces, Shane became caught up in them.

What had the man been like who had first blown that bugle? It would have been shiny then, and undented. A boy, she thought, with peach fuzz on his face. Had he been frightened? Exhilarated? Fresh off the farm, she imagined, and sure his cause was the right one. Whichever side he had fought for, he had blown the bugle into battle.

With a sigh, she took it down and set it in a packing box. Carefully, Shane wrapped and packed until the shelves were clear, but for the highest one. Standing back, she calculated how she would reach the pieces that sat several feet above her head. Not bothering to move the heavy ladder from across the room, she dragged over a nearby chair. As she stood on the seat, a knock sounded at the back door.

"Yes, come in," she called, stretching one arm up while balancing herself with a hand on one of the lower shelves. She swore and muttered as her reach still fell short. Just as she stood on tiptoe, teetering, someone grabbed her arm. Gasping as she overbalanced, Shane found herself gripped firmly by Vance Banning. "You scared me to death!" she accused.

"Don't you know better than to use a chair like that?" He kept his hands firmly at her waist as he lifted her down. Then, though he'd had every intention of doing so, he didn't release her. There was a smudge of dust on her cheek, and her hair was tousled. Her small, narrow hands rested on his arms while she smiled up at him. Without thinking, Vance lowered his mouth to hers.

Shane didn't struggle, but felt a jolt of surprise. Then she relaxed. Though she hadn't expected the kiss then, she had known the time would come. She let the first stream of pure pleasure run its course.

His mouth was hard on hers, with no gentleness, no trace of what kissing meant to her—a gesture of affection, love or comfort. Yet instinct told her he was capable of tenderness. Lifting a hand to his cheek, Shane sought to soothe the tur-

bulence she sensed. Immediately, he released her. The touch
of her hand had been too intimate.

Something told Shane to treat it lightly no matter how
her body ached to be held again. Tilting her head, she gave
him a mischievous smile. "Good morning."

"Good morning," he said carefully.

"I'm taking inventory," she told him with a sweeping gesture of the room. "I want to list everything before I haul it
upstairs for storage. I plan to use this room for the museum
and the rest of the first floor for the shop. Could you get
those things off the top shelf for me?" she asked, looking
around for her clipboard.

In silence, Vance moved the ladder and complied. The
fact that she'd made no mention of the turbulent kiss disconcerted him.

"Most of the work will be gutting the kitchen and putting one in upstairs," Shane went on, giving her lists another
glance. She knew Vance was watching her for some sort of
reaction. She was just as determined to give him none. "Of
course, some walls will have to be taken out, doorways widened. But I don't want to lose the flavor of the house in the
remodeling."

"You seem to have it all plotted out." Was she really so
cool? he wondered.

"I hope so." Shane pressed the clipboard to her breasts as
she looked around the room. "I've applied for all the necessary permits. What a headache. I don't have any natural
business sense, so I'll have to work twice as hard learning.
It's a big chance." Then her voice changed, became firm and
determined. "I'm going to make it work."

"When do you plan to open?"

"I'm shooting for the first part of December, but..." Shane shrugged. "It depends on how the work goes and how soon I can beef up my inventory. I'll show you the rest of the place. Then you can decide if you want to take it on."

Without waiting for his consent, Shane walked to the rear of the house. "The kitchen's a fairly good size, particularly if you include the pantry." Opening a door, she revealed a large shelved closet. "Taking out the counters and appliances should give me plenty of room. Then if this doorway is widened," she continued as she pushed open a swinging door, "and left as an archway, it would give more space in the main showroom."

They entered the dining room with its long diamond-paned windows. She moved quickly, he noted, and knew precisely what she wanted.

"The fireplace hasn't been used in years. I don't know whether it still works." Walking over, Shane ran a finger down the surface of the dining table. "This was my grandmother's prize. It was brought over from England more than a hundred years ago." The cherrywood stroked by sunlight, gleamed under her fingers. "The chairs are from the original set. Hepplewhite." Shane caressed the heart-shaped back of one of the remaining six chairs. "I hate to sell this, she loved it so, but..." Her voice was wistful as she unnecessarily straightened a chair. "I won't have anywhere to keep it, and I can't afford the luxury of storing it for myself." Shane turned away. "The china cabinet is from the same period," she continued.

"You could keep this and leave the house as it is if you took a job in the local high school," Vance interrupted. There was something valiant and touching in the way she kept her shoulders straight while her voice trembled.

"No." Shane shook her head, then turned back to him. "I haven't the character for it. It wouldn't take long before I'd be cutting classes just like my students. They deserve a better example than that. I love history." Her face brightened again. "*This* kind of history," she said as she walked back to the table. "Who first sat in this chair? What did she talk about over dinner? What kind of dress did she wear? Did they discuss politics and the upstart colonies? Maybe one of them knew Ben Franklin and was a secret sympathizer of the Revolution." She broke off laughing. "That's not the sort of thing you're supposed to teach in second-period eleventh-grade history."

"It sounds more interesting than reciting names and dates."

"Maybe. Anyway, I'm not going back to that." Pausing, Shane watched Vance steadily. "Did you ever find yourself caught up in something you were good at, something you'd been certain was the right thing for you, then woke up one morning with the feeling you were locked in a cage?"

The words hit home, and he nodded affirmatively.

"Then you know why I have to choose between something I love and my sanity." She touched the table again. After a deep breath, Shane took a circle around the room. "I don't want to change the architecture of this room except for the doorways. My great-grandfather built the chair rail." She watched Vance walk over to examine it. "He was a mason by trade," she told him, "but he must have been handy with wood as well."

"It's a beautiful job," Vance agreed, admiring the workmanship and detail. "I'd have a hard time duplicating this quality with modern tools. You wouldn't want to touch this, or any of the woodwork in this room."

In spite of himself he was becoming interested in the project. It would be a challenge—a different sort than the house he had chosen to test himself on. Sensing his change of attitude, Shane pressed her advantage.

"There's a small summer parlor through there." Indicating another door, she took Vance's arm to draw him with her. "It adjoins the living room, so I plan to make it the entrance to the shop, with the dining room as the main showroom."

The parlor was no more than twelve by twelve with faded wallpaper and a scarred wooden floor. Still, Vance recognized a few good pieces of Duncan Phyfe and a Morris chair. On the brief tour, he had seen no furniture less than a hundred years old, and unless they were excellent copies, a few pieces of Wedgwood. The furniture's worth a small fortune, he mused, and the back door's coming off the hinges.

"There's a lot of work here," Shane commented, moving over to open a window and dispel the faint mustiness. "This room's taken a beating over the years. I suppose you'd have a better idea than I would exactly what it needs to whip it into shape."

She watched his frowning survey of chipped floorboards and cracked trim. It was obvious to her that his professional eye missed little. It was also obvious the state of disrepair annoyed him. And, she thought, faintly amused, he hadn't seen anything yet.

"Maybe I shouldn't press my luck and take you upstairs just yet," she commented.

A quizzical brow shot up as he turned to her. "Why?"

"Because the second floor needs twice the attention this does, and I really want you to take the job."

"You sure as hell need somebody to do it," he muttered. His own place needed a major overhaul. Heavy physical work and a lot of time. This, on the other hand, needed a shrewd craftsman who could work with what was already there. Again, he felt the pull of the challenge.

"Vance…" After a moment's hesitation, Shane decided to take a chance. "I could make it six dollars an hour, throw in your lunches and all the coffee you can drink. The people who come in here will see the quality of your work. It could lead to bigger jobs."

He surprised her by grinning. Her heart leaped into her throat. More than the tempestuous kiss, the quick boyish grin drew her to him.

"All right, Shane," Vance agreed on impulse. "You've got a deal."

Three

Pleased with herself and Vance's abrupt good humor, Shane decided to show him the second floor. Taking his hand, she led him up the straight, steep stairway. Though she had no notion of what had prompted the amused gleam or sudden grin, Shane wanted to keep him with her while his mood lasted.

Against his work-hardened hand, her palm was baby soft. It made Vance wonder how the rest of her would feel—the slope of her shoulder, the length of her thigh, the underside of her breast. She wasn't his type, he reminded himself, and glanced at the hairline crack in the wall to his left.

"There are three bedrooms," Shane told him as they came to the top landing. "I want to keep my own room, and turn the master into a sitting room and the third into my kitchen. I can handle the painting and papering after the initial work is done." With her hand on the knob of the master bedroom door, she turned to him. "Do you know anything about drywall?"

"A bit." Without thinking, Vance lifted a finger and ran it down her nose. Their eyes met in mutual surprise. "You've dust on your face," he mumbled.

"Oh." Laughing, Shane brushed at it herself.

"Here." Vance traced the rough skin of his thumb down her cheekbone. Her skin felt as it looked: soft, creamy. It would taste the same, he mused, allowing his thumb to linger. "And here," he said, caught up in his own imagination. Lightly he ran a fingertip along her jawline. He felt her slight tremor as his gaze swept over her lips.

Her eyes were wide and fixed unblinkingly on his. Abruptly, Vance dropped his hand, shattering the mood but not the tension. Clearing her throat, Shane pushed open the door.

"This—umm…" Frantically, Shane gathered her scattered thoughts. "This is the master," she continued, combing nervous fingers through her hair. "I know the floor's in bad shape, and I'd like to skin whoever painted that oak trim." She let out a long breath as her pulse began to level. "I'm going to see if it can be refinished." Idly, she touched a section of peeling wallpaper. "My grandmother didn't like changes. This room hasn't altered one bit in thirty years. That's when her husband died," she added softly. "The windows stick, the roof leaks, the fireplace smokes. Basically, the house, except for the dining room, is in a general state of disrepair. She never had the inclination to do more than a patch job here and there."

"When did she die?"

"Three months ago." Shane lifted a corner of the patchwork coverlet, then let it fall. "She just didn't wake up one morning. I was committed to teaching a summer course and couldn't move back permanently until last week."

Clearly, he heard the sting of guilt in her words. "Could you have changed anything if you had?" he asked.

"No." Shane wandered to a window. "But she wouldn't have died alone."

Vance opened his mouth, then closed it again. It wasn't wise to offer personal advice to strangers. Framed against the window, she looked very small and defenseless.

"What about the walls in here?" he asked.

"What?" Years and miles away, Shane turned back to him.

"The walls," he repeated. "Do you want any of them taken down?"

For a moment, she stared blankly at the faded roses on the wallpaper. "No... No," she repeated more firmly. "I'd thought to take out the door and enlarge the entrance." Vance nodded, noting she had won what must be a continuing battle with her emotions. "If the woodwork cleans off well," she continued, "the entrance could be framed in oak to match."

Vance walked over to examine it. "Is this a bearing wall?"

Shane made a face at him. "I haven't the slightest idea. How do—" She broke off, hearing a knock at the front door. "Damn. Well, can you look around up here for a few minutes? You'll probably get the lay of things just as well without me." With this, Shane was dashing down the steps. Shrugging, Vance took a rule out of his back pocket and began to take measurements.

Shane's instinctively friendly smile faded instantly when she opened the door.

"Shane."

"Cy."

His expression became faintly censorious. "Aren't you going to ask me in?"

"Of course." With a restraint unnatural to her, Shane stepped back. Very carefully, she shut the door behind him, but moved no farther into the room. "How are you, Cy?"

"Fine, just fine."

Of course he was, Shane thought, annoyed. Cy Trainer Jr., was always fine—permanent-pressed and groomed. And prosperous now, she added, giving his smart-but-discreet suit a glance.

"And you, Shane?"

"Fine, just fine," she said, knowing the sarcasm was both petty and wasted. He'd never notice.

"I'm sorry I didn't get by last week. Things have been hectic."

"Business is good?" she asked without any intonation of interest. He failed to notice that too.

"Money's loosening up." He straightened his tie unnecessarily. "People are buying houses. Country property's always a good investment." He gave her a quick nod. "The real estate business is solid."

Money was still first, Shane noticed with irony. "And your father?"

"Doing well. Semiretired now, you know."

"No," she said mildly. "I didn't." If Cy Trainer Sr. relinquished the reins to Trainer Real Estate six months after he was dead, it would have surprised Shane. The old man would always run the show, no matter what his son liked to think.

"He likes to keep busy," Cy told her. "He'd love to see you though. You'll have to drop by the office." Shane said nothing to that. "So…" Cy paused as he was wont to do before a big statement. "You're settling in."

Shane lifted a brow as she watched him glance around at her packing cases. "Slowly," she agreed. Though she knew it was deliberately rude, she didn't ask him to sit. They remained standing, just inside the door.

"You know, Shane, this house isn't in the best of shape, but it is a prime location." He gave her a light, condescending smile that set her teeth on edge. "I'm sure I could get you a good price for it."

"I'm not interested in selling, Cy. Is that why you came by? To do an appraisal?"

He looked suitably shocked. "Shane!"

"Was there something else?" she asked evenly.

"I just dropped by to see how you were." The distress in both his voice and eyes had an apology forming on her lips. "I heard some crazy story about your trying to start an antique shop."

The apology slipped away. "It's not a story, crazy or otherwise, Cy. I am going to start one."

He sighed and gave her what she termed his paternal look. She gritted her teeth. "Shane, have you any idea how difficult, how risky it is to start a business in today's economy?"

"I'm sure you'll tell me," she muttered.

"My dear," he said in calm tones, making her blood pressure rise alarmingly. "You're a certified teacher with four years' experience. It's just nonsense to toss away a good career for a fanciful little fling."

"I've always been good at nonsense, haven't I, Cy?" Her eyes chilled. "You never hesitated to point it out to me even when we were supposed to be madly in love."

"Now, Shane, it was because I cared that I tried to curb your...impulses."

"Curb my impulses!" More astonished than angry, Shane ran her fingers through her hair. Later, she told herself, later she would be able to laugh. Now she wanted to scream. "You haven't changed. You haven't changed a whit. I bet you still roll your socks into those neat little balls and carry an extra handkerchief."

He stiffened a bit. "If you'd ever learned the value of practicality—" he began.

"You wouldn't have dumped me two months before the wedding?" she finished furiously.

"Really, Shane, you can hardly call it that. You know I was only thinking of what was best for you."

"Best for me," she muttered between clenched teeth. "Well, let me tell you something." She poked a dusty finger at his muted striped tie. "You can stuff your practicality, Cy, right along with your balanced checkbook and shoe trees. I might have thought you hurt me at the time, but you did me a big favor. I *hate* practicality and rooms that smell like pine and toothpaste tubes that are rolled up from the bottom."

"I hardly see what that has to do with this discussion."

"It has *everything* to do with this discussion," she flared back. "You don't see anything unless it's listed in neat columns and balanced. And I'll tell you something else," she continued when he would have spoken. "I'm going to have my shop, and even if it doesn't make me a fortune, it's going to be fun."

"Fun?" Cy shook his head hopelessly. "That's a poor basis for starting a business."

"It's mine," she retorted. "I don't need a six-digit income to be happy."

He gave her a small, deprecating smile. "You haven't changed."

Flinging open the door, Shane glared at him. "Go sell a house," she suggested. With a dignity she envied and despised, Cy walked through the door. She slammed it after him, then gave in to temper and slammed her hand against the wall.

"Damn!" Putting her wounded knuckles to her mouth, she whirled. It was then she spotted Vance at the foot of the stairs. His face was still and serious as their eyes met. With angry embarrassment, Shane's cheeks flamed. "Enjoy the show?" she demanded, then stormed back to the kitchen.

She gave vent to her frustration by banging through the cupboards. She didn't hear Vance follow her. When he touched her shoulder, she spun around, ready to rage.

"Let me see your hand," he said quietly. Ignoring her jerk of protest, he took it in both of his.

"It's nothing."

Gently, he flexed it, then pressed down on her knuckles with his fingers. Involuntarily, she caught her breath at the quick pain. "You didn't manage to break it," he murmured, "but you'll have a bruise." He was forced to control a sudden rage that she had damaged that small, soft hand.

"Just don't say anything," she ordered through gritted teeth. "I'm not stupid. I *know* when I've made a fool of myself."

He took a moment to bend and straighten her fingers again. "I apologize," he said. "I should have let you know I was there."

After letting out a deep breath, Shane drew her hand from his slackened hold. The light throbbing gave her a perverse pleasure. "It doesn't matter," she muttered as she turned to make tea.

He frowned at her averted face. "I don't enjoy embarrassing you."

"If you live here for any amount of time, you'll hear about Cy and me anyway." She tried to make a casual shrug, but the quick jerkiness of the movement showed only more agitation. "This way you just got the picture quicker."

But he didn't have the full picture. Vance realized, with some discomfort, that he wanted to know. Before he could speak, Shane slammed the lid onto the kettle.

"He always makes me feel like a fool!"

"Why?"

"He always dots his *i*'s and crosses his *t*'s." With an angry tug, she pulled open a cabinet. "He carries an umbrella in the trunk of his car," she said wrathfully.

"That should do it," Vance murmured, watching her quick, jerky movements.

"He never, never, *never* makes a mistake. He's always reasonable," she added witheringly as she slammed two cups down on the counter. "Did he shout at me just now?" she demanded as she whirled on Vance. "Did he swear or lose his temper? He doesn't *have* a temper!" she shouted in frustration. "I swear, the man doesn't even sweat."

"Did you love him?"

For a moment, Shane merely stared; then she let out a small broken sigh. "Yes. Yes, I really did. I was sixteen when we started dating." As she went to the refrigerator, Vance turned the gas on under the kettle, which she had forgotten to do.

"He was so perfect, so smart and, oh...so articulate." Pulling out the milk, Shane smiled a little. "Cy's a born salesman. He can talk about anything."

Vance felt a quick, unreasonable dislike for him. As Shane set a large ceramic sugar bowl on the table, sunlight shot into her hair. The curls and waves of her hair shimmered briefly in the brilliance before she moved away. With an odd tingling at the base of his spine, Vance found himself staring after her.

"I was crazy about him," Shane continued, and Vance had to shake himself mentally to concentrate on her words. The subtle movements of her body beneath the snug T-shirt had begun to distract him. "When I turned eighteen, he asked me to marry him. We were both going to college, and Cy thought a year's engagement was proper. He's very proper," she added ruefully.

Or a cold-blooded fool, Vance thought, glancing at the faint outline of her nipples against the thin cotton. Annoyed, he brought his eyes back to her face. But the warmth in his own blood remained.

"I wanted to get married right away, but he told me, as always, that I was too impulsive. Marriage was a big step. Things had to be planned out. When I suggested we live together for a while, he was shocked." Shane set the milk on the table with a little bang. "I was young and in love, and I wanted him. He felt it his duty to control my more...primitive urges."

"He's a damn fool," Vance muttered under the hissing of the kettle.

"Through that last year, he molded me, and I tried to be what he wanted: dignified, sensible. I was a complete failure." Shane shook her head at the memory of that long, frustrating year. "If I wanted to go out for pizza with a bunch of other students, he'd remind me we had to watch our pennies. He already had his eye on this little house outside of Boonsboro. His father said it was a good investment."

"And you hated it," Vance commented.

Surprised, Shane looked back at him. "I despised it. It was the perfect little rancher with white aluminum siding and a hedge. When I told Cy I'd smother there, he laughed and patted my head."

"Why didn't you tell him to get lost?" he demanded.

Shane shot him a brief look. "Haven't you ever been in love?" she murmured. It was her answer, not a question, and Vance remained silent. "We were constantly at odds that year," she went on. "I kept thinking it was just the jitters of a long engagement, but more and more, the basic personality conflicts came up. He'd always say I'd feel differently once we were settled. Usually, I'd believe him."

"He sounds like a boring jackass."

Though the icy contempt in Vance's voice surprised her, Shane smiled. "Maybe, but he could be gentle and sweet." When Vance gave a derisive snort, she only shrugged. "I'd forget how rigid he was. Then he'd get more critical. I'd get angry, but I could never win a fight because he never lost control. The final break came over the plans for the honeymoon. I wanted to go to Fiji."

"Fiji?" Vance repeated.

"Yes," she said defiantly. "It's different, exotic, romantic. I was barely nineteen." On a fresh wave of fury, Shane slammed down her spoon. "He had plans for this—this plastic little resort hotel in Pennsylvania. The kind of place where they plan your activities, have contests and an indoor pool.

Shuffleboard." She rolled her eyes before she gulped down tea. "It was a package deal—three days, two nights, meals included. He'd inherited a substantial sum from his mother, and I had some savings, but he didn't want to waste money. He'd already outlined a retirement plan. I couldn't stand it!"

Vance sipped his own tea where he stood and studied her. "So you called off the wedding." He wondered if she would take the opportunity he was giving her to claim the break had been her idea.

"No." Shane pushed her cup aside. "We had a terrible fight, and I stormed off to spend the rest of the evening with friends at this little club near the college. I had told Cy I wouldn't spend my first night as a married woman watching a tacky floor show or playing bingo."

Vance's lips twitched but he managed to control his grin. "That sounds remarkably sensible," he murmured.

On a weak laugh, Shane shook her head. "After I'd calmed down, I decided where we went wasn't important, but that we'd finally be together. I told myself Cy was right. I was immature and irresponsible. We needed to save money. I still had two more years of college and he was just starting in his father's firm. I was being frivolous. That was one of his favorite adjectives for me."

Shane frowned down at her cup but didn't drink. "I went by his house ready to apologize. That's when he very reasonably, very calmly jilted me."

There was a long moment of silence before Vance came to the table to join her. "I thought you told me he never made mistakes."

Shane stared at him a moment, then laughed. It was a quick, pure sound of appreciation. "I needed that." Impulsively, she leaned her head against his shoulder. The anger had vanished in the telling, the self-pity with the laugh.

The tenderness that invaded him made Vance cautious. Still, he didn't resist the urge to stroke his hand down her disordered cap of hair. The texture of her hair was thick and unruly. And incredibly soft. He wasn't even aware that he twisted a curl around his finger.

"Do you still love him?" he heard himself ask.

"No," Shane answered before he could retract the question. "But he still makes me feel like an irresponsible romantic."

"Are you?"

She shrugged. "Most of the time."

"What you said to him out there was right, you know." Forgetting caution in simple wanting, he drew her closer.

"I said a lot of things."

"That he'd done you a favor," Vance murmured as his fingers roamed to the back of her neck. Shane sighed, but he couldn't tell if the sound came from pleasure or agreement. "You'd have gone crazy rolling up his socks in those little balls."

Shane was laughing as she tilted her head back to look at his face. She kissed him lightly in gratitude, then again for herself.

Her mouth was small and very tempting. Wanting his fill, Vance cupped his hand firmly on the back of her neck to keep her there. There was nothing shy or hesitant in her response to the increased pressure. She parted her lips and invited.

On a tiny moan of pleasure, her tongue met his. Suddenly hot, suddenly urgent, his mouth moved over hers. He needed her sweetness, her uncomplicated generosity. He wanted to saturate himself with the fresh, clean passion she offered so willingly. When his mouth crushed down harder, she only yielded; when his teeth nipped painfully at her lip, she only drew him closer.

"Vance," she murmured, leaning toward him.

He rose quickly, leaving her blinking in surprise. "I've got work to do," he said shortly. "I'll make a list of the materials I'll need to start. I'll be in touch." He was out the back door before Shane could form any response.

For several moments, she stared at the screen door. What had she done to cause that anger in his eyes? How was it possible that he could passionately kiss her one second and turn his back on her the next? Miserably, she looked down at her clenched hands. She had always made too much of things, she reminded herself. A romantic? Yes, and a dreamer, her grandmother had called her. For too long she'd been waiting for the right man to come into her life, to complete it. She wanted to be cherished, respected, adored.

Perhaps, she mused, she was looking for the impossible— to keep her independence and to share her dreams, to stand on her own and have a strong hand to hold. Over and over she had warned herself to stop looking for that one perfect love. But her spirit defied her mind.

From the first instant, she had sensed something different about Vance. For the flash of a second when their eyes had first held, her heart had opened and shouted, *Here he is!* But that was nonsense, Shane reminded herself. Love meant understanding, knowledge. She neither knew nor understood Vance Banning.

With a jolt, she realized she might have offended him. She was going to be his employer, and the way she had kissed him…he might think she wanted more than carpentry for her money. He might think she intended to seduce him while dangling a few much-needed dollars under his nose.

Abruptly, she burst into laughter. As her mirth grew, she threw back her head and pounded both fists on the table. Shane Abbott, seductress. Oh Lord! she thought, wiping tears of hilarity from her eyes. That was rich. After all, what red-blooded man could withstand a woman with dirt on her face who tries to punch holes in walls?

She sighed with the effort of laughing. Her imagination, she decided, needed a rest. Shane went back to her inventory.

Four

Vance couldn't sleep. He had worked until late in the evening, sweating off anger and frustrated desire. The anger didn't worry him. He knew that emotion too well to lose sleep over it. Neither was he a stranger to desire, but having to acknowledge he felt it for a snippy little history buff infuriated him...and made him restless.

He should never have agreed to take the job, he told himself yet again. What devil had provoked him into doing it? Annoyed with himself, Vance wandered outside to stand on the porch.

The air had cooled considerably with nightfall. Overhead, the stars were spread in a wide, brilliant pattern around a white half-moon. Venus was as clear as he'd ever seen it. An army of crickets sent out their high, monotonous signal while fireflies danced, tiny yellow lights, over the fallow field to his right. When he looked straight ahead, he could see to the edge of the trees but no farther. The woods were dark, mysterious, secret. Shane slept on the other side in a room with faded wallpaper and a Jenny Lind bed.

He imagined her cuddled under the wedding-ring quilt he'd seen on the bed. Her window would be open to let in the sounds and scents of night. Did she sleep in one of those fussy cotton nightgowns that would cover her from neck to feet, he wondered, or would she slip under the quilt in solitary nakedness?

Furious with the direction of his thoughts, Vance cursed himself. No, he should never have taken the damn job. It had appealed to his ego and his humor. Six dollars an hour. He laughed shortly, startling an owl in a nearby tree. Leaning on a post, he continued to stare into the woods, seeing nothing but silhouettes and shadows.

When was the last time he'd worked for an hourly wage? To answer his own question, Vance looked back, trying to remember. Fifteen years? Good God, he thought with a shake of his head. Had so much time passed?

He'd been a teenager starting out at the bottom of his mother's highly successful construction firm. "Learn the ropes," she had told him, and he'd eagerly agreed. Vance had wanted nothing more than to work with his hands, and with wood. He'd had his share of youthful confidence—and youthful arrogance. Administration was for old men in business suits who wouldn't know how to miter a corner. He'd wanted no part of their stuffy business meetings or complicated contract negotiations. Shuffle papers? No, he was too clever to fall into that trap.

How long had it taken before he had been pulled in—chained behind a desk? Five years? he thought. Six? With a shrug, he decided it didn't matter. He'd gone beyond the time when a year made much difference.

Sighing, Vance walked the length of the porch. Under his hand, the rail he had built himself was rough and sturdy. What choice had there been? he asked himself. There had been his mother's sudden stroke and long painful recovery. She had begged him to take over as president of Riverton. As a widow with only one child, she had been desperate not to see her business run by strangers. It had mattered to her, perhaps too much, that the firm she had inherited, had struggled to keep during the lean years, stay in the family. Vance knew that she had fought prejudices, taken chances and worked nearly half her life to turn a mediocre firm into an exemplary one. Then she had been all but helpless, and asking him.

If he had been a failure at it, he could have delegated the responsibilities and stayed a figurehead without a qualm. He could have picked up his tools again. But he hadn't been a failure—there was too much of his mother in him.

Riverton Construction had thrived and expanded under his leadership. It had grown beyond the prestigious Washington concern into a national conglomerate. It was his own misfortune that he had the same knack with administration that he had with a hammer. He had bolted the lock on his own cage.

Then there had been Amelia. Vance's mouth tightened into a cynical smile. Soft, sexy Amelia, he mused, with hair like a sunset and a quiet Virginia drawl. She had kept him yapping at her heels for months, drawing him in, holding him off, until he had been mad to have her. Mad, Vance thought again. A very apt word. If he had been sane, he would have seen through that beautiful, cultured mask to the calculat-

ing scrambler she had been—before he had put the ring on
her finger.

Not for the first time, he wondered how many men had
envied him his lovely, dignified wife. But they hadn't seen
the face unmasked—the perfect face with a rotted shell beneath. Cold. In all of his experience, Vance had known no
one as cold as Amelia Ryce Banning.

The owl in the oak to his left set up a steady hooting: two
short calls then a long—two short, then a long. Vance listened to the monotonous sound as he thought over the years
of his marriage.

Amelia had spent his money lavishly those first months—
clothes, furs, cars. That had mattered little to him as he had
felt her unearthly beauty demanded the finest. And he had
loved her—or the woman he had thought she'd been. He
had thought she was a woman made for diamonds, for soft,
exotic furs and silks. It had pleased him to surround her with
them, to see her sulky beauty glow. For the most part, he had
ignored the excessive bills, paying them without a murmur.
Once or twice he had commented on her extravagance and
had received her sweet distress and apologies. He'd hardly
noticed that the bills had continued to flow in.

Then he had discovered she was draining his bank account
to feed her brother's teetering construction firm in Rich-
mond. Amelia had been tearful and helpless when confronted
with it. She had pleaded prettily for her brother. She had
claimed she couldn't bear to have him almost facing bank-
ruptcy while she lived so well.

Because he'd believed her familial concern, Vance had
agreed to a personal loan, but he'd refused to siphon money
from Riverton into an unstable and mishandled company.

Amelia had been far from satisfied, had pouted and cajoled. Then when he'd remained adamant, she had attacked him like a crazed tigress, raking his face with her well-manicured nails, spewing out obscenities through her tinted cupid's-bow mouth. Her anger had driven her to strike out and tell him why she had married him—for his money and position, and what both could do for her and her own family business. Then Vance had looked beneath the beauty and the careful charm to see what she was. It had been only the first of many shocks and disillusionments.

Her warm passion had become frigidity; her adoring smiles had become sneers. She had refused to consider having children. It would have spoiled her figure and restricted her freedom. For more than two years Vance had struggled to save his failing marriage, to salvage something of the life he had planned to have with Amelia. But he had come to know that the woman he thought he had married was an illusion.

Ultimately, he'd demanded a divorce and Amelia had laughed and agreed. She would happily give him his freedom for half of everything he owned—including his share of Riverton. She had promised him an ugly court battle and plenty of publicity. After pointing out that she would be the injured party, Amelia had vowed to play her part of the cast-off wife to the hilt.

Trapped, Vance had lived with her for another year, keeping up the pretense of marriage in public, avoiding her privately. When he had discovered Amelia was taking lovers, he'd seen the first ray of hope.

He had felt no pain on being betrayed, for there had been no emotion in him for her. Slowly, discreetly, Vance had begun to compile the evidence that would give him his freedom. He was willing to face the humiliation and publicity of a messy court battle to free himself and his company. Then there had been no more need. One of Amelia's discarded lovers put a bullet through her heart and ended it.

It had been due to Vance's wealth and influence that the publicity hadn't been worse than it had been. Still, the whispers and speculation had been ugly enough. Yet there had been a staggering relief in him rather than grief. The guilt this had brought had caused him to bury himself even more in his work. There were condominiums to be built in Florida, a large medical complex in Minnesota, an addition to a university in Texas. But there had been no peace for him.

Determined to find Vance Banning again, he'd bought the dilapidated house in the mountains and had taken an extended leave of absence. Time, solitude and the work he loved had been his prescription. Then, just when he had thought he had found the answer, he had met Shane Abbott.

She was no smoldering hothouse beauty as Amelia had been, no poised sophisticate as were the women he had taken to his bed over the last two years. She was fresh and vital. Instinctively, he was attracted to her good-natured generosity. But his wife's legacy to him had been cynicism and distrust. Vance knew that only a fool fell for the innocent act twice. And he was no fool.

He had taken the job with Shane on impulse, and now he would see it through. It would be a challenge to learn if he was still capable of the fine precision work she required. And he knew how to be cautious with a woman now. It was true her fresh looks and artless charm had appealed to him. He admired her way of dealing with her former fiancé. She'd been hurt, yet she had held her own and booted Cy out the door.

It might be interesting, he decided, to spend his vacation remodeling Shane's house and learning what she hid under her mask. Everyone wore masks, he thought grimly. Life was one long masquerade. It wouldn't take long to discover what went on behind her big brown eyes and bubbling laugh.

With a sound of disgust, Vance hurled himself back into the house. He wasn't going to lose any sleep over a woman. Nevertheless, he tossed and turned much of the night.

It was a perfect morning. In the west, the mountains rose into a paintbrush blue sky. Birds chattered in noisy jubilation as Shane tossed open the windows. The air that rushed in was warm, laced with the scent of zinnias. It was all but impossible for one of her nature to remain inside on such a day, cooped up with dust and a clipboard. But there were ways, Shane decided as she leaned on the windowsill, of doing her duty *and* having fun.

After dressing in an old T-shirt and faded red shorts, she rummaged through the basement storage closet and unearthed a can of white paint and a roller. The front porch, she knew, needed more repair than her meager talents could provide, but the back was still sturdy enough. All it required was a coat or two of paint to make it bright and cheerful again.

Picking up a portable radio on her way, Shane headed outside. She fiddled with the tuner until she found a station that matched her mood; then, after turning the volume up, she went to work.

In thirty minutes, the porch was swept clean and hosed down. In the bright sun, it dried quickly while Shane pried the lid off the paint can. She stirred it, enjoying the day and the prospect of work. Once or twice, she glanced toward the old logging path, wondering when Vance would "keep in touch." She would have liked to have seen him coming down the path toward her. He had a long, loose-limbed stride she admired, and a way of looking as though he were in complete command of himself and anything that might get in his way. Shane liked that—the confidence, the hint of controlled power.

She had always admired people of strength. Her grandmother, through all her hardships and disappointments, had remained a strong woman right to the end. Shane would have admitted, for all their disagreements, that Cy was a strong man. What he lacked, in her opinion, was the underlying kindness that balanced strength and kept it from being hard. She sensed there was kindness in Vance, though he was far from easy with it. But the fact that the trait existed at all made the difference for Shane.

Turning away from the path, she took her bucket, roller and pan to the end of the porch. She poured, knelt, then took a deep breath and began to paint.

When Vance came to the end of the path, he stopped to watch her. She had nearly a third of the porch done. Her arms were splattered with tiny specks of white. The radio blared, and she sang exuberantly along with it. Her hips kept the beat. As she moved, the thin, faded material of her shorts strained over her bottom. That she was having a marvelous time with the homey chore was as obvious as her lack of skill. A smile tugged at his mouth when Shane leaned over for the bucket and rested her palm on the wet paint. Cheerfully, she swore, then wiped her hand haphazardly on the back of her shorts.

"I thought you said you could paint," Vance commented.

Shane started, nearly upsetting the contents of the bucket

as she turned. Still on all fours, she smiled at him. "I said I could paint. I didn't say I was neat." Lifting her hand, she shielded her eyes against the sun and watched him walk to her. "Did you come to supervise?"

He looked down at her and shook his head. "No, I think it's already too late for that."

Shane lifted a brow. "It's going to be just fine when I've finished."

Vance made a noncommittal sound. "I've got a list of materials for you, but I need to make a few more measurements."

"That was quick." Shane sat back on her haunches. Vance shrugged, not wanting to admit he'd written it out in the middle of the night when sleep had eluded him. "There was something else," she continued, stretching her back muscles. Leaning over, she turned down the volume on the radio so that it was only a soft murmur. "The front porch."

Vance glanced down at her handiwork. "Have you painted that too?"

Correctly reading his impression of her talents, Shane made a face. "No, I didn't paint that too."

"That's a blessing. What stopped you?"

"It's falling apart. Maybe you can suggest what I should do about it. Oh, look!" Shane grabbed his hand, forgetting the paint as she spotted a family of quail bobbing single file across the path behind them. "They're the first I've seen since I've been home." Captivated, she watched them until they were out of sight. "There's deer too. I've seen the signs, but I haven't been able to catch sight of any yet." She gave a contented sigh as the quail rustled in the woods. All at once, she remembered the condition of her hand.

"Oh, Vance, I'm sorry!" Releasing him, she jumped to her feet. "Did I get any on you?"

For an answer, he turned his palm up, studying the white smear ironically.

"I really am sorry," she managed, choking on a giggle. He shot her a look as she struggled to swallow the irrepressible laughter. "No, really I am. Here." Taking the hem of her T-shirt, Shane lifted it to rub unsuccessfully at his palm. Her stab at assistance exposed the pale, smooth skin of her midriff.

"You're rubbing it in," Vance said mildly, trying not to be affected by the flash of skin or the glimpse of her narrow waist.

"It'll come off," she assured him while she fought a desperate battle with laughter. "I must have some turpentine or something." Though Shane pressed the back of her hand against her mouth, the giggle escaped. "I *am* sorry," she claimed, then dropped her forehead on his chest. "And I wouldn't laugh if you'd stop looking at me that way."

"What way?"

"Patiently."

"Does patience usually send you into uncontrollable laughter?" he asked. Her hair carried the scent of her shampoo, a faint tang of lemon. It was odd that he would think just then of the honey-sweetness of her mouth.

"Too many things do," she admitted in a strangled voice. "It's a curse." She drew a deep breath, but left her hand on his chest as she tried to compose herself. "One of my students drew a deadly caricature of his biology teacher. When I saw it, I had to leave the room for fifteen minutes before I could pretend I disapproved."

Vance drew her away, unnerved by his unwanted, unreasonable response to her. "Didn't you?"

"Disapprove?" Grinning, Shane shook her head. "I wanted to, but it was so good. I took it home and framed it."

Suddenly, she became aware that he was holding her arms, that his thumbs were caressing her bare skin while his eyes watched her in the deep, guarded way he had. Looking at him, Shane was certain he was unaware of the gentle, intimate gesture. There was nothing gentle in his eyes. If she had followed her first instinct, she would have risen to her toes and kissed him. It was what she wanted—what she sensed he wanted as well. Something warned her against making the move. Instead, she stood still. Her eyes met his calmly, with no secrets to be seen in them. All of the secrets were his, and at that moment, they both knew it.

Vance would have been more comfortable with secrets than candor. When he realized that he was holding her, that he wanted to go on holding her, he released her.

"You'd better get back to your painting," he said. "I'll take those measurements."

"All right." Shane watched him walk to the door. "There's hot water in the kitchen if you want some tea."

What a strange man, she thought, frowning after him. Unconsciously, she lifted a finger to the warm spot on her arm where his flesh had touched hers. What had he been looking for, she wondered, when he had searched her eyes so deeply? What did he expect to find? It would be so much simpler if he would only ask her the questions he had. Shrugging, Shane went back to her painting.

Vance paused by the foot of the stairs and glanced at the living room. Surprised, he walked in for a closer look. It was clean as a whistle, with every vase, lamp and knickknack packed away in labeled boxes.

She must have really worked, he thought. That compact little body stored a heavyweight energy. She had ambition, he concluded, and the guts to carry it through. Whatever her former fiancé termed her, Vance would hardly characterize Shane Abbott as frivolous. Not from what he had seen so far, he reminded himself. He felt another flash of admiration for her as he mounted the stairs.

She'd been at work on the second floor as well, Vance discovered. She must move like a whirlwind, he concluded as he looked at the labeled boxes in the master bedroom. After taking his measurements and notations, he moved into Shane's room.

It was a beehive of activity, with none of the meticulous organization he had found in the other rooms. Papers, lists, notes, scrawled tablets and bills sat heaped on the open slant top of a Governor Winthrop desk. They fluttered a bit from the breeze through the open windows. On the floor beside it were dozens of catalogs on antiques. A nightgown—not the one he had envisioned her in, but a thigh-length chemise— was tossed inside out over a chair. A pair of worn sneakers sat propped against the closet as if they had been kicked there then forgotten.

In the center of the room was a large box of books, which he remembered seeing the day before. Then they had been in the third bedroom. Obviously, Shane had dragged them into her own room the night before to sort through them. Several were piled precariously on the floor; others littered her nightstand. It was apparent that her style of working and style of living were completely at variance.

Oddly, Vance thought of Amelia and the elegant order of

her private rooms. They had been decorated in pinks and ivories, without the barest trace of dust or clutter. Even the army of bottles of creams and scents on her vanity had been carefully arranged. Shane had no vanity at all, and the bureau top held only a small enameled box, a framed photo and a single bottle of scent. He noted the photo was a color snapshot of a teenaged Shane beside a very erect, white-haired woman.

So this is the grandmother, Vance mused. She had a prim, proper smile on her face, but he was certain her eyes were laughing out of the lined face. He observed none of the softness of old age about her, but a rather leathery toughness that contrasted well with the girl beside her.

They stood on the summer grass, their backs to the creek. The grandmother wore a flowered housedress, the girl a yellow T-shirt and cut-off jeans. This Shane was hardly different from the woman outside. Her hair was longer, her frame thinner, but the look of unbridled amusement was there. Though her arm was hooked through the old woman's, the impression was of camaraderie, not of support.

She was more attractive with her hair short, Vance decided as he studied her. The way it curled and clung to the shape of her face accented the smoothness of her skin, and the way her jaw tapered...

He found himself wondering if Cy had taken the picture and was immediately annoyed with the idea. He disliked Cy on principle, though he'd certainly employed a good many men like him over the years. They plotted their way through life as though it were a tax return.

What the hell had she seen in him? Vance thought in disgust as he turned away to take more measurements. If she had tied herself up with him, she would be living in some stuffy house in the suburbs with 2.3 children, the Ladies Auxiliary on Wednesdays and a two-week vacation in a rented beach cottage every year. Fine for some, he thought, but not for a woman who liked to paint porches and wanted to see Fiji.

That buttoned-down jerk would have picked on her for the rest of her life, Vance concluded before he headed back downstairs. She'd had a lucky escape. Vance thought it was a pity he hadn't had one himself. Instead he had spent an intolerable four years wishing his wife out of existence and another two dealing with the guilt of having his wish come true.

Shaking off the mood, Vance walked outside to take a look at Shane's front porch.

Later, when he was measuring and muttering, Shane came out with a mug of tea in each hand. "Pretty bad, huh?"

Vance looked up with an expression of disgust. "It's a wonder someone hasn't broken a leg on this thing."

"No one uses it much." Shane shrugged as she worked her way expertly around the uncertain boards. "Gran always used the back door. So does anyone who comes to visit."

"Your boyfriend didn't."

Shane shot him a dry look. "Cy wouldn't use the back door, and he's not my boyfriend. What do you think I should do about it?"

"I thought you'd already done it," he returned, and pocketed his rule. "And very well."

Shane eyed him a moment, then laughed. "No, not about Cy, about the porch."

"Tear the damn thing down."

"Oh." Gingerly, Shane sat on the top step. "All of it? I was hoping to replace the worst boards, and—"

"The whole thing's going to collapse if three people stand on it at the same time," Vance cut in, frowning at the sagging wood. "I can't understand how anyone could let something get into this condition."

"All right, don't get riled up," she advised as she held out a mug of tea. "How much do you think it'll cost me?"

Vance calculated a moment, then named a price. He saw the flicker of dismay before Shane sighed.

"Okay." It killed her last hope of holding on to her grand-mother's dining-room set. "If it has to be done. I suppose it's first priority. The weather might turn cold anytime." She managed a halfhearted smile. "I wouldn't want my first cus-tomer to fall through the porch and sue me."

"Shane." Vance stood in front of her. As she sat on the top step, their faces were almost level. Her look was direct and open, yet still he hesitated before speaking. "How much do you have? Money," he added bluntly when she gave him a blank look.

She drew her brows together at the question. "Enough to get by," she said, then made a sound of annoyance as he continued to stare at her. "Barely," she admitted. "But it'll hold until my business makes a few dollars. I've got so much budgeted for the house, so much for buying stock. Gran left me a nest egg, and I had my own savings."

Vance hesitated again. He had promised himself not to become involved, yet he was being drawn in every time he saw her. "I hate to sound like your boyfriend," he began.

"Then don't," Shane said quickly. "And he's not."

"All right." Vance frowned down at his mug. It was one thing to take on a job as a lark, and another to take money from a woman who was obviously counting her pennies.

He sipped, trying to find a reasonable way out of his hourly wage. "Shane, about my salary—"

"Oh, Vance, I can't make it any more right now." Distress flew into her eyes. "Later, after I've gotten started…"

"No." Embarrassed and annoyed, he put a hand on hers to stop her. "No, I wasn't going to ask you to raise it."

"But—" Shane stopped. Realization filled her eyes. Tears followed it. Swiftly, she set down the mug and rose. Shaking her head, she descended the stairs. "No, no, that's very kind of you," she managed as she walked away from him. "I—I appreciate it, really, but it's not necessary. I didn't mean to make it sound as though—" Breaking off, she stared at the surrounding mountains. For a moment there was only the sound of the creek bubbling on its way behind them.

Cursing himself, Vance went to her. After a brief hesitation, he put his hands on her shoulders. "Shane, listen—"

"No, please." Swiftly, she turned to face him. Though the tears hadn't brimmed over, her eyes still swam with them. When she lifted her hands to his forearms, he found her fingers surprisingly strong. "It's very kind of you to offer."

"No, it's not," Vance snapped. Frustration, guilt and something more ran through him. He resented all of it. "Damn it, Shane, you don't understand. The money isn't—"

"I understand you're a very sweet man," she interrupted. Vance felt himself become tangled deeper when she put her arms around him, pressing her cheek to his chest.

"No, I'm not," he muttered. Intending to push her away and find a way out of the mess he'd gotten himself into, Vance put his hands back on her shoulders. The last thing he wanted was misplaced gratitude. But his hands found their way into her hair.

He didn't want to push her away, he realized. No, by God,

he didn't. Not when her small firm breasts were pressed against him. Not when her hair curled riotously around his fingers. It was soft, so soft, and the color of wild honey. Her mouth was soft, he remembered, aching. Surrendering to need, Vance buried his face in her hair, murmuring her name.

Something in the tone, the hint of desperation, made Shane long to comfort him. She didn't yet sense his desire for her, only his trouble. She pressed closer, wanting to ease it while she ran soothing hands over his back. At her touch, his blood leaped. In a swift, almost brutal move, Vance pulled her head back to savage her mouth with his.

Shane's instinctive cry of alarm was silenced. Her struggles went unnoticed. A fire consumed him—so great, so unbearably hot, he had no thought but to quench it. She felt fear, then, greater than fear, passion. The fire spread, engulfing her until her mouth answered his wildly.

No one, nothing had ever brought her to this—this madness of need, terror of desire. She moaned in panicked excitement as his teeth nipped into her bottom lip. Along her skin, quick thrills raced to confuse and inflame. There was never a thought to deny him. She knew she was already his.

He thought he would go mad if he didn't touch her, learn just one of the secrets of her small, slim body. For countless hours the night before, his imagination had tormented him. Now, he had to satisfy it. Never stopping his assault on her mouth, he reached beneath her shirt to find her breast. Her heart pounded beneath his hand. She was firm and small. His appetite only increased, making him groan while his thumb and finger worked the already erect peak.

Colors exploded inside her head like a blinding, brilliant rainbow. Shane clutched at him, afraid, enthralled, while her lips and tongue continued with a demand equal to his. Against her smooth skin his palm was rough and callused. His thumb scraped her, lifting her to a delirium of excitement. There was no smoothness, no softness in him. His mouth was hard and hot with the stormy taste of anger. Crushed to hers, his body was taut and tense. Some raw, turbulent passion seemed to pour out of him to dare her to match it.

She felt his arms tighten around her convulsively; then she was free so quickly she staggered, grabbing his arm to steady herself.

In her eyes, Vance saw the clouds of passion, the lights of fear. Her mouth was bruised and swollen from the fierceness of his. He frowned at it. Never before had he been rough with a woman. For the most part, he was a considerate lover, perhaps indifferent at times but never ungentle. He took a step back from her. "I'm sorry," he said stiffly.

Shane lifted her fingers to her still-tender lips in a nervous gesture. Her reaction, much more than Vance's technique, had left her shaken. Where had all that fire and feeling been hiding all this time? she wondered. "I don't..." Shane had to clear her throat to manage more than a whisper. "I don't want you to be sorry."

Vance studied her steadily for a moment. "It would be better all around if you did." Reaching in his back pocket, he drew out a list. "Here are the materials you'll need. Let me know when they're delivered."

"All right." Shane accepted the list. When he started to walk away, she drew up all of her courage. "Vance..." He paused and turned back to her. "I'm not sorry," she told him quietly.

He didn't answer, but walked around the side of the house and disappeared.

Five

S hane decided she had worked harder over the following three days than she had ever worked in her life. The spare bedroom and dining room were loaded with packing boxes, labeled and listed and sealed. The house had been scrubbed and swept and dusted from top to bottom. She had pored through catalogs on antiques until the words ran together. Every item she owned was listed systematically. The dating and pricing was more grueling for her than the manual work and often kept her up until the early hours of the morning. She would be up to start again the moment the sunlight woke her. Yet her energy never flagged. With each step of progress she made, the excitement grew, pushing her to make more.

As the time passed, she became more convinced, and more confident, that what she was doing was right. It *felt* right. She needed to find her own way—the sacrifices and the financial risk were necessary. She didn't intend to fail.

For her, the shop would be not only a business but an adventure. Though Shane was impatient for the adventure to begin, as always, the planning and anticipation were just as stimulating to her. She had contracted with a roofer and a plumber, and had chosen her paints and stains. Just that afternoon, in a torrent of rain, the materials she had ordered from Vance's list had been delivered. The mundane, practical occurrences had given her a thrill of accomplishment. Somehow, the lumber, nails and bolts had been tangible evidence that she was on her way. Shane told herself that Antietam Antiques and Museum became a reality when the first board was set in place.

Excited, she had phoned Vance, and if he were true to his word, he would begin work the next morning.

Over a solitary cup of cocoa in the kitchen, Shane listened to the constant drumming rain and thought of him. He had been brief and businesslike on the phone. She hadn't been offended. She had come to realize that moodiness was part of his character. This made him only more attractive.

The windows were dark as she stared out, with a ghostly reflection of the kitchen light on the wet panes. She thought idly about starting a fire to chase away the damp chill, but she had little inclination to move. Instead, she rubbed the bottom of one bare foot over the top of the other and decided it was too bad her socks were all the way upstairs.

Sluggishly, a drip fell from the ceiling into a pot on the floor. It gave a surprising ping now and again. There were several other pots set at strategic places throughout the house. Shane didn't mind the rain or the isolation. The sensation of true loneliness was almost foreign to her. Content with her own company, the activity of her own mind, she craved no companionship at that moment, nor would she have shunned it. Yet she thought of Vance, wondering if he sat watching the rain through a darkened window.

Yes, she admitted, she was very much attracted to him. And it was more than a physical response when he held her, when he kissed her in that sudden, terrifyingly exciting way. Just being in his presence was stimulating—sensing the storm beneath the calm. There was an amazing drive in him. The drive of a man uncomfortable, even impatient, with idleness. The lack of a job, she thought with a sympathetic sigh, must frustrate him terribly.

Shane understood his need to produce, to be active, although her own spurts of frantic energy were patchworked with periods of unapologetic laziness. She moved fast but didn't rush. She could work for hours without tiring, or sleep until noon without the least blush of guilt. Whichever she did, she did wholeheartedly. It was vital to her to find some way to enjoy the most menial or exhausting task. She concluded that while Vance would work tirelessly, he would find the enjoyment unnecessary.

The basic difference in their temperaments didn't trouble her. Her interest in history, plus her teaching experience, had given her insight into the variety of human nature. It wasn't necessary to her that Vance's thoughts and moods flow along the same stream as hers. Such comfortable compatibility would offer little excitement and no surprises at all. Absolute harmony, she mused, could be lovely, rather sweet and very bland. There were more...interesting things.

She'd seen a spark of humor in him, perhaps an almost forgotten sense of the ridiculous. And he was far from cold.

While she accepted his faults and their differences, these qualities caused her to accept her own attraction to him.

What she had felt from the first meeting had only intensified. There was no logic in it, no sense, but her heart had known instantly that he was the man she'd waited for. Though she'd told herself it was impossible, Shane knew the impossible had an uncanny habit of happening just the same. Love at first sight? Ridiculous. But...

Impossible or not, ridiculous or not, Shane's heart was set. It was true she gave her affections easily, but she didn't give them lightly. The love she had felt for Cy had been a young, impressionable love, but it had been very real. It had taken her a long time to get over it.

Shane had no illusions about Vance Banning. He was a difficult man. Even with spurts of kindness and humor, he would never be anything else. There was too much anger in him, too much drive. And while Shane could accept the phenomenon of love at first sight on her part, she was practical enough to know it wasn't being reciprocated.

He desired her. She might puzzle over this, never having thought of herself as a woman to attract desire, but she recognized it. Yet, though he wanted her, he kept his distance. This was the reserve in him, she decided, the studied caution that warred with the passion.

Idly, she sipped her drink and stared out into the rain. The problem as Shane saw it was to work her way through the barrier. She had loved before and faced pain and emptiness. She could accept pain again, but she was determined not to face emptiness a second time. She wanted Vance Banning. Now all she had to do was to make him want her. Smiling a little, Shane set down her cup. She'd been raised to succeed.

The glare of headlights against the window surprised her. Rising, Shane went to the back door to see who'd come visiting in the rain. Cupping her hands on either side of her face, she peered through the wet glass. She recognized the car and immediately threw open the door. Cold rain hurled itself into her face, but she laughed, watching Donna scramble around puddles with her head lowered.

"Hi!" Still laughing, Shane stepped back as her friend dashed through the door. "You got a little wet," she observed.

"Very funny." Donna stripped off her raincoat to hang it over a peg near the back door. With the casualness of an old friend, she stepped out of her wet loafers. "I figured you were hibernating. Here." She handed Shane a pound can of coffee.

"A welcome home present?" Shane asked, turning the can over curiously. "Or a hint that you'd like some?"

"Neither." Shaking her head, Donna ran her fingers through her wet hair. "You bought it the other day, then left it at the store."

"I did?" Shane thought about it a moment, then laughed. "Oh, that's right. Thanks. Who's minding the store while you're out making deliveries?" Turning, she popped the can into a cupboard.

"Dave." With a sigh, Donna plopped onto a kitchen chair. "His sister's babysitting, so he kicked me out."

"Aw, out in the storm."

"He knew I was restless." She glanced out the window. "It doesn't seem as though this rain's ever going to let up." With a shiver, she frowned at Shane's bare feet. "Aren't you cold?"

"I thought about starting a fire," she said absently, then grinned. "It seemed like an awful lot of trouble."

"So's the flu."

"The cocoa's still warm," Shane told her, automatically reaching for another cup. "Want some?"

"Yes, thanks." Donna ran her fingers through her hair again, then folded her hands, but she couldn't keep them still. Suddenly, she gave Shane a glowing smile. "I have to tell you before I burst."

Mildly curious, Shane looked over her shoulder. "Tell me what?"

"I'm having another baby."

"Oh, Donna, that's wonderful!" Shane felt a twinge of envy. Hurriedly dismissing it, she went to hug her friend. "When?"

"Not for another seven months." Laughing, Donna wiped the rain from her face. "I'm just as excited as I was the first time. Dave is too, though he's trying to be very nonchalant." She sent Shane a beaming look. "He's managed to mention it, very casually, to everyone who came into the store this afternoon."

Shane gave her another quick hug. "You know how lucky you are?"

"Yes, I do." A little sheepishly, she grinned. "I've spent all day thinking up names. What do you think of Charlotte and Samuel?"

"Very distinguished." Shane moved back to the stove. After pouring cocoa, she brought two cups to the table. "Here's to little Charlotte or Samuel."

"Or Andrew or Justine," Donna said as they touched rims.

"How many kids are you planning to have?" Shane asked wryly.

"Just one at a time." Donna gave her stomach a proud little pat.

The gesture made Shane smile. "Did you say Dave's sister was watching Benji? Isn't she still in school?"

"No, she graduated this summer. Right now she's hunting for a new job." With a contented sigh, Donna sat back. "She was planning to go to college part-time, but money's tight and the hours she's working right now make it next to impossible." Her brow creased in sympathy. "The best she can manage this term is a couple of night classes twice a week. At that rate it's going to take her a long time to earn a degree."

"Hmm." Shane stared into her cocoa. "Pat was a very bright girl as I remember."

"Bright and pretty as a picture."

Shane nodded. "Tell her to come see me."

"You?"

"After the shop's set up, I'm going to need some part-time help." She glanced over absently as the wind hurled rain at the windows. "I wouldn't be able to do anything for her for a month or so, but if she's still interested, we should be able to work something out."

"Shane, she'll be thrilled. But are you sure you can afford to hire someone?"

With a toss of her head, Shane lifted her drink. "I'll know within the first six months if I'm going to make it." As she considered, she twisted a curl around her finger—a gesture Donna recognized as nerves. She drew her brows together but said nothing. "I want to keep the place open seven days a week," Shane continued. "Weekends are bound to be the busiest time if I manage to lure in any tourists. Between sales and bookkeeping, inventory and the buying I have to do, I won't be able to manage alone. If I'm going down," she murmured, "I'm going down big."

"I've never known you to do anything halfway," Donna observed with a trace of admiration vying with concern. "I'd be scared to death."

"I am a little scared," Shane admitted. "Sometimes I imagine this place the way it's going to look, and I see customers coming in to handle merchandise. I see all the rooms and records I'm going to have to keep…" She rolled her eyes to the ceiling. "What makes me think I can handle all that?"

"As long as I can remember, you've handled everything that came your way." Donna paused a moment as she considered Shane carefully. "You're going to try this no matter how many pitfalls I point out?"

A grin had Shane's dimples deepening. "Yes."

"Then I won't point out any," Donna said with a wry smile. "What I will say is that if anyone can make it work, you can."

After frowning into her cocoa, Shane raised her eyes to Donna's. "Why?"

"Because you'll give it everything you've got."

The simplicity of the answer made Shane laugh. "You're sure that'll be enough?"

"Yes," Donna said so seriously that Shane sobered.

"I hope you're right," Shane murmured, then shook off the doubts. "It's a little late in the game to start worrying about it now. So," she continued in a lighter tone, "what's new besides Justine or Samuel?"

After a moment's hesitation, Donna plunged ahead. "Shane, I saw Cy the other day."

"Did you?" Shane lifted a brow as she sipped. "So did I."

Donna moistened her lips. "He seemed very…ah, concerned about your plans."

"Critical and concerned are entirely different things," Shane pointed out, then smiled as the color in Donna's cheeks deepened. "Oh, don't worry about it, Donna. Cy's never approved of any of my ideas. It doesn't bother me anymore. In fact, the less he approves," she continued slowly, "the more I'm sure it's the right thing to do. I don't think he's ever taken a chance in his entire life." Noting that Donna was busy gnawing on her bottom lip, Shane fixed her with a straight look. "Okay, what else?"

"Shane." Donna paused, then began running her fingertip around and around the rim of her cup. Shane recognized the stalling gesture and kept silent. "I think I should tell you before—well, before you hear it from someone else. Cy..."

Shane waited patiently for a few seconds. "Cy what?" she demanded. Miserably, Donna looked up.

"He's been seeing quite a lot of Laurie MacAfee." Seeing Shane's eyes widen, Donna continued in a rush. "I'm sorry, Shane, so sorry, but I did think you should know. And I figured it might be easier hearing it from me. I think...well, I'm afraid it's serious."

"Laurie..." Shane broke off and seemed to stare, fascinated, at the water dripping into the pot. *"Laurie MacAfee?"* she managed after a strangled moment.

"Yes," Donna said quietly, and she stared down at the table. "Rumor is they'll be married next summer." Donna waited, unhappily, for Shane's reaction. When she heard the burst of wild laughter, she looked up, fearing hysterics.

"Laurie MacAfee!" Shane pounded her palms on the table and laughed until she thought she would burst. "Oh, it's wonderful, it's perfect! Oh God. Oh God, what an *admirable* couple!"

"Shane…" Concerned with the damp eyes and rollicking laughter, Donna searched for the right thing to say.

"Oh, I wish I had known before so I could have congratulated him." Almost beside herself with delight, Shane laid her forehead on the table. Taking this as a sign of a broken heart, Donna put a comforting hand on her hair.

"Shane, you mustn't take on so." Her own eyes filled as she gently stroked Shane's hair. "Cy isn't for you. You deserve better."

The statement sent Shane into a fresh peal of laughter. "*Oh, Donna!* Oh, Donna, do you remember how she always wore those neat little coordinates to school? And she got straight A's in home economics." Shane was forced to take deep breaths before she could continue. "She did a term paper on planning household budgets."

"Please, darling, don't think about it." Donna cast her eyes around the kitchen, wondering if there were any medicinal brandy in the house.

"She'll have her own shoe trees," Shane said weakly. "I just know it. And she'll label them so they don't get them mixed up. Oh, Cy!" On a new round of giggles, she pounded a fist on the table. "Laurie. Laurie MacAfee!"

Almost frantic with concern, Donna gently lifted Shane's face. "Shane, I…" With a jolt she saw that rather than being devastated, her friend was simply overcome with amusement. For a moment, Donna stared into round dancing eyes. "Well," she said dryly, "I knew you'd be upset."

Shane howled with laughter. "I'm going to give them a Victorian whatnot as a wedding present. Donna," she added with grinning gratitude, "you've made my day. Absolutely made it."

"I knew you'd take it badly," Donna said with a baffled smile. "Just try not to weep in public."

"I'll keep my chin up," Shane promised, then smiled. "You're sweet. Did you really think I was carrying a torch for Cy?"

"I wasn't sure," Donna admitted. "You were…well, an item for so long, and I knew how crushed you were when the two of you broke up. You'd never talk about it after that."

"I needed some time to lick my wounds," Shane told her. "They've been healed over for a long while. I was in love with him, but I got over it. He put a large dent in my pride. I survived."

"I could have killed him at the time," Donna muttered darkly. "Two months before the wedding."

"Better than two months after," Shane pointed out logically. "We would never have made a go of it. But now, Cy and Laurie MacAfee…"

This time they both broke out into laughter.

"Shane." Donna gave her a sudden sober look. "A lot of people are going to be thinking you still care for Cy."

Shane shrugged it off. "You can't do anything about what people think."

"Or what they say," Donna murmured.

"They'll find something more interesting to talk about before long," Shane returned carelessly. "Besides, I have too much to do to be worried about it."

"So I noticed from the pile of stuff on the porch. What's under that tarp?"

"Lumber and materials."

"Just what are you going to do with it?"

"Nothing. Vance Banning's going to do it. Want some more cocoa?"

"Vance Banning!" Stunned, then fascinated, Donna leaned forward. "Tell me."

"There's not much to tell. You didn't answer me," Shane reminded her.

"What? No, no, I don't want any more." Impatiently, she brushed the offer away. "Shane, what is Vance Banning going to do with your lumber and materials?"

"The carpentry work."

"Why?"

"I hired him to do it."

Donna gritted her teeth. "Why?"

"Because he's a carpenter."

"Shane!"

Valiantly, Shane controlled a grin. "Look, he's out of work, he's talented, I needed someone who'd work under union scale, so…" She spread her hands.

"What have you found out about him?" Donna demanded the right to fresh news.

"Not much." Shane wrinkled her nose. "Nothing, really. He doesn't say much."

Donna gave her a knowing smirk. "I already knew that."

A quick grin was Shane's response. "Well, he can be downright rude when he wants to. He has a lot of pride and a marvelous smile that he doesn't use nearly enough. Strong hands," she murmured, then brought herself back. "And a streak of reluctant kindness. I think he can laugh at himself but he's forgotten how. I know he's a workhorse because when the wind's right I can hear him hammering and sawing at all hours." She glanced out the window in the direction of the path. "I'm in love with him."

"Yes, but what—" Donna caught her breath and choked on it. *"What!"*

"I'm in love with him," Shane repeated with an amused smile. "Would you like some water?"

For nearly a full minute, Donna only stared at her. *She's joking,* she told herself. But by Shane's expression, she saw her friend was perfectly serious. It was her duty, Donna decided, as a married woman starting on her second child, to point out the dangers of this kind of thinking.

"Shane," she began in a patient, maternal tone, "you only just met the man. Now—"

"I knew it the minute I set my eyes on him," Shane interrupted calmly. "I'm going to marry him."

"Marry him!" Beyond words, Donna could only come up with sputters. Indulgently, Shane rose to pour her some water. "He—he asked you to marry him?"

"No, of course not." Shane chuckled at the idea as she handed Donna a glass. "He only just met me."

In an attempt to understand Shane's logic, Donna closed her eyes and concentrated. "I'm confused," she said at length.

"I said I was going to marry him," Shane explained, taking her seat again. "He doesn't know it yet. First I have to wait for him to fall in love with me."

After setting the untouched water aside, Donna gave her a stern look. "Shane, I think you're under more strain than you realize."

"I've been giving this a lot of thought," Shane answered, ignoring Donna's comment. "Number one, why would I have fallen in love with him in the blink of an eye if it wasn't right? It must be right, so number two, sooner or later he's going to fall in love with me."

Donna followed the pattern of thought and found it filled with snags. "And how are you going to make him do that?"

"Oh, I can't make him," Shane said reasonably. Her voice was both serene and confident. "He'll have to fall in love with me just as I am and in his own time—the same way I fell in love with him."

"Well, you've had some nutty ideas before, Shane Abbott, but this is the top." Donna folded her arms over her chest. "You're planning on marrying a man you've known barely a week who doesn't know he's going to marry you, and you're just going to sit patiently by until he gets the idea."

Shane thought for a moment, then nodded. "That's about it."

"It's the most ridiculous thing I've ever heard," Donna stated, then let out a surprised laugh. "And knowing you, it'll probably work."

"I'm counting on it."

Leaning forward, Donna took Shane's hands in hers. "Why do you love him, Shane?"

"I don't know," she answered immediately. "That's another reason I'm sure it's right. I know almost nothing about him except he's not a comfortable man. He'll hurt me and make me cry."

"Then why—"

"He'll make me laugh too," Shane interrupted. "And make me furious." She smiled a little, but her eyes were very serious. "I don't think he'll ever make me feel—inadequate. And when I'm near him, I *know*. That's enough for me."

"Yes." Donna nodded, giving Shane's hands a squeeze. "It would be. You're the most loving person I've ever known. And the most trusting. Those are wonderful traits, Shane, and—well, dangerous. I only wish we knew more about him," she added in a mutter.

"He has secrets," Shane murmured, and Donna's eyes sharpened. "They're his until he's ready to tell me about them."

"Shane..." Donna's fingers tightened on hers. "Be careful, please."

A little surprised by the tone, Shane smiled. "I will. Don't worry. Maybe I am more trusting than most, but I have my defenses. I'm not going to make a fool of myself." Unconsciously, she glanced out the window again, seeing the path to his house in her mind's eye. "He's not a simple man, Donna, but he is a good one. That much I'm sure of."

"All right," Donna agreed. Silently, she vowed to keep a close eye on Vance Banning.

For a long time after Donna left, Shane sat in the kitchen. The rain continued to pound. The steady drip from the ceiling plopped musically into the pan. She was aware of how reckless her words to Donna had been, yet she felt better having said them out loud.

No, she wasn't as blindly confident as she appeared. Inside, she was terrified by the knowledge that she loved so irrationally. She was trusting, yes, but not naive. She understood there was a price to pay for trust, and that often it was a dear one. Yet she knew her choice had already been made—or perhaps she'd never had one.

Rising, Shane switched off the lights and began to wander through the darkened house. She knew its every twist and turn, every board that creaked. It was everything familiar and comforting to her. She loved it. She knew none of Vance's twists and turns, none of his secret corners. He was everything strange and disturbing. She loved him.

If it had been a quiet, gentle love, she could have accepted it easily. But there was nothing quiet in the storm churning inside her. For all her energy and love of adventure, Shane had grown up in a slow, peaceful world where excitement was a run through the woods or a ride on the back of a tractor at haymaking. To fall suddenly in love with a stranger might seem romantic and wonderful in a story, but when it happened in real life, it was simply terrifying.

Shane walked upstairs, habitually avoiding the steps that creaked or groaned. The rain was a hollow, drumming sound all around her, whipped up occasionally by the wind to fly at the windows. Her bare feet met bare wood with a quiet patter. A small bucket caught the drip in the center of the hall. Expertly, she skirted around it.

Who was she to think all she had to do was to sit patiently by until Vance fell in love with her? she asked herself. After flipping on the light in her room, she went to stare at herself in the mirror. Was she beautiful? Shane asked her reflection. Alluring? With a half laugh, she rested her elbows on the dresser to look closer.

She saw the dash of freckles, the large dark eyes and cap of hair. She didn't see the stunning vitality, the temptingly smooth skin, the surprisingly sensual mouth.

Was that a face to send a man into raptures? she asked herself. The thought amused her so, that the reflection grinned back with quick good humor. Hardly, Shane decided, but she wouldn't want a man who looked only for a perfect face. No, she hadn't the face or figure to lure a man into love had she wanted to. She had only herself and the love in her heart.

Shane flashed the mirror a smile before she turned away to prepare for bed. She'd always thought love the ultimate adventure.

Six

Weak sunlight filtered through the bad-tempered clouds. The creek was swollen from the rainfall so that it ran its course noisily, hissing and complaining as it rounded the bend at the side of Shane's house. Shane was doing some complaining of her own.

The day before, she had moved her car out of the narrow driveway so that the delivery truck could have easy access to the back porch. Not wanting to ruin the grass, she had parked in the small square of dirt her grandmother had used as a vegetable garden. Once the car had been moved, Shane had become involved with the unloading of lumber and had promptly forgotten it. Now, it was sunk deep in mud, firmly resisting all efforts to get it out.

She pressed the gas lightly, tried forward, then reverse. She gunned the engine and swore. Slamming out of the driver's side, Shane sloshed ankle-deep in mire as she stomped back to the rear tire. She gave it an accusing stare, then kicked it.

"That's not going to help," Vance commented. He had been watching her for the last few minutes, torn somewhere between amusement and exasperation. And pleasure. There was a simple pleasure in just seeing her. He'd stopped counting the times over the last few days that he'd thought of her.

Out of patience, Shane turned to him, hands on hips. Her predicament was annoying enough without the added benefit of an audience. "You might have let me know you were there."

"You were…involved," he said, glancing pointedly at her mired car.

She sent him a cool look. "You've got a better idea, I suppose."

"A few," he agreed, moving across the lawn to join her. Her eyes snapped with temper while her mouth pouted. Her boots were caked with mud past the ankle. Her jeans, rolled up to the calf, had fared little better. She looked ready to boil over at the first wrong word. A cautious man would have said nothing.

"Who the hell parked it in this mud hole?" Vance demanded.

"*I* parked it in this mud hole." Shane gave the tire another fierce kick. "And it wasn't a mud hole when I did."

He lifted a brow. "I suppose you noticed it rained all night."

"Oh, get out of my way." Incensed, Shane pushed him aside and stomped back to the driver's seat. She turned on the ignition, shoved the shift into first, then stepped heavily on the gas. Mud flew like rain. The car groaned and sank deeper.

For a moment, Shane could only pound on the steering wheel in enraged impotence. She would have dearly loved to tell Vance that she didn't require any assistance. There was nothing more infuriating than an amused, superior male…especially when you needed one. Forcing herself to take a deep breath, she climbed back out of the car to meet Vance's grin with icy composure. "What's the first of your few ideas?" she asked coolly.

"Got a couple of planks?"

Even more annoyed that she hadn't thought of it herself, Shane went to the shed and found two long, thin boards. Without fuss or conversation, Vance took them and secured them just under the front wheels. Shane folded her arms and tapped one muddy boot as she watched him.

"I'd have thought of that in a minute," she muttered.

"Maybe." Vance stood again to walk to the rear of the car. "But you wouldn't get anywhere the way your back wheels are stuck."

Shane waited for him to make some comment on feminine stupidity. Then she would have an excuse to give him the full force of her temper. He merely studied her flushed face and furious eyes. "So?" she said at length.

Something suspiciously like a smile tugged at his mouth. Shane's eyes narrowed. "So, get back in and I'll push," he said, then put a restraining hand on her arm. "Gentle on the gas this time, hot rod. Just put it in Drive and easy does it."

"It's a four-speed," she told him with dignity.

"I beg your pardon." Vance waited until she had waded her way back to the front of the car. For the first time in months, perhaps years, he had to make a concentrated effort to control laughter. "Let the clutch out slow," he instructed after clearing his throat.

"I know how to drive," she snapped, and slammed the door smartly. Frowning into the rearview mirror, Shane watched him until he gave her a nod. With meticulous care, she engaged the clutch and gently pressed on the gas. The front wheels crept slowly onto the planks. The back tires slid, then stuck, then ponderously moved again. Shane kept the speed slow and even. It was humiliating, she thought, glaring straight ahead, absolutely humiliating that he was going to get her out without a hitch.

"Just a little more," Vance called to her, shifting his weight. "Keep it slow."

"What?" Shane rolled down the window, then stuck her head out to hear his answer. As she did, her foot slipped and fell heavily on the gas. The car shot out of the mud like a banana squeezed from its peel. With a gasp, Shane hit the brake, rocking to an abrupt halt.

Closing her eyes, she sat for a moment and considered making a run for it. She didn't dare glance in the rearview mirror now. It wouldn't be difficult, she reflected, to make a U-turn, then keep right on going. But cowardice wasn't her way. She swallowed, bit her lip, then climbed out of the car to face the music.

Vance was kneeling in the mud. He was thoroughly splattered and hopping mad. *"You idiot!"* he shouted before Shane could say a word. Even as she started to agree with him, he continued. "What the hell did you think you were doing? Pea-brained little twit, I told you to take it *slow.*"

He didn't stop there. He swore at length, and fluently, but Shane lost track of the content. It was enough to know he was in a justifiable high rage, while she was fighting a desperate battle with laughter. She did her best, her very best, to keep her face composed and penitent. Feeling it would be unwise, as well as useless to interrupt with apologies, she folded her lips, bit the bottom one and swallowed repeatedly.

At first she concentrated on keeping her eyes directly on his, hoping the fury there would kill the urge to giggle. But the sight of his mud-splattered face had her sides aching with restrained mirth. She hung her head, ostensibly from shame.

"I'd like to know who the hell told you you could drive," Vance went on furiously. "And what person with a brain cell working would have parked the car in a swamp to begin with?"

"It was my grandmother's garden," Shane managed in a strangled voice. "But you're right. You're absolutely right. I'm so sorry, really…" She broke off here as a gurgle of laughter rose dangerously. Clearing her throat, she hurried on. "Sorry, Vance. It was very—" she had to look over his head in order to compose herself "—careless of me."

"Careless!"

"Stupid," she amended quickly, thinking that might placate him. "Absolutely stupid. I'm really sorry." Helplessly, she pressed both hands to her mouth, but the giggles came through. "I *am* sorry," she insisted, giving up as he glared at her. "I don't mean to laugh. It's terrible." Dizzy with the effort of trying to hold back, Shane bent over double. "Really awful," she added on a howl of laughter.

"Since you think it looks like fun…" he muttered grimly, and grabbed her hand. Shane landed on her seat with a gentle splash and kept on laughing.

"I didn't—I didn't thank you," she said on a peal of giggles, "for getting my car out."

"Think nothing of it." Most women, he mused, would have been infuriated to find themselves sitting in a pile of mud. Shane was laughing just as hard at herself as she had at him. His grin was completely unexpected and spontaneous. "Brat," he accused, but Shane shook her head.

"Oh no, no, I'm not, really." She pressed the back of her hand to her mouth. "It's just this terrible habit of laughing at the wrong time. Because I really am sorry." The last word was drowned in a flood of laughter.

"I can see you are."

"Anyway, I didn't get it *all* over you." Scooping up some mud, she wiped it across his cheek. "I missed that part right there." She made a little choking sound in her throat. "That's much better," she approved.

"You aren't wearing nearly enough," Vance returned. He trailed both muddy palms down her face. Trying to avoid him, Shane slid, ending up flat on her back. Vance's boom of laughter broke into her shriek. "Much better," he agreed, then spotting the handful of mud she was about to heave, he made a grab for her arm. "Oh, no, you don't!"

As he laughed, she shifted. Vance landed half on his chest, half on his side. With a muttered curse, he propped himself up, studying her out of narrowed eyes.

"City boy," she mocked on a whoop of appreciation. "Probably never been in a mud fight in your life." She was too pleased with her maneuver to see the next one coming.

In a flash, Vance had her by the shoulders. Rolling her over, he straddled her, holding a hand to the back of her head. Lying full length, Shane looked wide-eyed at the mud inches away from her face.

"Oh, Vance, you *wouldn't!*" The helpless laughter bubbled still as she struggled.

"The hell I wouldn't." He pushed her face an inch closer.

"Vance!" Though she was slippery as an eel by this time, Vance held her firmly, clamping his knees around her while his hand urged her down. As the distance between revenge and her nose lessened, Shane closed her eyes and held her breath.

"Give?" he demanded.

Cautiously, Shane opened one eye. She hesitated a moment, torn between the desire to win and the image of having her face pushed into the mud. She didn't doubt he'd do it. "Give," she said reluctantly.

Abruptly, Vance rolled her over so that she lay in his lap. "City boy, huh?"

"You wouldn't have won if I weren't out of practice," she told him. "It was just beginner's luck."

Her eyes were mocking him. Her face was streaked with mud from his own fingers. The hands pressed against his chest were slippery with it. The grip on the back of her neck lightened until it was a caress. The hand at her hip roamed absently down her thigh as he lowered his eyes to her mouth. Slowly, without any conscious thought of doing so, Vance began to draw her closer.

Shane saw the change in his eyes and was suddenly afraid. Did she really have the defenses she had bragged to Donna about? Now that she was certain she loved him, could there be any defense? It was too fast, she thought frantically. It was all happening too fast. Breathless from the race of her heart, she scrambled up.

"I'll beat you to the creek," she challenged, then was off in a flash.

Pondering on her abrupt retreat, Vance watched her run around the side of the house. Normally, he would have considered it a ploy, but he found it didn't fit this time. Nothing about her fit, he concluded as he rose. Oddly, he realized he didn't seem to fit either. He hadn't realized he could find anything amusing or enjoyable about wrestling in the mud. Nor had he realized he could find a woman like Shane Abbott both intriguing and desirable. Trying to organize his thoughts, Vance walked around the side of the house to find her.

She had stripped off her boots and was wading knee-deep in the rushing creek water. "It's freezing!" she called out, then lowered herself to her waist. At the shock of cold, she sucked in her breath. "If it was warmer, we could walk down to Molly's Hole and take a quick swim."

"Molly's Hole?" Watching her, Vance sat on the grass to pull off his own boots.

"Right around the bend." She pointed vaguely in the direction of the main road. "Great swimming hole. Fishing too." Shivering a bit, she rubbed at the front of her shirt to help the water take off the worst of the mud. "We're lucky it rained, or else the creek wouldn't be high enough to do any good."

"If it hadn't rained, your car wouldn't have been stuck in the mud."

Shane shot him a grin. "That's beside the point." She watched him step into the water. "Cold?" she said sweetly when he winced.

"I should have pushed your face in," he decided. Stripping off his shirt, Vance tossed it on the grassy bank before scrubbing at his hands and arms.

"You'd have felt really bad if you had." Shane rubbed her face with creek water.

"No, I wouldn't have."

Glancing up, Shane laughed. "I like you, Vance. Gran would have called you a scoundrel."

He lifted a brow. "Is that praise?"

"Her highest," Shane agreed, rising to rub at the thighs of her jeans. They were plastered against her, molding her legs while her shirt clung wetly to her breasts. The cold had her nipples taut, straining against the thin cotton. Involved with cleaning off her clothes, she chattered, sublimely unaware they left her as good as naked.

"She loved scoundrels," Shane continued. "I suppose that's why she put up with me. I was always getting into one scrape or another."

"What kind?" Vance's torso was wet, cleaned of mud now, but he stayed where he was. Her body was exquisitely formed. He wondered how he hadn't noted before how perfectly scaled it was—small round breasts, wasp-thin waist, narrow hips, lean thighs.

"I don't like to brag." Shane worked the mud from the slippery sleeves of her shirt. "But I can show you the best way into old man Trippet's orchard if you want to snitch a few green apples. And I used to have a great time riding Mr. Poffenburger's dairy cows." Shane sloshed over to him. "Here, you haven't got it all off your face." Cupping some water in her hand, she lifted it and began to clean his face herself. "I tore my britches on every farmer's fence for three miles," she went on. "Gran would patch them up saying she despaired of my being any more than a hooligan."

With one small, smooth hand, she methodically scrubbed Vance's face. The other she held balanced against his naked chest. He made no protest, but stood still, watching her.

"'That Abbot girl,' they'd say," Shane told him, rubbing at a spot on his jawline. "Now I have to convince them I'm an upstanding citizen so they'll forget I filched their apples and buy my antiques. No one takes a hooligan very seriously. There, that's better." Satisfied, Shane started to lower her hand. Vance caught it in his. Her eyes didn't waver from his, but she became very still.

Without speaking, he began to wash the few lingering traces of mud from her face. He worked in very slow, very deliberate circles, his eyes fixed on hers. Though his palm was rough, his touch was gentle. Shane's lips trembled apart. With something like curiosity, Vance took a damp finger to trace their shape. He felt her quick, convulsive shudder. Still slow, still inquisitive, he ran his fingertip along the inside of her bottom lip. Under his thumb, the pulse in her wrist began to hammer. The sun broke briefly through the clouds, so that the light shifted and brightened before it dimmed again. He watched it play over her face.

"You won't run away this time, Shane," he murmured, as if to himself.

She said nothing, afraid to speak while his finger lingered on her lips. Slowly, he traced it down, over her chin, over the throbbing pulse in her throat. He paused there a moment, as if gauging and enjoying her response to him. Then he allowed his fingertip to sweep up over the swell of her breast and lie lightly on the erect peak covered only by the thin wet shirt.

Heat and cold shot through her; her skin was chilled from the water, her blood flamed at his touch. Vance watched the color drain from her face while her eyes grew impossibly large and dark. Yet she didn't draw away or protest the intimacy. He heard the sharp intake of her breath, then the slow, ragged expulsion.

"Are you afraid of me?" he asked, bringing his hand up to cup the back of her neck.

"No," she whispered. "Of me."

Puzzled, he drew his brows together. For a moment he looked hard and very fierce. Though his eyes weren't cold, they were piercing—full of questions, full of suspicion. Still Shane felt no fear of him, only of the needs and longing running through her. "An odd answer, Shane," he murmured thoughtfully. "You're an odd woman." With his fingers, he kneaded the back of her neck while he searched her face for answers. "Is that why you excite me?"

"I don't know," she said, struggling for breath. "I don't want to know. Just kiss me."

He lowered his lips, but only tested hers with the same lightness as his fingertip. "I wonder," he said softly against her mouth, "what it is about you I can't quite shake. Your taste?" He dug his teeth almost experimentally into her bottom lip. A low moan of pleasure was wrenched from her. "Fresh as rain one minute and honey soaked the next." Lightly, languidly, he traced her lips with his tongue. "Is it the way you feel? That skin of yours…like the underside of a rose petal." He ran his hands down her arms, then up again, gradually bringing her to him until she was caught close. The thud of her heart sounded like thunder in her ears.

"Why do you have to know?" The question was low and shaky. "Feeling's enough." They might have been naked, pressed body to body with only wet clinging clothes between them. "Kiss me, Vance, just kiss me. It's enough."

"You smell like rain now," he murmured, telling himself to resist her but knowing he wouldn't. "Pure and honest. When I look in your eyes, I'd swear there isn't a lie in you. Is there?" he demanded, but he crushed his mouth to hers before she could answer.

Shane reeled from the impact. Even as she gasped, his tongue was probing and exploring. The anger she had sensed in him before was now pure passion. Hunger, the rawness of his hunger, thrilled her. The water ran swiftly, grumbling as it hurried on its way to the river, but Shane heard only her own heartbeat. She no longer felt the stinging cold, only the warmth of his hand as it ran up her spine and down again.

He wasn't content with only her lips now, but took his own wild journey of her face. It was still wet, tasting of the cold freshness of the creek. But wherever his kisses wandered, he was drawn back again to the soft sweet taste of her mouth. It seemed always to be waiting for him, ready to open, invite, demand. Beneath the pliancy, beneath the willingness was a passion as great as his own and a strength he was just beginning to measure.

Vance told himself he needed a woman. That was why he was so desperate for Shane. He needed a woman's softness and flavor, and she was here. There was no exclusivity to it. How could there be? Yet there was something about her slight body, her fascinatingly different taste that drove every other woman to some dark corner of his mind, leaving only Shane in the light.

He could take her now, on the bank of the creek, in the dim daylight on the rain-damp grass. As her mouth moved, moist and warm under his, Vance could imagine how it would be to take full possession of her body. Her energy and hunger would match his own. There would be no false, foolish pretense of seduction, but an honest meeting of desires.

Her small round breasts pressed into his naked chest. Vance thought he could feel the aching need in them—or was it his own need? It raged in him, drove at him, until she was all he craved. Her mouth was small too, but avid, never retreating from the savageness of his. Instead, she matched it, propelling him further and further, pulling him closer and closer. All women or one woman, he was no longer certain, but she was overpowering him.

Somehow he knew that if he took her, he would never walk away easily. The reasons might not be fully clear yet, but she wasn't like the other women he had known and bedded. He was afraid her eager hands and mouth could hold him—and he wasn't yet ready to chance it.

Vance drew her away, but Shane dropped her head on his chest. There was something vulnerable in the gesture though the arms around his waist were strong. The contrast aroused him, as did the lightning fast beat of her heart. For a moment, he stood holding her while the water ran cold and fast around their legs and hazy sunlight drifted through the trees.

She'd once told him that a snowfall had made her feel a complete isolation. Vance felt it now. There might have been nothing, no one beyond the rushing creek and fringe of trees. And to his own confusion, he felt a need for none.

He wanted only her. Perhaps they were alone… The thought both excited and disturbed him. Perhaps there was nothing beyond that forgotten little spot, and no reason not to take what he wanted.

Shane shivered, making him realize she must be chilled to the bone. It brought him back to reality in a rush. His arms dropped away from her.

"Come on," he muttered. "You should get inside." Vance pulled her up the slippery bank.

Shane bent over to pick up her boots. When she was certain she could do so calmly, she met his eyes. "You're not coming in." It wasn't a question. She had sensed all too well his change of attitude.

"No." His tone was cool again though his blood still throbbed for her. "I'll go change, then come back and get started on the porch."

Shane had known he would bring her pain, but she hadn't thought it would be so soon. The old wounds of rejection opened again. "All right. If I'm not here, just do whatever you have to do."

Vance could feel the hurt, yet she met his eyes and her voice was steady. Recriminations he could have dealt with easily. Anger he would have welcomed. For the first time in years, he was completely baffled by a woman.

"You know what would happen if I came in now." The words were rough with impatience. Vance found himself wanting to shake her.

"Yes."

"Is that what you want?"

Shane said nothing for a moment. When she smiled, the light didn't reach her eyes. "It's not what you want," she said quietly. Turning, she started back to the house, but Vance caught her arm, spinning her around. He was furious now, all the more furious when he saw the effort her composure was costing her.

"Damn it, Shane, you're a fool if you think I don't want you."

"You don't want to want me," she returned evenly. "That's more important to me."

"What difference does it make?" he ground out impatiently. Frustrated by the calmness of her answer, he did shake her. How could she look at him with those big quiet eyes when she'd driven him to the wall only moments before? "You know how close I came to taking you right here on the ground. Isn't it enough to know you can push me to that? What more do you want?"

She gave him a long searching look. "Push you to it," she repeated quietly. "Is that really how you see it?"

The conflict raged in him. He wanted badly to get away from her. "Yes," he said bitterly. "How else?"

"How else," she agreed with a shaky laugh that started a new ache moving in him. "I suppose for some that might be a compliment of sorts."

"If you like," he said curtly as he picked up his shirt.

"I don't," she murmured. "But then, you said I was odd." With a sigh, she stared into his eyes. "You've cut yourself off from your feelings, Vance, and it eats at you."

"You don't know a damn thing," he tossed back, only more enraged to hear her speak the truth.

As he glared at her, Shane heard a bird set up a strident song in the woods behind her. The high, piercing notes suited the air of tension and anger. "You're not nearly as hard or cold as you'd like to think," she said calmly.

"You don't know anything about me," he countered furiously, grabbing her arms again.

"And it infuriates you when the guard slips," Shane continued without breaking rhythm. "It infuriates you even more that you might actually feel something for me." His fingers loosened on her arms, and Shane drew away. "I don't push you, but something else certainly does. No, I don't know what it is, but you do." She took a long steadying breath as she studied him. "You've got to fight your own tug-of-war, Vance."

Turning, she walked to the house, leaving him staring after her.

Seven

He couldn't stop thinking of her. In the weeks that passed, the mountains became a riot of color. The air took on the nip of fall. Twice, Vance spotted deer through his own kitchen window. And he couldn't stop thinking of her.

He split his time between the two houses. His own was taking shape slowly. Vance calculated he would be ready to start the more detailed inside work by winter.

Shane's was progressing more quickly. Between roofers and plumbers, the house had been bedlam for more than a week. The old kitchen had been gutted and stood waiting for new paint and trim. Shane had waited patiently for rain after the roof had been repaired. Then she had checked all the familiar spots for signs of leaks. Oddly, she found herself a trifle sad that she didn't have to set out a single pan or bucket.

The museum area was completely finished. While Vance

worked elsewhere, Shane busied herself arranging and filling the display cases that had been delivered.

At times she would be gone for hours, hunting up treasures at auctions and estate sales. He always knew the moment she returned because the house would spring to life
again. In the basement, she'd set up a workroom where she
refinished certain pieces or stored others. He saw her dash
out, or dash in. He saw her carting tables, dragging packing
boxes, climbing ladders. He never saw her idle.

Her attitude toward him was just as it had been from the
first—friendly and open. Not once did she mention what
had happened between them. It took all of his strength of
will not to touch her. She laughed, brought him coffee and
gave him amusing accounts of her adventures at auctions. He
wanted her more every time he looked at her.

Now, as he finished up the trim on what had been the
summer parlor, Vance knew she was downstairs. He went
over his work critically, checking for flaws, while the simple awareness of her played havoc with his concentration. It
might be wise, he thought, to take a trip back to Washington.
So far, he had handled everything pertaining to his company
by phone or mail. There was nothing urgent that required
his attention, but he wondered if it wouldn't be wise to have
a week of distance. She was haunting him. Plaguing him,
Vance corrected. On a wave of frustration he packed his tools.
The woman was trouble, he decided. Nothing but trouble.

Still, as he got ready to leave, Vance detoured to the basement steps. He hesitated, cursed himself, then started down.

Dressed in baggy cord jeans and a hip-length sweater, she
was working on a tilt-top table. Vance had seen the table
when Shane had first brought it in. It had been scarred and

scratched and dull. Flushed with excitement, she had claimed to have bought it for a song, then had hustled it off to the basement. Now, the grain of mahogany gleamed through the thin coats of clear lacquer she had applied. She was industriously buffing it with paste wax. The basement smelled of tung oil and lemon.

Vance would have turned to go back upstairs, but Shane raised her head and saw him. "Hi!" Her smile welcomed him before she gestured him over. "Come take a look. You're the expert on wood." As he crossed the room, Shane stood back to survey her work. "The hardest thing now," she muttered as she twisted a curl around her finger, "is going to be parting with it. I'll make a nice profit. I only paid a fraction of its worth."

Vance ran a fingertip over the surface. It was baby smooth and flawless. His mother had a similar piece in the drawing room of her Washington estate. Since he had purchased it for her himself, he knew the value. He also knew the difference between an amateur job of refinishing and an expert one. This hadn't been done haphazardly. "Your time's worth something," he commented. "And your talent. It would have cost a good deal to have this done."

"Yes, but I enjoy it, so it doesn't count."

Vance lifted his eyes. "You're in business to make money, aren't you?"

"Yes, of course." Shane snapped the lid back on the can of paste wax. "I love the smell of this stuff."

"You won't make a lot of money if you don't consider your own time and labor."

"I don't need to make a lot of money." She placed the can on a shelf, then examined the ladder-back chair, which needed recaning. "I need to pay bills and stock my shop and have a bit left over to play with." Turning the chair upside down, she frowned at the frayed hole in the center of the seat. "I wouldn't know what to do with a lot of money."

"You'd find something," Vance said dryly. "Clothes, furs."

Shane glanced up, saw he was serious, then burst out laughing. "Furs? Oh, yes, I can see myself waltzing into the general store to buy milk in a mink. Vance, you're a riot."

"I've never known a woman who didn't appreciate a mink," he countered.

"Then you've known the wrong women," she said lightly as she set the chair upright again. "I know this man in Boonsboro who does caning and rushing. I'll have to give him a call. Even if I had the time, I wouldn't know where to begin on this."

"What kind of woman are you?"

Shane's thoughts came back from her ladder-back chair. When she looked at him again, she noted that Vance's expression was cynical. She sighed. "Vance, why do you always look for complications?"

"Because they're always there," he returned.

She shook her head, keeping her hands on the top rung of the chair's back. "I'm exactly the kind of woman I seem to be. Perhaps that's too simple for you, but it's true."

"The kind who's content to work twelve hours a day just for enough money to get by on?" Vance demanded. "The kind who's willing to slave away hour after hour—"

"I don't slave," Shane interrupted testily.

"The hell you don't. I've watched you. Dragging furniture, lugging boxes, scrubbing on your hands and knees." Remembering only made him angrier. She was too small to labor the way he had seen over the past weeks. The fact that he wanted to insist she stop only infuriated him further. "Damn it, Shane, it's too much for you to handle by yourself."

"I know what I'm capable of," she tossed back, springing to her own defense. "I'm not a child."

"No, you're a woman who doesn't crave furs or all the niceties an attractive female can have if she plays her cards right." The words were cool with sarcasm.

Temper sprang into Shane's eyes. Struggling not to explode, she turned away from him. "Do you think everyone has a game to play, Vance?"

"And some play better than others" was his response.

"Oh, I feel sorry for you," she said tightly. "Really very sorry."

"Why?" he demanded. "Because I know that grabbing all they can get is what motivates people? Only a fool settles for less."

"I wonder if you really believe that," she murmured. "I wonder if you really could."

"I wonder why you pretend to believe otherwise," he retorted.

"I'm going to tell you a little story." When she turned back, her eyes were dark with anger. "A man like you will probably find it corny and a bit boring, but you'll just have to listen anyway." Stuffing her hands into her pockets, she paced the low-ceilinged room until she was certain she could continue.

"Do you see these?" Shane demanded, indicating a row of shelves that held filled mason jars. "My grandmother—technically, she was my great-grandmother—canned these. Putting by, she always called it. She'd dig and hoe and plant and weed, then spend hours in a hot, steamy kitchen canning. Putting by," Shane repeated more quietly as she studied the colorful glass jars. "When she was sixteen, she lived in a mansion in southern Maryland. Her family was very wealthy. They still are," Shane added with a shrug. "The Bristols. The Leonardtown Bristols. You might have heard of them."

He had, and though his eyes registered surprise, he said nothing. Bristols Department Stores were scattered strategically all over the country. It was a very old, very prestigious firm that catered to the wealthy and the prominent. Even now, Vance's firm was contracted to build another branch in Chicago.

"In any case," Shane continued, "she was a young, beautiful, pampered girl who could have had anything. She'd been educated in Europe, and there were plans for her to be finished in Paris before a London debut. If she had followed her parents' plans, she would have married well, had her own mansion and her own staff of servants. The closest she would have come to planting would have been watching her gardener prune a rosebush."

Shane gave a little laugh as though the thought both amused and baffled her. "She didn't follow the plan, though. She fell in love with William Abbott, an apprentice mason who had been hired to do some stonework on the estate. Of course, her family would have none of it. They were already planning the groundwork for a marriage between Gran and the heir to some steel company. The moment they got wind of what was happening, they fired him. To keep it brief, Gran made her choice and married him. They disowned her. Very dramatic and Victorian. The I-have-no-daughter sort of thing you read in a standard Gothic."

Vance said nothing as she stared at him, almost daring him to comment. "They moved here, back with his family," Shane continued. "They had to share this house with his parents because there wasn't enough money for one of their own. When his father died, they cared for his mother. Gran never regretted giving up all the *niceties*. She had such tiny hands," she murmured, looking down at her own. "You wouldn't have thought they could be so strong." She shook off the mood and turned away. "They were poor by the standards she had grown up with. What horses they had were for pulling a plow. Some of your land was hers at one time, but with the taxes and no one to work it…" She trailed off, lifting down a mason jar, then setting it back. "The only gesture her parents ever made was when her mother left Gran the dining-room set and a few pieces of china. Even that was done through lawyers after her mother had died." Shane plucked up her polishing cloth and began to run it through her hands.

"Gran had five children, lost two in childhood, another in the war. One daughter moved to Oklahoma and died childless about forty years ago. Her youngest son settled here, married and had one daughter. Both he and his wife were killed when the daughter was five." She paused a moment, brooding up at the small window set near the ceiling. Light poured through it to lie in a patch on the concrete floor. "I wonder if you can appreciate how a mother feels when she outlives every one of her children."

Vance said nothing, only continued to watch as Shane moved agitatedly around the room. "She raised her granddaughter, Anne. Gran loved her. Maybe part of the love was grief, I don't know. My mother was a beautiful child—there are pictures of her upstairs—but she was never content. The stories I've heard came mostly from people in town, though once or twice Gran talked to me. Anne hated living here, hated not having enough. She wanted to be an actress. When she was seventeen, she got pregnant."

Shane's voice altered subtly, but he heard the change. It was flat now, devoid of emotion. He'd never heard that tone from her before. "She didn't know—or wouldn't admit—who the father was," she said simply. "As soon as I was born, she took off and left me with Gran. From time to time, she came back, spent a few days and talked Gran out of more money. At last count she's been married three times. I've seen her in furs. They don't seem to make her happy. She's still beautiful, still selfish, still discontented."

Shane turned and looked at Vance for the first time since she had begun. "My grandmother only grabbed for one thing in her life, and that was love. She spoke French beautifully, read Shakespeare and tilled a garden. And she was happy. The only thing my mother ever taught me was that *things* meant nothing. Once you have a *thing,* you're too busy looking for the next one to be happy with it. You're too worried that someone might have a better one to be able to enjoy it. All the games my mother played never brought anything but pain to the people who loved her. I don't have the time or the skill for those games."

As she started to walk to the stairs, Vance stepped in front of her to bar her way. She lifted her chin to stare with eyes that glittered with anger and tears. "You should have told me to go to hell," he said quietly.

Shane swallowed. "Go to hell then," she muttered, and tried to move past him again.

Vance took her shoulders, holding her firmly at arm's length. "Are you angry with me, Shane, or with yourself for telling me something that was none of my business?" he asked.

After taking a deep breath, Shane stared at him, dry-eyed. "I'm angry because you're cynical, and I've never been able to understand cynicism."

"Any more than I understand an idealist."

"I'm not an idealist," she countered. "I simply don't automatically assume there's someone waiting to take advantage of me." She felt calmer suddenly, and sadder. "I think you miss a lot more by not trusting people than you risk by trusting them."

"What happens when the trust is violated?"

"Then you pick up and go on," she told him simply. "You're only a victim if you choose to be."

His brows drew together. Is that what he considered himself? A victim? Was he continuing to allow Amelia to blight his life two years after she'd died? And how much longer would he look over his shoulder for the next betrayal?

Shane felt his fingers relax, saw the puzzled consideration on his face. She lifted a hand to touch his shoulder. "Were you hurt very badly?" she asked him.

Vance focused on her again, then released her. "I was… disillusioned."

"That's the worst kind of hurt, I think." In compassion, she laid a hand on his arm. "When someone you love or care for turns out to be dishonest, or an ideal turns to glass, it's difficult to accept. I always set my ideals high. If they're going to crumble, I'd just as soon take the long fall." She smiled, slipping her hand down so it linked with his. "Let's go for a drive."

His thoughts were so bound up in her words, it took him a moment to understand the suggestion. "A drive?" he repeated.

"We've been cooped up for weeks," Shane stated as she pulled him toward the stairs. "I don't know about you, but I haven't done anything but work until I tumbled into bed. It's a beautiful day, maybe the last of Indian summer." She shut the basement door behind them. "And I bet you haven't had a tour of the battlefield yet. Certainly not with an expert guide."

"Are you," he asked with the beginnings of a smile, "an expert guide?"

"The best," she said without modesty. As she had hoped, the tension went out of the fingers that were laced with hers. "There's nothing about the battle I can't tell you, or as some of my critics would claim, won't tell you."

"As long as I don't have to take a quiz afterward," Vance agreed as she pulled him out the back door.

"I'm retired," she reminded him primly.

"The Battle of Antietam," Shane began as she drove down a narrow, winding road lined with monuments, "though claimed as a clear victory for neither side, resulted in the repulse of Lee's first effort to invade the North." Vance gave a quick grin at her faintly lecturing tone, but didn't interrupt. "Near Antietam Creek here in Sharpsburg," she continued, "on September 17, 1862, Lee and McClellan engaged in the bloodiest single day of the Civil War. That's Dunker Church." Shane pointed to a tiny white building set off the road. "Some of the heaviest fighting went on there. I have some pretty good prints for the museum."

Vance glanced back at the peaceful little spot as Shane drove by. "Looks quiet enough now," he commented, and earned a mild look.

"Lee divided his forces," she went on, ignoring him, "sending Jackson to capture Harper's Ferry. A Union soldier picked up a copy of Lee's orders, giving McClellan an advantage, but he didn't move fast enough. Even when he engaged Lee's much smaller army in Sharpsburg, he failed to smash through the line before Jackson returned with support. Lee lost a quarter of his army and withdrew. McClellan still didn't capitalize on his advantage. Even so, twenty-six thousand men were lost."

"For a retired schoolteacher, you don't seem to have forgotten the facts," Vance remarked.

Shane laughed, taking a bend in the road competently. "My ancestors fought here. Gran didn't let me forget it."

"For which side?"

"Both." She gave a small shrug. "Wasn't that the worst of it really? The choosing sides, the disintegration of families. This is a border state. Though it went for the North, sympathies this far south leaned heavily toward the Confederacy as well. It isn't difficult to imagine a number of people from this area cheering secretly or openly for the Stars and Bars."

"And with this section being caught between Virginia and West Virginia—"

"Exactly," she said, very much like a teacher approving of a bright student. Vance chuckled but she didn't seem to notice. Shane pulled off the side of the road into a small parking area. "Come on, let's walk. It's beautiful here."

Around them mountains circled in the full glory of fall. A few leaves whipped by—orange, scarlet, amber—to be caught by the wind and carried off. There were rolling hills, gold in the slanting sunlight, and fields with dried, withering stalks of corn. The air was cooler now as the sun dropped toward the peaks of the western mountains. Without thinking, Vance linked his hand with hers.

"Bloody Lane," Shane said, bringing his attention to a long, narrow trench. "Gruesome name, but apt. They came at each other from across the fields. Rebs from the north. Yanks from the south. Artillery set up there—" she pointed "—and there. This trench is where most of them lay after it was over. Of course, there were engagements all around— at the Burnside Bridge, the Dunker Church—but this…"

Vance shot her a curious look. "War really fascinates you, doesn't it?"

Shane looked out over the field. "It's the only true obscenity. The only time killing's glorified rather than condemned. Men become statistics. I wonder if there's anything more dehumanizing." Her voice became more thoughtful. "Haven't you ever found it odd that to kill one to one is considered man's ultimate crime, but the more a man kills during war, the more he's honored? So many of these were farm boys," she continued before Vance could form an answer. "Children who'd never shot at anything more than a weasel in the henhouse. They put on a uniform, blue or gray, and marched into battle. I doubt if a fraction of them had any idea what it was really going to be like. I'll tell you what fascinates me." Shane looked back at Vance, too wrapped up in her own thoughts to note how intensely he watched her. "Who were they really? The sixteen-year-old Pennsylvania farm boy who rushed across this field to kill a sixteen-year-old boy from a Georgia plantation—did they start out looking for adventure? Were they on a quest? How many pictured themselves sitting around a campfire like men and raising some hell away from their mothers?"

"A great many, I imagine," Vance murmured. Affected by the image she projected, he slipped an arm around her shoulders as he looked out over the field. "Too many."

"Even the ones who got back whole would never be boys again."

"Then why history, Shane, when it's riddled with wars?"

"For the people." She tossed back her head to look at him. The lowering sun shining on her eyes seemed to accentuate the tiny gold flecks that he sometimes couldn't see at all. "For the boy I can imagine who came across that field in September more than a hundred and twenty years ago. He was seventeen." She turned back to the field as if she could indeed see him. "He'd had his first whiskey, but not his first woman. He came running across that field full of terror and glory. The bugles were blaring, the shells exploding, so that the noise was so huge, he never heard his own fear. He killed an enemy that was so obscure to him it had no face. And when the battle was over, when the war was over, he went home a man, tired and aching for his own land."

"What happened to him?" Vance murmured.

"He married his childhood sweetheart, raised ten kids and told his grandchildren about his charge to Bloody Lane in 1862."

Vance drew her closer, not in passion, but in camaraderie. "You must have been a hell of a teacher," he said quietly.

That made Shane laugh. "I was a hell of a storyteller," she corrected.

"Why do you do that?" he demanded. "Why do you underrate yourself?"

She shook her head. "No, I know my capabilities and my limitations. And," she added, "I'm willing to stretch them both a bit to get what I want. It's much smarter than thinking you're something you're not." Before he could speak, she laughed, giving him a friendly hug. "No, no more philosophizing. I've done my share for the day. Come on, let's go up in the tower. The view's wonderful from there." She was off in a sprint, pulling Vance with her. "You can see for miles," she told him as they climbed the narrow iron steps.

The light was dim though the sun shot through the small slits set in the sides of the stone tower. It grew brighter as they climbed, then poured through the opening at the top. "This is the part I like best," she told him, while a few annoyed pigeons fluttered away from their roost in the roof. She leaned over the wide stone, pleased to let the wind buffet her face. "Oh, it's beautiful, the perfect day for it. Look at those colors!" She drew Vance beside her, wanting to share. "Do you see? That's our mountain."

Our mountain. Vance smiled as he followed the direction of her hand. The way she said it, it might have belonged to the two of them exclusively. Beyond the tree-thick hills, the more distant mountains were cast in blue from the falling afternoon light. Farmhouses and barns were set here and there, with the more closely structured surrounding towns quiet in the early evening hush. Just barely, he could hear the whiz of a car on the highway. As he looked over a cornfield, he saw three enormous crows take flight. They argued, taunting each other as they glided across the sky. The air was very still after they passed, so quiet he could hear the breeze whisper in the dry stalks of corn.

Then he saw the buck. It stood poised no more than ten yards from where Shane had parked her car. It was still as a statue, head up, ears pricked. Vance turned to Shane and pointed.

In silence, hands linked, they watched. Vance felt something move inside him, a sudden sense of belonging. He wouldn't have been amused now if Shane had said "our mountain." Remnants of bitterness washed from him as he realized his answer had been staring him in the face. He'd kept himself a victim, just as Shane had said, because it was easier to be angry than to let go.

The buck moved quickly, bounding over the grassy hill, taking a low stone fence with a graceful leap before he darted out of sight. Vance felt rather than heard Shane's long, slow sigh.

"I never get used to it," she murmured. "Every time I see one, I'm struck dumb."

Shane turned her face up to his. It seemed natural to kiss her here, with the mountains and fields around them, with the feeling of something shared still on both of them. Above their heads a pigeon cooed softly, content now that the intruders were quiet.

Here was the tenderness Shane had sensed but had not been sure of. His mouth was firm but not demanding, his hands strong but not bruising. Her heart seemed to flutter to her throat. Everything warm and sweet poured through her until she was limp and pliant in his arms. She had been waiting for this—this final assurance of what she knew he held trapped inside him: a gentle goodness she would respect as much as his strength and confidence. Her sigh was not of surrender but of joy in knowing she could admire what she already loved.

Vance drew her closer, changing the angle of the kiss, reluctant to break the moment. Emotions seeped into him, through the cracks in the wall he had built so long ago. He felt the soft give of her mouth, tasted its moist generosity. With care, he let his fingertips reacquaint themselves with the texture of her skin.

Could she have been there all along, he wondered, waiting for him to stumble onto her through a curtain of bitterness and suspicion?

Vance drew her against his chest, holding her tightly with both arms as if she might vanish. Was it too late for him to fall in love? he wondered. Or to win a woman who already knew the worst of him and had no notion of his material advantages? Closing his eyes, he rested his cheek on her hair. If it wasn't too late, should he take the chance and tell her who and what he was? If he told her now, he might never be fully certain, if she came to him, that she came only to him. He needed that—to be taken for himself without the Riverton Banning fortune or power. He hesitated, torn and indecisive. That alone shook him. Vance was a man who ruled a multimillion-dollar company by being decisive. Now a slip of a woman whose hair curled chaotically under his cheek was changing the order of his life.

"Shane." Vance drew her away to kiss her brow.

"Vance." Laughing, she kissed him soundly, more like a friend than a lover. "You look so serious."

"Have dinner with me." It came out too swiftly and he cursed himself. What had become of his finesse with women?

Shane pushed at her windblown hair. "All right. I can fix us something at the house."

"No, I want to take you out."

"Out?" Shane frowned, thinking of the expense.

"Nothing fancy," he told her, thinking she was worried about her bulky sweater and jeans. "As you said, neither of us has done anything but work in weeks." He brushed his knuckles over the back of her cheek. "Come with me."

She smiled, pleasing him. "I know a nice little place just over the border in West Virginia."

Shane chose the tiny, out-of-the-way restaurant because it was inexpensive and she had some fond memories of an abbreviated career as a waitress there. She'd worked the summer after her high school graduation in order to earn extra money for college.

After they had settled into a cramped booth with a sputtering candle between them, she shot him a grin. "I knew you'd love it."

Vance glanced around at the painted landscapes in vivid colors and plastic frames. The air smelled ever so faintly of onion. "Next time, I choose."

"They used to serve a great spaghetti here. It was Thursday's special, all you can eat for—"

"It's not Thursday," Vance pointed out, dubiously opening the plastic-coated menu. "Wine?"

"I think they probably have it." Shane smiled at him when he peered over the top of the menu. "We could go next door and get a whole bottle for two ninety-seven."

"Good vintage?"

"Just last week," she assured him.

"We'll take our chances here." He decided next time he would take her somewhere he could buy her champagne.

"I'll have the chili," Shane announced, bringing his thoughts back.

"Chili?" Vance frowned at the menu again. "Is it any good?"

"Oh, no!"

"Then why are you—" He broke off as he lowered his menu and saw Shane buried behind her own. "Shane, what—"

"They just came in," she hissed, turning her menu toward the entrance and peeping around the side of it.

Curiously, he glanced over. Vance spotted Cy Trainer with a trim brunette in a severely tailored tan suit and sensible pumps. His first reaction was annoyance; then, looking the woman over again and noting the way her hand rested on Cy's arm, he turned back to Shane. She was fully hidden behind the menu.

"Shane, I know it must upset you, but you're bound to run into him from time to time and…" He heard a muffled sound from behind the plastic-coated cardboard. Instinctively, Vance reached for her hand. "We could go somewhere else, but we can't leave now without his seeing you."

"It's Laurie MacAfee." She squeezed Vance's fingers convulsively. He returned the pressure, furious that she still had feelings for the man who had hurt her.

"Shane, you've got to face this and not let him see you make a fool of yourself."

"I know, but it's so hard." Cautiously, she tilted the menu to the side. With a jolt, Vance saw she was convulsed not with tears but with laughter. "As soon as he sees us," she began confidentially, "he's going to come over and be polite."

"I can see that's going to cause you a lot of pain."

"Oh, it is," she agreed. "Because you've got to promise to kick me under the table or stomp on my foot the minute you see I'm going to laugh."

"My pleasure," he assured her.

"Laurie used to keep her dolls lined up according to height and she sewed little name tags on all their clothes," Shane explained, taking deep breaths to prepare herself.

"That certainly clears everything up."

"Okay, now I'm going to put the menu down." She swallowed, lowering her voice a bit more. "Whatever you do, don't look at them."

"I wouldn't dream of it."

After a final cleansing breath, Shane set the menu on the table. "Chili?" she said in a normal tone. "Yes, it's always been good here. I believe I'll have it too."

"You're an idiot."

"Oh yes, I agree." Smiling, she picked up her water glass. Out of the corner of her eye, she spotted Cy and Laurie crossing the room toward them. To kill the first bubble of laughter, she cleared her throat violently.

"Shane, how nice to see you."

Looking up, Shane managed to feign surprise. "Hello, Cy. Hello, Laurie. How've you been?"

"Very well," Laurie answered in her carefully modulated voice. She's really very pretty, Shane thought. Even if her eyes are just a fraction too close together.

"I don't think you know Vance," she continued. "Vance, this is Cy Trainer and Laurie MacAfee, old school friends of mine. Vance is my neighbor."

"Ah, of course, the old Farley place." Cy extended his

hand. Vance found it soft. The grip was correctly firm and brief. "I hear you're fixing the place up."

"A bit." Vance allowed himself to study Cy's face. He was passable, Vance decided, considering he had a weak jaw.

"You must be the carpenter who's helping Shane set up her little shop," Laurie put in. Her glance slipped over his work clothes before it shifted to Shane's sweater. "I must say, I was surprised when Cy told me your plans."

Seeing Shane's lip quiver, Vance set his foot firmly on top of hers. "Were you?" Shane said as she reached for her water again. Her eyes danced with suppressed amusement as they met Vance's over the rim. "Well, I've always liked to surprise people."

"We couldn't imagine you with your own business, could we, Cy?" Laurie went on without giving him a chance to answer. "Of course, we wish you the very best of luck, Shane, and you can count on both of us to buy something to help you get started."

The laughter was a pain in her stomach. Shane had to press a hand against it while Vance increased the pressure on her foot. "Thank you, Laurie. I can't tell you what that means to me... I really can't."

"Anything for an old friend, right, Cy? You know we wish you every success, Shane. I'll be sure to tell everyone I know about your little shop. That should help bring a few people in. Though of course," she sighed apologetically, "the selling's up to you."

"Y-yes. Thank you."

"We'll just be running along now. We want to order before it gets too crowded. So nice meeting you." Laurie sent Vance a brief smile and drew Cy away.

"Oh, God, I think I'm going to burst!" Shane drank down the whole glass of water without a breath.

"Your boyfriend got just what he deserved," Vance murmured, glancing after them. "She'll regiment everything right down to their sex life." Thoughtfully, he looked after them. "Do you think they have one yet?"

"Oh, stop," Shane begged, savaging her lip in defense. "I'll be hysterical in a minute."

"Do you suppose she picked out that tie he's wearing?" Vance asked.

Giving up, Shane burst into laughter. "Oh, damn you, Vance," she whispered when Laurie turned her head. "I was doing so well too."

"Want to give them something to talk about over dinner?" Before she could answer, Vance pulled her across the narrow booth and planted a long, lingering kiss on her lips. To keep Shane from ending it too soon, he caught her chin in his hand and held her still. He drew her away for only seconds, tilting her head, then pressing his mouth to hers again at a fresh angle. He heard her give a tiny moan of distress. Though she lifted a hand to his shoulder to push him away, when he deepened the kiss, she allowed it to lie unresisting until he took his lips from hers.

"Now you've done it," she said when she gathered her wits again. "By noon tomorrow it'll be all over Sharpsburg that we're lovers."

"Will it?" Smiling, he lifted her hand to his lips, then slowly kissed her fingers one by one. It satisfied him to feel the faint tremor of arousal.

"Yes," Shane answered breathlessly, "and I don't…" She

trailed off when he turned her palm up to press another long kiss in its center.

"Don't what?" he asked softly, taking his lips to the inside of her wrist. Her pulse pounded against the light trace of his tongue.

"Think it's—it's wise," she managed, forgetting the restaurant and Cy and Laurie and everything else.

"That we're lovers or that it's all over Sharpsburg?" Vance enjoyed the confusion in her eyes and the knowledge that he had put it there.

Her pulse beat jerkily. He was different. Reckless? she thought, and felt a fresh thrill race down her spine. Smooth? How could he be both at once? Yet he was. The recklessness was in his eyes, but the romantic moves were smooth with experience.

She hadn't been afraid of the hard, angry man she had met, but she felt a skip of fear for the one who even now traced his thumb over the speeding pulse at her wrist.

"I'm going to have to give that some thought," she murmured.

"Do that," he said agreeably.

Eight

Shane opened the doors of Antietam Antiques and Museum the first week of December. As she had expected, for the first few days the shop and museum were crowded, for the most part with people she knew. They had come to buy or browse out of curiosity or affection. Others came to see what "that Abbott girl" had up her sleeve this time. It amused Shane to hear her past crimes discussed as though they had taken place the day before. Cy's name was dropped a time or two, causing her to force back a chuckle and change the subject. Still, after the initial novelty had worn off, she had a steady trickle of customers. That was enough to satisfy her.

As planned, she hired Donna's sister-in-law, Pat, on a part-time basis. The girl was eager and willing, and not opposed to giving Shane weekend hours. Shane considered the additional expense well worth it when Pat, flushed with triumph,

rang up her first sale. With her coaching, and Pat's own en-
thusiastic studying, Shane's assistant had learned enough to
classify certain articles in the shop and to handle questions in
the museum section.

Shane found herself busier than ever, managing the shop,
watching for ads for estate sales and overseeing the remodeling
still under way on the second floor. The long, chaotic hours
stimulated her, and helped her deal with the slow but steady
loss of her grandmother's treasures. It was business, Shane reminded herself again and again as she sold a corner cabinet
or candle holder. It was necessary. The bills in her desk had
mounted over the weeks of preparation, and they had to be
paid.

She saw Vance almost daily as he came to hammer and saw
and trim on the second floor. Though he wasn't as withdrawn
as he once had been, the intimacy they had shared for an afternoon and evening had faded. He treated her as a casual friend,
not a woman whose palm he would kiss in a restaurant.

Shane concluded that he had taken on a loverlike aspect
for Cy's benefit, and now it was back to business as usual. She
wasn't discouraged. In fact, the man she had dined with had
made her nervous and uncertain. She was more confident
with Vance's temper than with soft words and tender caresses.
Knowing herself well, Shane was aware it would be difficult
not to make a fool of herself over him if he continued to treat
her with gentleness. She had little defense against romance.

Daily, her love for him grew. It only made her more certain than ever that he was the only man for her. It would
only be a matter of time, she decided, before he realized she
was the woman for him.

It was late afternoon when Shane carried her latest acquisition up the new front steps and into the shop. She was flushed with cold and highly pleased with herself. She was learning to be ruthless when bargaining. After pushing the door open with her bottom, she carried the table through the entrance sideways.

"Just look what I've got!" she said to Pat before she closed the door behind her. "It's a Sheridan. Not a scratch on it either."

Pat stopped washing the glass on the display case. "Shane, you were supposed to take the afternoon off." Automatically she polished off a lingering smear before giving Shane her full attention. "You've got to take some time for yourself," she reminded her with a hint of exasperation. "That's why you hired me."

"Yes, of course," Shane said distractedly. "There's a mantel clock in the car and a complete set of cut-glass saltcellars." Pat sighed, smart enough to know when she was being ignored, and followed Shane into the main showroom.

"Don't you ever quit?" she demanded.

"Uh-uh." After setting the table beside a Hitchcock chair, Shane stepped back to view the results. "I don't know," she said slowly. "It might look better in the front room, right under the window. Well, I want to polish it first anyway." She darted to the work counter, rummaging for the furniture polish. "How'd we do today?"

Pat shook her head. The first thing she had learned on the job was that Shane Abbott was a powerhouse. "I'll do that," she said, taking the polish and rag from Shane's hands. Shane grinned at Pat's weighty sigh but said nothing. "You had seven people come through the museum," Pat told her as she began to polish the Sheridan. "I sold some postcards and a print of the Burnside Bridge. A woman from Hagerstown bought the little table with the fluted edges."

Shane stopped unbuttoning her coat. "The rosewood piecrust?" It had sat in the summer parlor for as long as she could remember.

"Yes. And she was interested in the bentwood rocker." Pat tucked a strand of hair behind her ear while Shane struggled to be pleased. "I think she'll be back."

"Good."

"Oh, and you had a nibble on Uncle Festus."

"Really?" Shane grinned, thinking of the portrait of a dour Victorian man she'd been unable to resist. She had bought it because it amused her, though she had had little hope of selling it. "Well, I'll be sorry to lose him. He gives the place dignity."

"He gives me the creeps," Pat said baldly as Shane headed for the front door to fetch the rest of her new stock. "Oh, I nearly forgot. You didn't tell me you'd sold the dining-room set."

"What?" Puzzled, Shane stopped with her hand on the knob.

"The dining-room set with the heart-shaped chairs," Pat explained. "The Hepplewhite," she added, pleased that she was beginning to remember makes and periods. "I nearly sold it again."

"Again?" Shane released the knob and faced Pat fully. "What are you talking about?"

"There were some people in here a few hours ago who wanted it. It seems their daughter's getting married, and they were going to buy it as a wedding gift. They must be rich," she added with feeling. "The reception's going to be at a Baltimore country club…with an orchestra." She began to daydream about this a bit, but then she noted Shane's hard look. "Anyway," she continued quickly, "I'd nearly finalized the sale when Vance came downstairs and explained it was taken already."

Shane's eyes narrowed. "Vance? Vance said it was already sold?"

"Well, yes," Pat agreed, puzzled by the tone. If she had known Shane better, she would have recognized the beginnings of rage. Innocently, she continued. "It was a lucky thing too, or else they'd have bought it and arranged for the shipping right then and there. I guess you'd have been in a fix."

"A fix," Shane repeated between set teeth. "Yeah, somebody's in a fix all right." Abruptly, she turned to stride toward the rear of the shop while Pat looked after her, wide-eyed.

"Shane? Shane, what's wrong?" Confused, she trotted after her. "Where are you going?"

"To settle some business," she said tightly. "Get the rest of the stuff out of my car, will you?" she called back without slackening her pace. "And lock up. This might take a while."

"Sure, but…" Pat trailed off when she heard the back door slam. She puzzled a moment, shrugged, then went to follow orders.

"A fix," Shane muttered as she crushed dead leaves underfoot. "Lucky thing he came down." Furiously, she kicked at a fallen branch and sent it skidding ahead of her, waiting to be kicked again. Grinding her teeth, she stormed purposefully down the path between denuded trees. "Already taken!" Enraged, she made a dangerous sound in her throat. A hapless squirrel started across the path, then dashed in the other direction.

Through the bare trees, she could see his house, with smoke puffing from the chimney to struggle up into a hard blue sky. Shane set her jaw and increased her pace. Into the quiet came a steady thump, pause, thump. Without hesitation, she skirted around to the back of the house.

Vance put another log on the tree stump he used as a chopping block, then bore down with his axe to split it neatly in two. Without a pause in rhythm, he set a new log. Shane took no time to admire the precision or grace of the movement.

"You!" she spat, and stuck her fists on her hips.

Vance checked his next swing. Glancing over, he saw Shane glaring at him with glittering eyes and a flushed face. He thought idly that she looked her best when in a temper, then followed through. The next log split to fall in two pieces on either side of the stump. The generous pile was evidence that he had been working for some time.

"Hello, Shane."

"Don't you 'hello Shane' me," she snapped, closing the distance between them in three quick strides. "How dare you?"

"Most people consider it an acceptable greeting," he countered as he bent down for another log. Shane knocked it off the stump with a sweep of her hand.

"You had no right to interfere, no right to cost me a sale. An important sale," she added furiously. Her breath puffed out visibly in the frigid air. "Just who the hell do you think you are, telling my customers something's already taken? Even if it had been, which it wasn't, it's hardly your place to add your two cents."

Calmly, Vance picked up the log again. He had been expecting her—and her anger. He had acted on impulse but didn't regret it. Very clearly, he could recall the look on her face when she had first shown him her grandmother's pride and joy. There was no way he was going to stand by and do nothing while she watched it being carted out the door.

"You don't want to sell it, Shane."

Her eyes only became more furious. "It's none of your business what I want to do. I have to sell it. I'm *going* to sell it. If you hadn't opened your big mouth, I *would* have sold it."

"And spent several hours hating yourself and crying over the invoice," he tossed back, slamming the blade of the axe into the stump before he faced her. "The money isn't worth it."

"Don't you tell me what it's worth," she retorted, and poked a finger into his chest. "You don't know how I feel. You don't know what I have to do. *I* do. I need the money, damn it."

With strained calm, he curled his hand around the finger that dug into his chest, held it aloft a moment, then let it drop. "You don't need it enough to give up something that's important to you."

"Sentiment doesn't pay bills." The color in her cheeks heightened. "I've got a desk full of them."

"Sell something else," he shouted back at her. Her face was lifted to his, her eyes glowing with anger. He felt conflicting urges to protect her and to throttle her. "You've got the damn place packed with junk as it is."

"Junk!" He had just declared war. *"Junk!"* Her voice rose.

"Unload some of the other stuff you've got piled in there," he advised with a coolness that would have rattled his business associates. A dangerous hissing sound escaped through Shane's teeth.

"You don't know the first thing about it," she fumed,

poking him again so that he stepped back. "I stock the very best pieces I can find, and *you*—" she poked again "—you don't know a Hepplewhite from a—a piece of pressboard. You keep your city nose out of my affairs, Vance Banning, and play with your planes and drill bits. I don't need some flatlander to hand out empty advice."

"That's it," he said grimly. In one swift move, he swept Shane off her feet and dumped her over his shoulder.

"What the hell do you think you're doing?" she screamed, thrashing and pounding him with her fists.

"I'm taking you inside to make love to you," he stated between his teeth. "I've had enough."

In absolute astonishment, Shane stopped thrashing. "You're *what?*"

"You heard me."

"You're crazy!" More furious than frantic, she renewed her efforts to inflict pain wherever she could land a hit. Vance continued through the back door. "You're not taking me inside," she raged, even as he carted her through the kitchen. "I'm not going with you."

"You're going exactly where I take you," he countered.

"Oh, you're going to pay for this, Vance," she promised as she pounded against his back.

"I don't doubt that," he muttered, starting up the stairs.

"You put me down this minute. I'm not putting up with this."

Weary of being kicked, he pulled off her shoes, tossed them over the banister, then tightened an arm around the back of her knees. "You're going to put up with a hell of a lot more in a few minutes."

With her legs effectively pinned, she wiggled uselessly as he continued up the stairs. "I'm telling you, you're in big trouble. I'll get you for this," she warned, beating furiously against him as he strode down the hall and into a bedroom. "If you don't put me down this minute, *right this minute,* you're fired!" Shane let out a shriek as she tumbled through the air, then a whoosh as she thudded heavily on the bed. Breathless and infuriated, she scrambled to her knees. "You idiot!" she raged, puffing a bit. "Just what do you think you're doing?"

"I told you what I was doing." Vance stripped off his jacket and tossed it aside.

"If you think for one minute you can toss me over your shoulder like a bale of hay and get away with it, you're sadly mistaken." Shane watched with mounting fury as he unbuttoned his shirt. "And you stop that right now. You can't *make* me make love with you."

"Watch me." Vance peeled off his shirt.

"Oh no, you don't." Though she stuck her hands on her hips, the indignant pose lost something as she knelt on the bed. "Just put that right back on."

Watching her coolly, Vance dropped it to the floor, then bent to pull off his boots.

Shane glared at him. "You think you can just dump me on the bed and that's all there is to it?"

"I haven't even started yet," he informed her as the second boot dropped with a clatter.

"You simpleminded clod," she returned, heaving a pillow at him. "I wouldn't let you touch me if—" She searched for something original and scathing but settled on the standby. "If you were the last man on earth!"

Vance sent her a long, glittering look before he unbuckled his belt.

"I told you to stop that." Shane pointed a warning finger. "I mean it. Don't you dare take another thing off. Vance!" she added threateningly as he reached for the snap of his jeans. "I'm serious." The word ended on a giggle. His hands paused; his eyes narrowed. "Put your clothes back on this minute," she ordered, but pressed the back of her hand to her mouth. Over it, her eyes were wide and brilliant with amusement.

"What the hell's so funny?" he demanded.

"Nothing, not a thing." With this, Shane collapsed on her back, helpless with laughter. "Funny? No, no, this is a very grave situation." Convulsed with giggles, she pounded her fists on the bed. "The man is standing there, pulling off his clothes and looking fit for murder. Nothing could be more serious."

Shane glanced over at him, then covered her mouth with both hands. "*That* is the face of a man overcome by lust and desire." She laughed until tears came to her eyes.

Damn her, Vance thought as a grin tugged at his mouth. He crossed to the bed; then, sitting beside her, he planted his hands on either side of her head. The harder she tried to control her amusement, the more her eyes laughed at him. "Glad you're having a good time," he commented.

She swallowed a chuckle. "Oh no, I'm furious, absolutely furious, but it was *so* romantic."

"Was it?" His grin widened as he considered her.

"Oh yes, why you just swept me off my feet." Her laughter rang through the room. "I don't know when I've been more *aroused*," she managed.

"Is that so?" Vance murmured as Shane gave herself wholly to mirth. Very deliberately, he lowered his lips to brush her chin.

"Yes, unless it was when Billy Huffman pushed me into

the briars in second grade. Obviously I inflame males into violent seizures of passion."

"Obviously," Vance agreed, tucking her hair behind her ear. "I've had several since I tangled with you." Her fit of giggles ceased abruptly when he caught her earlobe between his teeth. "I think I'm bound to have several more," he murmured, moving down to her neck.

"Vance—"

"Soon," he added against her throat. "Any minute."

"I have to get back," she began breathlessly. As she attempted to sit up, he pressed a hand to her shoulder to keep her still.

"I wonder what else might arouse you." He nibbled at the cord of her neck. "This?"

"No, I…"

"No?" He gave a deep, quiet laugh, feeling her pulse hammer against his lips. "Something else then." Her coat was unzipped, and deftly he loosened the range of buttons on her blouse. "This?" Very gently, he touched the tip of her breast with his tongue.

On a gasp, Shane arched against him. Vance drew her nipple into his mouth to let her taste seep through him. He savored it a moment as Shane dug her nails into his bare shoulders. But when the heat shot into him, he knew he had to pull back before he took her too quickly. He'd been careful since the night they had dined together to keep some space between them. He hadn't wanted to rush her. Now that he had her in his bed, he intended to savor every moment.

Vance lifted his head and looked down at her. Her eyes were wide and fixed on his. For a moment, they both looked for answers. Very slowly, Shane smiled. "This," she whispered, and drew his mouth down to hers.

She hadn't been prepared for the sweetness of the kiss. His lips moved gently over hers. Their breath merged and matched rhythm. With light kisses he roamed her face, only to return over and over to her waiting mouth. To linger, to savor, to make each moment, each taste last; that was his only thought. The fiery needs were banked by the simple knowledge that she was his to touch, to kiss, to love. For the first time in his memory, he wanted to bring a woman pleasure much more than he wanted to take his own. He could give her that with the slow kisses that made his own blood thunder. Until he sensed she craved more, he used only his lips and tongue to arouse her.

Hardly touching her, Vance drew her jacket over her shoulders and arms, lifting her slightly to slip it from under her. His touch was so sure, so gentle, she remained unaware of his inner conflict between passion and tenderness. Without hurry, he drew off her shirt, following its progress over her shoulders with his lips. Shane sighed as his kisses ranged down her arm to nibble at the inside of her elbow. Fighting the growing need to rush, Vance trailed his lips down to her wrist.

If the wind still blew outside the windows, if leaves still rustled along the ground, Shane was unaware. There was only the play of Vance's fingertips, only the warm trace of his mouth. Content, almost sleepy, she ran her fingers through his thick mane of hair as his teeth tugged lightly at the cord of her neck. The lazy friction of his skin against hers had her pulse beating thickly. She felt she could stay forever, floating in a world halfway between passion and serenity.

He began the downward journey slowly, hardly seeming to move at all. With kisses and light love bites, he circled her breast, moving inward until he captured the peak. It grew hot and hard in his mouth while she began to move under him. He suckled, using his tongue to bring them both to the edge of delirium. Her breathing was as raspy as his. Now he could feel the energy flowing from her, pouring out in passion and urgency. Moaning his name, she pressed him closer to her.

But there was so much more to give, so much more to take. With deliberate care, Vance repeated the same aching journey around her other breast, feeling her shudders, listening to the storm of her heartbeat under his hungry, seeking lips.

"So soft," he murmured. "So beautiful." For a moment he merely buried his face against her breast, struggling to hang on to his control. On a moan of need, Shane reached for him as if to bring his mouth back to hers, but he slipped lower.

Taking her arching hips in his hands, Vance traced his tongue down her quivering skin. Shane felt her jeans loosen at the waist and shifted to help him. But he only pressed his mouth deep into the vee of exposed flesh. Again she shifted, curving her back to offer herself, but he lingered, tracing lazy circles with his tongue.

When he worked the jeans over her hips, she felt each searing brush of his fingers. Down her thighs he journeyed, pausing to caress their soft inner flesh, over her calves to nibble gently at the taut muscles, then to her ankles, sending a devastating flush of heat up her body with a quick flick of his tongue.

He found points of pleasure she had been unaware existed. Then he was at the core of her, his tongue stabbing inside her to catapult her beyond all bounds of reason. She moaned his name, moving with him, moving for him, with mind and body tormented by dark, pulsing delights.

Vance heard his name come huskily through her lips and thrilled to it. Her energy, her wellspring of passion inflamed him, driving him to take her deeper before he took all. The sweet, sweet taste of her made him greedy. Somewhere in the back of his clouded mind he knew he was no longer gentle with her, but needs whipped at him.

Madness overcame him. His mouth roamed wildly over her body as his fingers took her from peak to staggering peak. Her breath was heaving when he found her breast. If she had been capable of words, Shane would have pleaded with him to take her. Her world was spinning at a terrifying speed, a speed far beyond the scope of her imagination. When his mouth crushed hers, she answered blindly. He thrust into her.

The flow of energy came from nowhere—a power, a strength that hurled her beyond the reasonable and into the impossible. One fed the other, driving higher and faster until they found the apex. Together, they clung to it, shuddering.

How long he lay still, Vance was unsure. Perhaps he even dozed. When his mind began to clear, he found his mouth nuzzled against Shane's throat, her arms wrapped around him. He was still inside her and could feel the light pulses of lingering passion deep within her. For a moment longer he kept his eyes closed, wondering how it was possible to be both sated and exhilarated. When he started to move, thinking of her comfort, Shane tightened her hold to keep him close.

"No," she murmured. "Just a little longer."

He laughed as his lips grazed her ear. "Can you breathe?"

"I'll breathe later."

Content, he snuggled back into the curve of her neck. "I like the way you taste. I've had a problem with that since the first time I kissed you."

"A problem?" she said lazily, running experimental fingers over the muscles of his back. "That doesn't sound much like a compliment to me."

"Would you like one?" He pressed his mouth to her skin. "You're the most exquisite creature I've ever seen."

Shane received this news with a snort of laughter. "Your first compliment was a bit more credible."

Vance lifted his head and looked down at her. Though her eyes were still sleepy with passion, they were amused. "You really don't see it, do you?" he said thoughtfully. Did she really have no notion what big velvet eyes and satin skin could do to a man when combined with her kind of vivacity? Didn't she realize the kind of power there was in striking innocence when it was offset by a sensual mouth and an open, honest sexuality? "You might lose it if you did," he said half to himself. "What if I said I liked your nose?"

She eyed him warily for a moment. "If you say I'm cute, I'll hit you."

He chuckled, then kissed both dimpled cheeks. "Do you know how long I've wanted you like this?"

"From the first moment in the general store." She smiled when he lifted his head to stare down at her. "I felt it too. It was as though I'd been expecting you."

Vance laid his forehead on hers. "I was furious."

"I was stunned. I forgot my coffee."

They laughed before their mouths met. "You were terribly rude that day," she remembered.

"I meant to be." He lured her lips back to his. "I wanted to get rid of you."

"Did you really think you could?" Chuckling, she nipped at his bottom lip. "Don't you know a determined woman when you see one?"

"I *would* have gotten rid of you if I'd been able to close my eyes at night without seeing you."

"Did you really? Poor Vance." She gave him a sympathetic kiss.

"I'm sure you're very sorry I lost sleep over you."

She made a suspicious sound. Vance lifted his head again to see her bottom lip caught firmly between her teeth. "I would be sorry," she assured him, "if I didn't think it was wonderful."

"I often wanted to strangle you at three o'clock in the morning."

"I'm sure you did," she returned soberly. "Why don't you kiss me instead?"

He did, roughly, as banked passions began to smolder again. "That day when you sat in the mud, laughing like a fool, I wanted you so badly I hurt. Damn you, Shane, I haven't been able to think straight for weeks." His mouth crushed down on hers again with a touch of the anger she remembered. She soothed the back of his neck with her fingers.

When he lifted his head, their eyes met in a long, deep look. Shane lifted her palm to his cheek.

So much turbulence, she thought. So many secrets.

So much sweetness, he thought. So much honesty.

"I love you," they said together, then stared at each other in amazement. For a moment, they neither moved nor spoke. It seemed even their breathing had halted at the same instant. Then, as one, they reached out, clinging heart to heart, mouth to mouth. What started as a desperate meeting of lips softened, then sweetened, then promised.

Vance closed his eyes on waves of relief and towering pleasure. When he felt Shane's shudders he drew his arms tighter around her. "You're trembling. Why?"

"It's too perfect," she said in a voice that shook. "It frightens me. If I were to lose you now—"

"Shh." He cut her off with a kiss. "It *is* perfect."

"Oh, Vance, I love you so much. I've been waiting all these weeks for you to love me back, and now..." She took his face in her hands and shook her head. "Now that you do, I'm scared."

Looking down at her, he felt a surge of passion and possession. She was his now; nothing was going to change it. No more mistakes, no more disillusionments. He heard her breath catch then shudder.

"I love you," he said fiercely. "I'm going to keep you, do you understand? We belong together. We both know it. Nothing, by God, nothing's going to interfere with that."

He took her on a wild surge of need and desperation, ignoring the shadow of trepidation that watched over his shoulder.

Nine

It was dark when Shane woke. She had no idea of time or place, only of deep inner contentment and security. The weight of an arm around her waist meant love; the quiet breathing near her ear meant her lover slept beside her. She needed nothing more.

Idly, she wondered how long they had slept. The sun had been setting when she had closed her eyes. The moon was up now. Its cool white light filtered in through the windows to slant across the bed. Shifting slightly, Shane tilted her head back to look at Vance's face. In the dim light, she could make out the sweep of cheekbone and outline of jaw, the strong straight nose. With a fingertip, she traced his mouth gently, not wanting to wake him. As long as he slept, she could look her fill.

It was a strong face, even a hard one, she mused, with its sharp angles and dark coloring. His mouth could be cruel, his eyes cold. Even in his loving there was a ruthless sort of power in him. While a woman might feel safe in his arms, she would never be completely comfortable. A life with him would be full of constant demands, arguments, passion.

And he loves me, Shane thought in a kind of terrified wonder.

In sleep, Vance shifted, drawing her closer. As their naked bodies pressed intimately close, a dull throb of need moved through her. Her skin heated against his, tingling with the contact. Against the slow, steady beat of his heart, hers began to thud erratically. Desire had never seemed more demanding, yet he did nothing more than lie quietly beside her, deep in his own dreams.

It would always be like this, she realized as she settled her head in the crook of his shoulder. He would give her very little peace. Though she was a woman who had always taken peace for granted, Shane would now forfeit it cheerfully. He was her fate; she had known it from the first instant. Now, she felt as bound to him as if she had been his wife for decades.

For a long time she lay awake, listening to him sleep, feeling the steady rise and fall of his chest against her breasts. This would never change, she told herself. This need to hold each other. She burrowed against him for a moment, filling herself with his scent. As long as she lived, Shane knew she would remember every second, every word spoken during their first time together. She would need no diary to remind her of young, churning fires when she was old. No passage of time would dull her memory or her feelings.

With a sigh, she brushed a whisper of a kiss over his lips. He didn't stir, but she wondered if he dreamed of her. She wanted him to, and closing her eyes, she willed him to. Carefully, she drew away from him, then moving lightly, slipped from the bed. Their clothes were in scattered heaps. Finding Vance's shirt, Shane slipped it on before she left the room.

Her scent lingered on the pillowcase. It was the first thing to penetrate Vance's senses as he drifted awake. It suited her so, the fresh, clean fragrance with a suggestion of lemon. Lazily, he allowed it to seep into him. Even in sleep, his mind was full of her. There was a slight stiffness in his shoulder where her head had rested. Vance flexed it before reaching out to bring her back to him. He found himself alone. Opening his eyes, Vance whispered her name.

He experienced the same sense of time disorientation that Shane had. The room was dim with moonlight, so that for a moment he thought he must have dreamed it all. But the sheets were still warm from her, and her scent still lingered. No dream. The relief he felt overwhelmed him. Softly, he called her name. It was then he smelled the bacon. In the dark, he grinned foolishly and settled back. As he lay quietly, he could just hear Shane's voice as she sang some silly popular song.

She was in the kitchen, he thought. Vance stayed where he was, listening. She was rooting through the cupboards, clattering something. Water was running. The scent of bacon grew stronger. How long, he wondered, had he waited to feel this way? *Complete*. He hadn't known he had been waiting, but he did know what he had found. She filled the emptiness that had nagged at him for years, healed an old, festering wound. She was all the answers to all the questions.

And what would he bring her? his conscience demanded. Vance closed his eyes. He knew himself too well to pretend he would give her a smooth, serene life. His temper was too volatile, his responsibilities too intrusive. Even with adjustments to both, he could paint her no soft pastoral scene. His life, past, present and future, had too many complications. Even this, their first night together, would have to be marred by one of his ghosts. He had to tell her about Amelia. There was a burst of rage followed by a prickle of fear.

No, he wouldn't accept the fear, he told himself as he rose quickly from the bed. Nothing, no one was going to interfere with him. No shadow of a dead wife or demands of a hungry business were going to take her from him. She was strong, he reminded himself, trying to override the apprehension. He could make her see his past as it was—something that had happened before her. It might shock her to learn he was president of a multimillion-dollar firm, but she could hardly be displeased once it was out in the open. He would tell Shane everything and wipe the slate clean. When it was done, he could ask her to marry him. If he had to make professional adjustments, he'd make them. He had sacrificed his own youthful dream for the good of the company, but he wouldn't sacrifice Shane.

As he pulled on his jeans, Vance tried to work out the best way to tell her and, perhaps more important, to explain why he had yet to tell her.

Shane added a dash of thyme to the canned soup she was heating. She rose on her bare toes to reach for a bowl on the shelf, the hem of Vance's shirt skimming her naked thighs. Her hair was tousled, her cheeks flushed. Vance stood for a moment in the doorway watching her.

Then in three strides, he was behind her, wrapping his arms around her waist and burying his face in the curve of her neck. "I love you," he murmured in a low, fierce whisper. "God, how I love you."

Before she could answer, he spun her around to take her mouth with his. Both stunned and aroused, Shane clung to him as her knees buckled. But she met the kiss with equal passion with soft, willing lips until he slowly drew her away. As the flame mellowed to a glow, Vance looked down at her and smiled.

"Any time you want to drive me crazy, just put on one of my shirts."

"If I'd known the kind of results I'd get, I'd have done it weeks ago." Returning his smile, Shane clasped her hands around his neck. "I thought you'd be hungry. It's after eight."

"I smelled food," he said with a grin. "That's why I came down."

"Oh." Shane lifted a brow. "Is that the only reason?"

"What else?"

Her retort ended on a laugh as he nuzzled her neck. "You could make something up," she suggested.

"If it makes you feel better, I could pretend it was because I couldn't keep away from you." He kissed her until she was limp and breathless. "That I woke up reaching for you, then lay listening to your clattering in the kitchen and knew I'd never been happier in my life. Will that do?"

"Yes, I…" She sighed as his hands slid down to caress beneath the loose shirt. Behind her, bacon popped and hissed. "If you don't stop, the food's going to burn."

"What food?" He chuckled, pleased that she was flushed and breathing unsteadily when she struggled away from him.

"My own specially doctored tomato soup and prize-winning BLTs."

He pulled her back to nuzzle her neck another moment. "Mmm, it does smell pretty good. So do you."

"It's your shirt," she claimed as she wiggled out of his arms again. "It smells like wood chips." Deftly, Shane took the sizzling bacon from the frying pan to let it drain. "If you want coffee, the water's still hot."

Vance watched her finish preparing the simple meal. She did more than fill the kitchen with the scents and sounds of cooking. He'd done that himself often enough in the past weeks. Shane filled it with life. He may have repaired and renovated and remodeled, but the house had always been empty. Vance realized now that without her, it would have always been unfinished.

There would be no living there without her—no living anywhere. Fleetingly, he thought of the large white house in an exclusive Washington suburb—the house he had bought for Amelia. There was an oval swimming pool sheltered by a white brick wall, a formal rose garden with flagstone paths, a clay tennis court. Two maids, a gardener and a cook. When Amelia had been alive there had been yet another maid to tend to her personally. Her dressing room alone had been larger than the kitchen where Shane was now fixing soup and sandwiches. There was a parlor with a rosewood cabinet Shane would adore, and heavy damask drapes she would detest.

No, Vance thought, he wouldn't go back there now, nor would he ask Shane to share his ghosts. He had no right to ask her to cope with something he was only beginning to resolve himself. But he would have to tell her something of his former marriage, and of his work, before yesterday could be buried.

"Shane…"

"Sit down," she ordered, busily pouring soup into bowls. "I'm starving. I skipped lunch this afternoon bargaining for this wonderful Sheridan table. I paid a bit more for the clock than I should have, but made it up on the table and the salt-cellars."

"Shane, I have to talk to you."

Deftly, she sliced a sandwich in half. "Okay, I can talk and eat at the same time. I'm going to have some milk. Even I can tell that instant coffee's dreadful."

She was bustling here and there, putting bowls and plates on the table, poking into the refrigerator. Vance was suddenly struck with the picture of his life before she had come into it—the rush, the demands, the work that had ultimately added up to nothing. If he lost her… He couldn't bear thinking about it.

"Shane." He stopped her abruptly, taking both of her arms in a strong grip. Looking up, she was surprised by the fierceness in his eyes. "I love you. Do you believe it?" His grip tightened painfully on the question, but she made no protest.

"Yes, I believe it."

"Will you take me just as I am?" he demanded.

"Yes." There was no hesitation in her, no wavering. Vance pulled her toward him.

A few hours, he thought, squeezing his eyes tight. Just a few hours with no questions, no past. It's not too much to ask.

"There are things I have to tell you, Shane, but not tonight." As the tension drained, he loosened his hold to a caress. "Tonight, I only want to tell you that I love you."

Sensing turmoil and wanting to soothe it, Shane tilted her face back to his. "Tonight it's all I need to know. I love you,

Vance. Nothing you tell me will change that." She pressed her lips to his cheek and felt some of the tightness in his body loosen. Part of her wanted to coax him to tell her what caused the storm inside him, but she was conscious of the same need for isolation that Vance had. This was their night. Problems were for the practical, for the daytime. "Come on," she said lightly, "the food's getting cold." The fierce hug she gave him made him laugh. "When I fix a gourmet meal, I expect it to be properly appreciated."

"I do," he assured her, kissing her nose.

"Do what?"

"Appreciate it. And you." He dropped a second kiss on her mouth. "Let's go into the living room."

"Living room?" Her brow creased, then cleared. "Oh, I suppose it would be warmer."

"Exactly what I had in mind," he murmured.

"I tossed a couple of logs onto the fire when I came downstairs."

"You're a clever soul, Shane," Vance said admiringly as he took her arm and steered her from the room.

"Vance, we have to take the food."

"What food?"

Shane laughed and started to turn back, but he propelled her into the sparsely furnished, firelit room. "Vance, the soup'll have to be reheated in a minute."

"It'll be terrific," he told her as he began to unbutton the oversize shirt she wore.

"Vance!" Shane brushed his fingers away. "Be serious."

"I am," he said reasonably, even as he pulled her down on the oval braided rug. "Deadly."

"Well, *I'm* not going to reheat it," she promised huffily while he leaned on an elbow to undo the rest of the buttons.

"No one would blame you," he told her as he parted the shirt. "It'll be fine cold."

She gave a snort. "It'll be dreadful cold."

"Hungry?" he asked lightly, cupping her breast.

Shane looked up at him. He saw the dimples flash. "Yes!" In a quick move, she was lying across his chest, her mouth fixed greedily on his.

The verve and speed of her passion stunned him. He had meant to tease her, to stoke her desires slowly, but she was suddenly and completely in command. Her mouth was avid, demanding, with her small teeth nibbling, her quick tongue arousing him so quickly he would have rolled her over and taken her at once had his limbs not been so strangely weak. Her weight was nothing, yet he couldn't move her when she shifted to do clever, torturous things to his ear. Her hands were busy too, stroking through his hair, skimming over his shoulders and chest to find and exploit small, devastating points of pleasure.

He reached to pull off her shirt, too dazed to realize his fingers shook, but he fumbled, dragging at it. High on her own power, Shane gave a quick, almost nervous laugh. "Too soon," she whispered into his ear. "Much too soon."

He swore, but the curse ended on a groan when she pressed her lips to his throat. She burned even as he did, but she was driven to heighten his pleasure to the fullest. It spun through her mind until she was giddy that her touch, her kisses were enough to make him weak and vulnerable. Under her roaming mouth, his skin grew hot and damp. He stroked her where he could reach, but there was something dream-like in the touch, as though he had passed the first feeling of desperation. For all his strength and power, he had surrendered to hers.

The light shifted and jumped with the crackling of the fire. A log broke apart, crumbling in a shower of sparks. The wind picked up, pushing a sluggish puff of smoke back down the chimney so that it struggled halfheartedly into the room to vie with the lingering scent of fried bacon. Neither of them was aware.

Shane heard the thunderous beat of his heart under her ear, the shallow, ragged sound of his breathing. Taking his mouth again, she kissed him deeply, filling herself on him, knowing she drained him. She luxuriated in him, experimenting with angles, allowing her tongue to twine with his. Then she began the journey down his throat.

Once, he murmured her name as though he were dreaming. She grew bolder. With firm, quick kisses, she ranged down his chest to the taut flat stomach. Vance jolted as though he had been scorched. Shane pressed her lips to the heated skin, wrenching a moan from him, then circled almost lazily with her tongue.

Her excitement was almost unbearable. He was hers, and she was learning his secrets. Her body felt weightless and capable of anything. The gnawing hunger in the pit of her stomach was growing, but the need to learn, to explore was greater. With a kind of greedy wonder, she took her hands and lips over him, reveling in a man's taste—*her* man's taste. The hair on his chest tapered down. Shane followed it.

Slowly, with a light touch, she loosened his jeans and began to draw them over his hips. Curious, Shane moved her lips over his hipbone and down to his thigh.

She heard him call out to her, hoarse, desperate, but she found the corded muscles of his thighs fascinating. So strong, she thought as her heart began to thud painfully. She ran fingers down his leg, aroused by the lean firmness and straining sinews. Testing, she replaced her fingers with her tongue, then her teeth. Vance shifted under her, murmuring something between his short, ragged breaths. His taste was everything male and mysterious. Shane felt she would never get her fill of him.

But he was on the point of madness. Her slender fingers, her curious tongue had him plunging down and rocketing up so that each breath he drew was an agony of effort. His body was alive with pleasure and pain, his blood swimming with passion that was both tantalized and frustrated. He wanted her to go on touching him, driving him mad. He wanted to take her quickly before he lost his mind. Then slowly, her small avid mouth roamed back up over his stomach, so that his skin quivered with fresh dampness. The heat was unbearable and more wonderful than anything he had ever known. Her breasts with their hard, erect points brushed over him, making him long to taste them. She gave him her mouth instead. Lying full length on his, her body was furnace hot and agile.

"Shane, in the name of God," he breathed, groping for her. Then she slid down, taking him inside her with a shuddering sigh of triumph.

His sanity shattered. Not knowing what he did, Vance seized her shoulders, rolling her over roughly, driving inside her with all the fierce, desperate strength that was pent up in him. Passion hammered through his core. Need was delirium.

She cried out as her hips arched to meet him, but he was far beyond any control. Harder and faster he took her, never feeling the bite of her nails on his flesh, barely hearing her harsh, quick breathing. She dragged him closer when he could get no closer. He drove her, drove himself to a crest that was dangerously high. Even the plummet was a shattering thrill.

She was shuddering beneath him, dazed, weak, powerful. Experimentally, Vance ran a hand over her arm, then linked his fingers around it. His thumb and forefinger met. "You're so small," he murmured. "I didn't mean to be rough."

Shane brushed a hand through his hair. "Were you?"

His sigh ended on a chuckle. "Shane, you make me crazy. I don't usually toss women around."

"I don't think this is a good time to go into that," she said dryly.

Shifting, he supported himself on his elbow so he could look down at her. "Would it be better to tell you that you inflame me into violent seizures of passion?"

"Infinitely."

"It appears to be true," he murmured.

She smiled at him, running her hand down his shoulder to the arm taut with muscle. "Would you rather I didn't?"

"No," he said definitely, then covered her laughing lips with his.

"Actually," she began in a considering tone, "since you do the same to me, it's only fair."

He liked seeing her with the sleepy, just-loved look on her face. Her eyes were soft and heavy, her mouth slightly swollen. With shifting shadows and a red glow, firelight danced over her skin. "I like your logic." Gently, he traced the shape of her face with a fingertip, imagining what it would be like to wake beside her every morning. Shane captured his hand, pressing his palm to her lips.

"I love you," she said softly. "Will you get tired of hearing that?"

"No." He kissed her brow, then her temple. Slipping an arm under her, he drew her close. "No," he said again on a sigh.

Shane snuggled, running a casual hand over his chest. "The fire's getting low," she murmured.

"Mmm."

"We should put some more wood on."

"Mmm-hmm."

"Vance." She tilted her face to look up at him. His eyes were closed. "Don't you dare go to sleep. I'm hungry."

"God, the woman's insatiable." After a long sigh, he cupped her breast. "I might find the energy with the right incentive."

"I want my dinner," she said firmly, but made no move to stop his caressing hand. "*You're* going to reheat the soup."

"Oh." Vance considered that a moment, running a lazy finger over the peak of her breast. "Aren't you afraid I might interfere with that special touch you have?"

"No," she told him flatly. "I have every confidence in you."

"I thought you might," he said as he sat up to tug on his jeans. Leaning over, he planted a quick kiss on her mouth. "*You* can toss some logs in the fire."

But after he had gone to the kitchen, Shane lay dreaming a moment. The hiss of the fire was comforting. She drew the soft flannel of Vance's shirt closer around her, smiling as his scent stayed with her. Could it really be true that he needed her so much? she wondered sleepily. Love, yes, and desire, but she had a deep, innate knowledge that he very simply needed her. Not just for lovemaking, for holding, but to *be* there. Though she was unsure what it was, Shane knew there was something she had—or something she was—that Vance needed. Whatever she brought to him, it was enough to balance his anger, his mistrust. Fleetingly, she wondered again what had caused him to retreat behind cynicism. Disillusioned, he had said. Who or what had disillusioned him? A woman, a friend, an ideal?

Shane watched the sizzling red coals in the fire and wondered. The anger was still there. She had sensed it when he had demanded to know if she would take him just as he was. Patience, she told herself. She had to be patient until he was ready to share his secrets with her. But it was difficult for Shane to love and not try to help. Shaking her head, she sat up to rebutton her shirt. She'd promised him that love was enough for tonight; she had to abide by it. Tomorrow would be soon enough for problems. Expertly, she arranged more wood on the coals before she went to the kitchen.

"About time," Vance said coolly as she walked in. "There's nothing I hate more than having food get cold."

Shane shot him a look. "How inconsiderate of me."

After setting the bowls back on the table, Vance shrugged. "Well, no harm done," he told her in a forgiving tone. His eyes brimmed with amusement as Shane sat. "Coffee?"

"Not yours," she said witheringly. "It's terrible."

"I suppose if someone really cared, they'd see to it that I had decent coffee in the morning."

"You're right." Shane lifted her spoon. "I'll buy you a percolater." Grinning, she began to eat. The soup was hot and tangy, causing her to close her eyes in appreciation. "Good grief, I'm starving!"

"You should know better than to miss meals," Vance commented before applying himself to the meal. He quickly discovered he was famished.

"It was worth it." Shane shot him another grin. "The Sheridan I bought is fabulous." When he only lifted a brow, she chuckled. "Then I had intended to have an early dinner...but I was distracted."

Vance reached over to take her hand. Gently, he lifted it to his lips, then bit her knuckle. "Ow!" Shane snatched her hand away as he picked up his sandwich. "I didn't say it wasn't an enjoyable distraction," she added after a moment. "Even if you did make me furious."

"The feeling was mutual," he assured her mildly.

"At least I control my temper," she said primly. She eyed him coolly as he choked over his soup. "I *wanted* to punch you," she explained. "Hard."

"Again the feeling was mutual."

"You're not a gentleman," she accused with her mouth full.

"Good God, no," he agreed. For a moment, he hesitated, wanting to choose his words carefully. "Shane, will you hold off for a little while on that dining-room set?"

"Vance," she began, but he took her hand again.

"Don't tell me I shouldn't have interfered. I love you."

Shane stirred her soup, frowning down at it. She didn't want to tell him how pressing her bills were. In the first place, she had every confidence that between her current stock and the small amount of capital she had left, she could straighten out her finances. And more, she simply didn't want to heap her problems on him.

"I know you did what you did because you cared," she began slowly. "I appreciate that, really. But it's important to me to make the shop work." She lifted her eyes now to meet the frown in his. "I didn't fail as a teacher, but I didn't succeed either. I have to make a go of this."

"By selling the one tangible thing you have left of your grandmother's?" Immediately, he saw he had hit a nerve. He tightened his fingers around hers. "Shane…"

"No. It is hard for me, I won't pretend it isn't." Wearily, she let out a long breath. "I'm not basically a practical person, but in this case I have to be. I have no place to keep that set and it's very valuable. The money it'll bring into the shop will keep me going for quite a while. And more than that…" She broke off with a little shake of her head. "If you can understand, it's more difficult for me having it there, knowing it has to be sold, than if it were already done."

"Let me buy it. I could—"

"No!"

"Shane, listen to me."

"No!" Pulling her hand from his, she rose to lean against the sink. For a moment she stared hard out the window at the trees splattered with moonlight. "Please, it's very sweet of you, but I couldn't allow it."

Frustrated, Vance rose. Taking her shoulders, he drew Shane back against him. And how, he wondered, was he going to begin to explain? "Shane, you don't understand. I can't bear watching you hurting, watching you work so hard when I could—"

"Please, Vance." Shane turned to him. Though her eyes were dry, they were eloquent. "I'm doing what I have to do, and what I want." She took his hands tightly in hers. "It's not that I don't love you even more for wanting to help. I do."

"Then let me help," he began. "If it's just a matter of the money right now—"

"It wouldn't make any difference if you were a millionaire," she said, giving him a little shake. "I'd still say no."

Not knowing whether to laugh or swear, Vance pulled her against him. "Stubborn little twit, I could make it easier for you. Let me try to explain."

"I don't want anyone, not even you, to make it easier." She gave him a fierce squeeze. "Please understand. All of my life I've been cute little Shane Abbott, Faye's sweet, slightly odd granddaughter. I need to prove something."

Remembering how frustrating it had been to be known as Miriam Riverton Banning's son, Vance sighed. Yes, he understood. And the understanding made him keep his silence on how simple it would be for him to help. "Well," he said, wanting to hear her laugh, "you are kind of cute."

"Oh, Vance," she moaned.

"And sweet," he added, tilting her face up for a kiss. "And slightly odd."

"That's no way to endear yourself to me," she warned. "I'll wash, you dry."

"Wash what?"

"The dishes."

He pulled her closer, wrapping his arms firmly around her waist. "I don't see any dishes. You have wonderful eyes, just like a cocker spaniel."

"Watch it, Vance," she said threateningly.

"I like your freckles." He placed a light kiss on the bridge of her nose. "I've always thought that Becky Thatcher had freckles."

"You're heading for trouble," she told him, narrowing her eyes.

"And your dimples," he continued blithely. "She probably had dimples too, don't you think?"

Shane bit her lips to hold back a smile. "Shut up, Vance."

"Yes," he continued, beaming down at her, "I'd say that's definitely a cute little face."

"Okay, that does it." Putting a good deal of effort into it, Shane tried to wiggle out of his hold.

"Going somewhere?"

"Home," she told him grandly. "You can do your own dishes."

He sighed. "I guess I have to get tough again."

Anticipating him, Shane began to struggle in earnest. "If you throw me over your shoulder again, you really are fired!"

Hooking an arm behind her knees, Vance swept her up. "How's this?"

She circled his neck. "Better," she said grudgingly. The smile was becoming impossible to control.

"And this?" Softly, he placed his lips on hers, letting the kiss deepen until he heard her sigh.

"Much better," she murmured as he carried her from the room. "Where are we going?"

"Upstairs," he told her. "I want my shirt back."

Ten

"Yes, of course you could convert it," Shane agreed, passing her fingertip over the porcelain base of a delicate oil lamp.

"That's just what I thought." Mrs. Trip, her potential customer, nodded her carefully groomed white head. "And my husband's very handy with electrical things too."

Shane managed a smile for Mr. Trip's prowess. It broke her heart to think that the sweet little lamp would be tampered with. "You know," she began, trying another tactic, "an oil lamp is a smart thing to have around in case of power failure. I keep a couple myself."

"Well yes, dear," Mrs. Trip said placidly, "but I have candles for that. This lamp's going to go right next to my rocker. That's where I do my crocheting."

Though she knew the value of a sale, Shane couldn't stop

herself from adding, "If you really want an electric lamp, Mrs. Trip, you could buy a good reproduction much cheaper."

Mrs. Trip sent her a vague smile. "But it wouldn't be a real antique then, would it? Do you have a box I can carry it in?"

"Yes, of course," Shane murmured, seeing it was useless to repeat that converting the lamp would decrease both its value and its charm. Resigned, she wrote out the sales slip, comforting herself with the thought that the profit from the lamp would help pay her own electric bill.

"Oh my, I didn't see this!"

Glancing up, Shane noted that Mrs. Trip was admiring a tea set in cobalt blue. The sun slanting in the windows fell generously on the dark, rich glass. There was a contrast of delicate gold leaf painted around the rim of each cup and the edge of each saucer.

"It's lovely, isn't it," Shane agreed, though she bit the underside of her lip as the lady began to handle the sugar bowl. When she found the discreet price tag, she lifted a brow. "It goes as a complete set," Shane began, knowing the price would seem staggering to someone unacquainted with valuable glass. "It's late nineteenth century and…"

"I must have it," Mrs. Trip said decisively, cutting off Shane's explanation. "It's just the thing for my corner cabinet." She sent a surprised Shane a grin. "I'll tell my husband he's just bought me a Christmas present."

"I'll wrap it for you," Shane decided, as pleased as Mrs. Trip with the idea.

"You have a lovely shop," the woman told her as Shane began to box the glass. "I must say, I only stopped in because the sign at the bottom of the hill intrigued me. I wondered what in the world I would find. But it wasn't a big barn of a place with nonsense packed around like a yard sale." She pursed her lips, glancing around again. "You've done very well." Shane laughed at the description and thanked her. "And it's so nice to have the little museum too," she went on. "A very clever idea, and so tidy. I believe I'll bring my nephew by the next time I'm in the area. Are you married, dear?"

Shane sent her a look of wary amusement. "No, ma'am."

"He's a doctor," Mrs. Trip disclosed. "Internal medicine."

Clearing her throat, Shane sealed the box. "That's very nice."

"A good boy," Mrs. Trip assured her as Shane adjusted the sales ticket to include the tea set. "Dedicated." She dug out her checkbook, pulling her wallet along with it. "I have a picture of him right here."

Politely, Shane examined the snapshot of a young, attractive man with serious eyes. "He's very good-looking," she told his aunt. "You must be proud of him."

"Yes," she said wistfully, tucking the wallet back into her purse. "Such a pity he hasn't found the right girl yet. I'm going to be sure to bring him by." Without a blink for the amount, Mrs. Trip wrote out a check.

It wasn't easy, but Shane maintained her composure until the door shut behind her customer. With a shout of laughter, she dropped into a button-back chair. Though she was uncertain if the nephew should be congratulated or pitied for having such a dedicated aunt, she did know what appealed to her sense of humor. Her next thought was how Vance would try not to grin when she told him of the lady's matchmaking attempts.

He'd lift a brow, Shane thought, and make some dry comment about her charming the old ladies so that they'd dangle their nephews under her nose. She was beginning to know him very well. Most of him, Shane corrected with a considering smile. The rest would come.

She checked her watch, finding herself impatient that two hours remained before he would be with her. She'd promised him dinner—a more elaborate dinner than the soup and sandwiches they had eaten the night before. Even now, the small rib roast was cooking gently in the oven upstairs. She considered closing early, calculating she had just about enough time to whip up some outrageous, elaborate dessert before he arrived. As the thought passed through her head, the door opened again.

Laurie MacAfee stepped in, buttoned to the neck in a long tan coat. "Shane," she said, observing her casual posture in the chair. "Not busy I see."

Though she smiled in greeting, some demon kept her seated. "Not at the moment. How are you, Laurie?"

"Just fine. I took off work early to go to the dentist, so I thought I'd drop by afterward."

Shane waited, half expecting Laurie to comment on her good checkup. "I'm glad you did," she said at length. "Would you like a tour?"

"I'd love to browse," Laurie told her, glancing around. "What sweet things you have."

Shane swallowed a retort and rose. "Thank you," she said with a humility Laurie never noticed. Shane thought again how well suited she was to Cy.

"I must say, the place looks so much different." In her slow, measured step, Laurie began to wander the old summer parlor. Though she hadn't expected to approve, she could find nothing to condemn in Shane's taste. The room was small, but light and airy with its ivory-toned walls, and the gleaming natural wood floor was scattered with hand-hooked rugs.

Furniture was set to advantage, with accessories carefully arranged to give the appearance of a tidy, rather comfortable room instead of a store. Loosening the first few buttons of her coat, she roamed to the main showroom, then stood perusing it from the doorway.

"Why, you've hardly changed this at all?" she exclaimed. "Not even the wallpaper."

"No," Shane agreed, unable to keep her eyes from skimming over the dining-room set. "I didn't want to. Of course, I had to set more stock in here, and widen the doorways, but I loved the room as it was."

"Well, I'll confess I'm surprised," Laurie commented as she wandered through to what had been the kitchen. "It's so organized, not jumbled up at all. Your bedroom was always a disaster."

"It still is," Shane replied dryly.

Laurie gave what passed for a laugh before continuing into the museum. "Yes, this I might have expected." She gave a quick nod. "You always were a whiz at this sort of thing. I could never understand it."

"Because I wasn't a whiz at anything else?"

"Oh, Shane." Laurie flushed, revealing how close Shane's words had been to her thoughts.

"I'm sorry." Immediately contrite, Shane patted her arm. "I was only teasing you. I'd show you the upstairs, Laurie, but it's not quite finished, and I shouldn't leave the shop in any case. Pat has classes this afternoon."

Mollified, Laurie strolled back into the shop. "I'd heard she was working for you. It was very kind of you to give her the job."

"She's been a big help. I couldn't manage it seven days a week all alone." Shane felt a twinge of impatience as Laurie began to browse again. There wasn't going to be time to whip up anything more than instant chocolate pudding at this rate.

"Oh well, this is very nice." Laurie's voice held the first true ring of admiration as she studied the Sheridan table Shane had bought the day before. "It doesn't look old at all."

That was too much for Shane. She gave a burst of appreciative laughter. "No, I'm sorry," she assured Laurie when she turned to frown at her. "You'd be surprised how many people think antiques should look moldy or dented. It's quite old, really, and it is lovely."

"And expensive," Laurie added, squinting at the price. "Still, it would look rather nice with the chair Cy and I just bought. Oh…" Turning, she gave Shane a quick, guilty look. "I wonder if you'd heard—that is, I'd been meaning to have a talk with you."

"About Cy?" Shane controlled the smile, noting Laurie was truly uncomfortable. "I know you're seeing quite a lot of each other."

"Yes." Hesitating, Laurie brushed some fictitious lint from her coat. "It's a bit more than that really. You see, we're—actually…" She cleared her throat. "Shane, we're planning to be married next June."

"Congratulations," Shane said so simply that Laurie's eyes widened.

"I hope you're not upset." Laurie began to twist the strap of her purse. "I know that you and Cy…well, it was quite a few years ago, but still, you were…"

"Very young," Shane said kindly. "I really do wish you the best, Laurie." But a demon of mischief had her adding, "You suit him much better than I ever could."

"I appreciate your saying that, Shane. I was afraid you might…" She flushed again. "Well, Cy's such a wonderful man."

She means it, Shane noted with some surprise. She really loves him. She felt simultaneous tugs of shame and amusement. "I hope you're happy, Laurie, both of you."

"We will be." Laurie gave her a beaming smile. "And I'm going to buy this table," she added recklessly.

"No," Shane corrected her. "You're going to take the table as an early wedding present."

Comically, Laurie's mouth dropped open. "Oh, I couldn't! It's so expensive."

"Laurie, we've known each other a long time, and Cy was a very important part of my—" she searched for the proper phrase "—growing up years. I'd like to give it to both of you."

"Well, I—thank you." Such uncomplicated generosity baffled her. "Cy will be so pleased."

"You're welcome." Laurie's flustered appreciation made her smile. "Can I help you out to the car with it?"

"No, no, I can manage." Laurie lifted the small table, then paused. "Shane, I really hope you have a tremendous success here. I really do." She stood awkwardly at the door a moment. "Goodbye."

"Bye, Laurie."

Shane closed the door with a smile, then immediately put Laurie and Cy out of her mind. After a glance at her watch, she noted that she had barely more than an hour now before Vance would be there. She hurried around to lock up the museum entrance. If she moved fast, she would have time to… The sound of an approaching car had her swearing.

Business is business, she reminded herself, and unlocked the door again. If Vance wanted dessert, he'd have to settle for a bag of store-bought cookies. Hearing the sound of foot-steps on the porch, she opened the door with a ready smile. It faded instantly, as did her color.

"Anne," she managed in a voice unlike her own.

"Darling!" Anne bent down for a quick brush of cheeks. "What a greeting. Anyone would think you weren't glad to see me."

It took only a few seconds to see that her mother was as lovely as ever. Her pale, heart-shaped face was unlined, her eyes the same deep china blue, her hair a glorious sweeping blond. She wore a casual, expensive blue fox stroller belted at the waist with black leather, and silk slacks unsuitable for an Eastern winter. Her beauty, as always, sent the same surges of love and resentment through her daughter.

"You look lovely, Anne."

"Oh, thank you, though I know I must look a wreck after that dreadful drive from the airport. This place is in the middle of nowhere. Shane, dear, when are you going to do something about your hair?" She cast a critical eye over it before breezing past. "I'll never understand why... Oh, my Lord, what *have* you done!"

Stunned, she gazed around the room, taking in the dis-play cases, the shelves, the racks of postcards. With a trill of laughter, she set down her exquisite leather bag. "Don't tell me you've opened a Civil War museum right in the living room. I don't believe it!"

Shane folded her hands in front of her, feeling foolish. "Didn't you see the sign?"

"Sign? No—or perhaps I did but didn't pay any attention." Her eyes slid, sharp and amused around the room. "Shane, what *have* you been up to?"

Determined not to be intimidated, she straightened her shoulders. "I've started a business," she said boldly.

"*You?*" Delighted, Anne laughed again. "But, darling, surely you're joking."

Stabbed by the utter incredulity in Anne's voice, Shane angled her chin. "No."

"Well, for heaven's sake." She gave a pretty chuckle and eyed Shane's dented bugle. "But what happened to your teaching job?"

"I resigned."

"Well, I can hardly blame you for that. It must have been a terrible bore." She brushed away Shane's former career as a matter of indifference. "But why in God's name did you come back here and bury yourself in Hicksville?"

"It's my home."

With a mild *hmm* for the temper in Shane's eyes, Anne spun the rack of postcards. "Everyone to his own taste. Well, what have you done with the rest of the place?" Before Shane could answer, Anne swept through the doorway and into the shop. "Oh, no, don't tell me, an antique shop! Very quaint and tasteful. Shane, how clever of you." Her eye was sharp enough to recognize a few very good pieces. She began to wonder if her daughter wasn't quite the fool she'd always considered her. "Well…" Anne unbelted her fur and dropped it carelessly over a chair. "How long has this been going on?"

"Not long." Shane stood rigid, knowing part of herself was drawn, as it always was, to the strange, beautiful woman who was her mother. Knowing too that Anne was deadly.

"And?" Anne prompted.

"And what?"

"Shane, don't be difficult." Masking quick annoyance,

Anne gave her a charming smile. She was an actress. Though she had never made the splash she had hoped for, she wrangled a bit part now and again. She felt she knew her trade well enough to handle Shane with a friendly smile. "Naturally I'm concerned, darling. I only want to know how you're doing?"

Uncomfortable with her own manners, Shane unbent. "Well enough, though I haven't been open long. I wasn't happy with teaching. Not bored," she explained, "just not suited for it. I am happy with this."

"Darling, that's wonderful." She crossed her nylon-clad legs and looked around again. It occurred to her that Shane might be useful after all. It had taken brains and determination to set up this kind of establishment. Perhaps it was time she started to take a little more interest in the daughter she had always thought of as a mild annoyance. "It helps to know you're settling your life, especially since mine's such a mess at the moment." Noting the wariness in Shane's eyes, she sent her a sad smile. If memory served her, the girl was very susceptible to an unhappy story. "I divorced Leslie."

"Oh?" Shane only lifted a brow.

Momentarily set back by Shane's coolness, Anne continued. "I can't tell you how mistaken I was in him, how foolish it feels to know I was deceived into thinking he was a kind, charming man." She didn't add that he had failed, again and again, to get her the kind of parts that would lead to the fame she craved—or that she'd already begun to cultivate a certain producer she felt would be more successful. In any event, Leslie had begun to bore her to distraction. "There's nothing more devastating than to have failed in love."

You've had practice, Shane thought, but held her tongue.

"These past few months," Anne added on a sigh, "haven't been easy."

"For any of us," Shane agreed, understanding Anne too well. "Gran died six months ago. You didn't even bother to come to the funeral."

She'd been ready for this. With a tiny sigh, she dropped her eyes to her soft, pampered hands. "You must know how badly I felt, Shane. I was finishing a film. I couldn't be spared."

"You couldn't find the time for a card, a phone call?" Shane asked. "You never even bothered to answer my letter."

As if on cue, Anne's lovely eyes filled with tears. "Darling, don't be cruel. I couldn't—I just couldn't put the words down on a piece of paper." She drew a delicate swatch of silk from her breast pocket. "Even though she was old, somehow I felt she would just live forever, always be here." Mindful of her mascara, she dabbed at the tears. "When I got your letter telling me she was... I was so devastated." She lifted beautifully drenched eyes to Shane's, waiting while a single tear trickled gently down her cheek. "You of all people must know how I feel. She raised me." A little sob caught in her throat. "I still can't believe she's not in the kitchen, fussing over the stove."

Because the image tore at her own grief, Shane knelt at her mother's feet. She'd had no family to mourn with her, no one to help her through the wrenching, aching hours after the numbness had passed. If she had been unable to share anything else with her mother throughout her life, perhaps they could share this. "I know," she managed in a thick voice. "I still miss her terribly."

Anne began to think the little scene had a great deal of possibility. "Shane, please forgive me." Anne gripped her hands, concentrating on adding a tremor to her voice. "I know it was wrong of me not to come, wrong to make excuses. I just wasn't strong enough to face it. Even now, when I thought I could…" She trailed off, bringing Shane's hand to her damp cheek.

"I understand. Gran would have understood too."

"She was so good to me always. If I could only see her one more time."

"You mustn't dwell on it." Those very thoughts had haunted Shane's mind a dozen times after the funeral. "I felt the same way, but it's better to remember all the good times. She was so happy here in this house, doing her gardening, her canning."

"She did love the house," Anne murmured, casting a nostalgic eye around the old summer parlor. "And I imagine she'd have been pleased with what you're doing here."

"Do you think so?" Earnestly, Shane looked up into her mother's damp eyes. "I was so sure, but still sometimes…" Trailing off, she glanced at the freshly painted walls.

"Of course she would," Anne said briskly. "I suppose she left the house to you?"

"Yes." Shane was looking around the room, remembering how it had been.

"There was a will then?"

"A will?" Distracted, Shane glanced back at her. "Yes, Gran had a will drawn up years ago. She had Floyd Arnette's son do it after he passed the bar. She was his first client." Shane smiled, thinking how proud Gran had been of the fancy legal terms that "sassy Arnette boy" had come up with.

"And the rest of the estate?" Anne prompted, attempting to curb her impatience.

"There was the house and land of course," Shane answered, still looking back. "Some stocks I sold to pay the taxes and the funeral expenses."

"She left everything to you?"

The tightness in Anne's voice didn't penetrate. "Yes. There was enough cash in her savings to handle most of the repairs on the place, and—"

"You're lying!" Anne shoved at her as she sprung to her feet. Shane grabbed the arm of the chair to keep from toppling; then, too stunned to move, she stayed on the floor. "She wouldn't have cut me off without a penny!" Anne exploded, glaring down at her.

The blue eyes were hard and glittery now, the lovely face white with fury. Once or twice before, Shane had seen her mother in this sort of rage—when her grandmother hadn't given her precisely what she had wanted. Slowly, she rose to face her. Anne's tantrums, she knew, had to be handled carefully before they turned violent.

"Gran would never have thought of it as cutting you off, Anne," Shane said with a calm she was far from feeling. "She knew you'd have no interest in the house or land, and there weren't that many extra pennies after taxes."

"What kind of fool do you think I am?" Anne demanded in a harsh, bitter voice. It was her temper more than a lack of talent that had snagged her career. Too often, she had let it rake over directors and other actors. Even now, when patience and the right words would have ensured success, she lashed out. "I know damn well she had money socked away, moldering in some bank. I had to pry every penny I got out of her when she was alive. I'm going to have my share."

"She gave you what she could," Shane began.

"What the hell do you know? Do you think I'm so stupid I don't know this property is worth a tidy sum on the market?" She glanced around once in disgust. "You want the place, keep it. Just give me the cash."

"There isn't any to give. She didn't—"

"Don't hand me that." Anne shoved her aside and strode toward the stairs.

For a moment, Shane stood still, caught in a turmoil of disbelief. How was it possible anyone could be so unfeeling? And how, she asked herself, was it possible for her to be taken in again and again? Well, she would end it this time, once and for all. On her own wave of fury, she raced after her mother.

She found Anne in her bedroom, pulling papers out of her desk. Without hesitation, Shane dashed across the room and slammed the desk lid shut. "Don't you touch my things," she said in a dangerous voice. "Don't you ever touch what belongs to me."

"I want to see the bankbooks, and this so-called will." Anne turned to leave the room, but Shane grabbed her arm in a surprisingly strong grip.

"You'll see nothing in this house. This is mine."

"There *is* money," Anne said furiously, then jerked away. "You're trying to hide it."

"I don't have to hide anything from you." Rage raced through Shane, fed by years of cast-aside love. "If you want to see the will and the status of the estate, get yourself a lawyer. But I own this house, and everything in it. I won't have you going through my papers."

"Well…" Anne's blue eyes became slits. "Not such a sweet simpleton after all, are you?"

"You've never known what I am," Shane said evenly. "You've never cared enough to find out. It didn't matter, because I had Gran. I don't need you." Though saying the words was a relief, they didn't bank her fury. "There were times I thought I did, when you came sweeping in, so beautiful I hardly believed you were real. That was closer to the truth than I knew, because there's nothing real about you. You never cared about her. She knew that and she loved you anyway. But I don't." Her breathing was coming quickly, but she was unaware of how close it was to sobbing. "I can't even work up a hate. I just want to be rid of you."

Turning, she pulled open the desk and drew out her checkbook. Quickly, she wrote out a check for half of the capital she had left. "Here." She held it out to Anne. "Take it; consider it from Gran. You'll never get anything from me."

After snatching the check, Anne scanned the amount with a smirk. "If you think I'll be satisfied with this, you're wrong." Still, she folded the check neatly, then slipped it into her pocket. She knew better than to press her luck, and her own financial status was far from solid. "I'll get that lawyer," she promised, though she had no intention of wasting her money on the slim chance of getting more. "And I'll contest the will. We'll just see how much I get from you, Shane."

"Do what you like," Shane said wearily. "Just stay away from me."

Anne tossed back her hair with a harsh laugh. "Don't think I'll spend any more time in this ridiculous house than I have to. I've always wondered how the hell you could possibly be my daughter."

Shane pressed a hand to her throbbing temple. "So have I," she murmured.

"You'll hear from my lawyer," Anne told her. Turning on her heel, she glided from the room, exiting gracefully.

Shane stood beside the desk until she heard the slam of the front door. Bursting into tears, she crumpled into a chair.

Eleven

Vance sat in the one decent chair he had in the living room. Impatiently, he checked his watch. He should have been with Shane ten minutes ago. And would have been, he thought with a glance at the front door, if the phone hadn't caught him as he'd been leaving the house. Resigned, he listened to the problems listed by the manager of his Washington branch. Though it wasn't said in words, Vance was aware there was some grumbling in the ranks that the boss had taken a sabbatical.

"...and with the union dispute, the construction on the Wolfe project is three weeks behind schedule," the manager continued. "I've been informed that there will be a delay in delivery of the steel on the Rheinstone site—possibly a lengthy one. I'm sorry to bother you with this, Mr. Banning, but as these two projects are of paramount importance to the firm, particularly with the bids going out on the shopping mall Rheinstone is planning, I felt…"

"Yes, I understand." Vance cut off what promised to be a detailed explanation. "Put a double shift on the Wolfe project until we're back on schedule."

"A double shift? But—"

"We contracted for completion by April first," Vance said mildly. "The increase in payroll will be less than the payment of the penalty clause, or the damage to the firm's reputation."

"Yes, sir."

"And have Liebewitz check into the steel delivery. If it's not taken care of satisfactorily by Monday, I'll handle it from here." Picking up a pencil, Vance made a scrawled note on a pad. "As to the Rheinstone bid, I looked it over myself last week. I see no problem." He scowled at the floor a moment. "Set up a meeting with the department heads for the end of next week. I'll be in. In the meantime," he added slowly, "send someone… Masterson," he decided, "up here to scout out locations for a new branch."

"New branch? Up there, Mr. Banning?"

The tone had a smile tugging at his mouth. "Have him concentrate on the Hagerstown area and give me a report. I want a list of viable locations in two weeks." He checked his watch again. "Is there anything else?"

"No, sir."

"Good. I'll be in next week." Without waiting for a reply, Vance broke the connection.

His last orders, he thought ruefully, would put them into quite a stir. Well, he reflected, Riverton had expanded before; it was going to expand again. For the first time in years, the company was going to bring him some personal happiness. He would be able to settle down with the woman he loved, where he chose to settle down, and still keep a firm rein on his business. If he had to justify the new branch to the board, which he would certainly have to do, he would point out that Hagerstown was the largest city in Maryland. There was also its proximity to Pennsylvania to consider… and to West Virginia. Yes, he mused, the expansion could be justified to the board easily enough. His track record would go a long way toward swaying them.

Rising, Vance shrugged back into his coat. All he had left to do now was to talk to Shane. Not for the first time, he speculated on her reaction. She was bound to be a bit stunned when he told her he wasn't precisely the unemployed carpenter she had taken him for. And he hadn't discounted the possibility that she might be angry with him for allowing her to go on believing him to be one. Vance felt a slight tug of apprehension as he stepped out into the cold, clear night.

There was a stiff breeze whipping in from the west. It sent stiff, dead leaves scattering and smelled faintly of snow. With his mind fully occupied, Vance never noticed the old stag fifty yards to his right, scenting the air and watching him.

He'd never set out to deceive her, he reminded himself. When they had first met, it had been none of Shane's business who he was. More, he added thoughtfully, he had simply wanted to shake loose of his company title for a while and be exactly what she had perceived him to be. Had there been any way of knowing she would become more important to him than anything else in his life? Could he have guessed that weeks after he met her he would be planning to ask her to marry him, finding himself ready to toss his company into a frenzy of rush and preparation so that she wouldn't have to give up her home or the life she had chosen for herself?

Once he'd explained the circumstances, Vance told himself as he crunched through frosted leaves, she'd understand. One of Shane's most endearing qualities was understanding. And she loved him. If he was sure of nothing else, he was sure of that. She loved him without questions, without demands. No one had ever given him so much for so little. He intended to spend the rest of his life showing her just what that meant to him.

He imagined that once the surprise of what he had to tell her had worn off, she would laugh. The money, the position he could offer her would mean nothing. She would probably find it funny that the president of Riverton had cut and hammered the trim in her kitchen.

Telling her about Amelia would be more difficult, but it would be done—completely. He wouldn't pass over his first marriage, but would tell her everything and rely on her to understand. He wanted to tell her that she had been responsible for softening his guilt, lightening his bitterness. Loving her was the only genuine emotion he'd felt in years. Tonight, he would open up his past long enough to let the air in; then he would ask Shane to share his future.

Still, Vance felt a twinge of apprehension as he approached her house. He might have ignored it if it hadn't been for the sudden realization that all the windows were dark. It was odd, he thought, unconsciously increasing his pace. She was certainly home, not only because her car was there, but because he knew she was expecting him. But why in God's name, he wondered, wasn't there a single light on? Vance tried to push away a flood of pure anxiety as he reached the back door.

It was unlocked. Though he entered without knocking, he called her name immediately. The house remained dark and silent. Hitting a switch, Vance flooded the rear showroom with light. A quick glance showed him nothing amiss before he continued through the first floor.

"Shane?"

The quiet was beginning to disturb him even more than the darkness. After making a quick circle of the lower floor, he went upstairs. At once he caught the scent of cooking. But the kitchen was empty. Absently turning off the oven, Vance went back into the hall. The thought struck him that she might have lain down after closing the shop and had simply fallen asleep. Amused more than concerned now, he walked quietly into her bedroom. All the amusement fled when he saw her curled up in the chair.

Though the room was in darkness, there was enough moonlight to make her out clearly. She wasn't asleep, but was curled up tightly with her head resting on the arm of the chair. He'd never seen her like that. His first thought was that she looked lost; then he corrected himself. Stricken. There was no innate vivacity in her eyes, and her face glowed palely in the silvery light of the moon. He might have thought her ill, but something told him that even in illness Shane wouldn't lose all of her spark. The thought ran through his mind in only seconds before he crossed the room to her. She made no sign that she saw him, nor was there any response when he spoke her name again. Vance knelt in front of her and took her chilled hands.

"Shane."

For a moment, she stared at him blankly. Then, as though a dam had burst, desperate emotion flooded her eyes. "Vance," she said brokenly, throwing her arms around his neck. "Oh, Vance."

She trembled violently, but didn't weep. The tears were dry as stone inside her. With her face pressed into his shoulder, she clung to him, breaking out of the numbed shock which had followed her earlier bout of tears. It was the warmth of him that made her realize how cold she had been. Without questions, with both strength and sweetness he held her to him.

"Vance, I'm so glad you're here. I need you."

The words struck him more forcibly than even her declaration of love. Up to that moment he had been almost uncomfortably aware that his needs far outweighed hers. Now it seemed there was something he could do for her, if it was only to listen.

"What happened, Shane?" Gently he drew her away only far enough to look into her eyes. "Can you tell me?"

She drew a raw breath, making him eloquently aware of the effort it cost her to speak. "My mother."

With his fingertips, he brushed the tousled hair from her cheeks. "Is she ill?"

"No!" It was a quick, furious explosion. The violence of the denial surprised him, but he took her agitated hands in his.

"Tell me what happened."

"She came," Shane managed, then fought to compose herself.

"Your mother came here?" he prompted.

"Near closing time. I didn't expect... She didn't come for the funeral or answer my letter." Her hands twisted in his, but Vance kept them in a gentle grip.

"This is the first time you've seen her since your grandmother died?" he asked. His voice was calm and quiet. Shane's eyes were still for a moment as she met his eyes directly.

"I haven't seen Anne in over two years," she said flatly. "Since she married her publicity agent. They're divorced now, so she came back." Shaking her head, Shane drew in a breath. "She almost made me believe she cared. I thought we could talk to each other. Really talk." She squeezed her eyes shut. "It was all an act, all the tears and grief. She sat there begging me to understand, and I believed—" Breaking off again, she shuddered with the effort of continuing. "She didn't come because of Gran or because of me." When she opened her eyes again Vance saw they were dull with pain. With a savage effort he kept his voice calm.

"Why did she come, Shane?"

Because her breathing was jerky again, she took a moment to answer. "Money," she said flatly. "She thought there would be money. She was furious that Gran left everything to me, and she wouldn't believe me when I told her how little there had been. I should have known!" she said in a quick rage, which then almost immediately subsided. "I did know." Her shoulders slumped as though she bore an intolerable weight. "I've always known. She's never cared about anyone. I'd hoped there might be some feeling in her for Gran, but... When she came running up here to paw through my papers, I said horrible things. I can't be sorry that I did." Tears sprang to her eyes, only to be swiftly controlled. "I gave her half of what's left and made her leave."

"You gave her money?" Vance demanded, incredulous enough to interrupt.

Shane gave him a weary look. "Gran would have given it to her. She's still my mother."

Disgust and rage rose in his throat. It took all the willpower he had not to give in to it. His anger wouldn't help Shane. "She's not your mother, Shane," he said matter-of-factly. When she opened her mouth to speak, he shook his head and continued. "Biologically, yes, but you're too smart to think that means anything. Cats have kittens too, Shane." He tightened his grip when he saw the flicker of pain on her face. "I'm sorry, I don't want to hurt you."

"No. No, you're right." Her hands went limp again as she let out a sigh. "The truth is, I very rarely think of her. Whatever feelings I have for her are mostly because Gran loved her. And yet…"

"And yet," he finished, "you make yourself sick with guilt."

"How can it be natural to want her to stay away?" Shane demanded in a rush. "Gran—"

"Your grandmother might have felt differently, might have given her money out of a sense of obligation. But think, who did she leave everything to? Everything important to her?"

"Yes, yes, I know, but…"

"When you think of the meaning of 'mother,' Shane, who comes to your mind?"

She stared at him. This time when the tears gathered, they brimmed over. Without a word, she dropped her head back onto his shoulder. "I told her I didn't love her. I meant it, but…"

"You don't owe her anything." He drew her closer. "I know something about guilt, Shane, about letting it tear at you. I won't let you do that to yourself."

"I told her to stay away from me." She gave a long, weary sigh. "I don't think she will."

Vance remained silent for a moment. "Is that what you want?"

"Oh God, yes."

He pressed his lips to her temple before lifting her into his arms. "Come on, you're exhausted. Lie down for a while and sleep."

"No, I'm not tired," she lied as her lids fluttered down. "I just have a headache. And dinner's—"

"I turned off the oven," he told her as he carried her to the bed. "We'll eat later." After flipping down the quilt, he bent to lay Shane between the cool sheets. "I'll go get you some aspirin." He slipped off her shoes, but as he started to pull the quilt over her, Shane took his hand.

"Vance, would you just…stay with me?"

Touching the back of his hand to her cheek, he smiled at her. "Sure." As soon as he had pulled off his boots, he slipped into bed beside her. "Try to sleep," he murmured, gathering her close. "I'll be right here."

He heard her long, quiet sigh, then felt the feather-brush of her lashes against his shoulder as her eyes shut.

How long they lay still, he had no idea. Though the grandfather clock which stood in Shane's sitting room struck the hour once, Vance paid no attention. She wasn't trembling anymore, nor was her skin chilled. Her breathing was slow and even. The fingers that absently soothed at her temple were gentle, but his thoughts were not.

No one, nothing, was ever going to put that look on Shane's face again. He would see to it. He lay staring at the ceiling as he thought out the best way to deal with Anne

Abbott. He'd let the money go, because that's the way Shane wanted it. But he couldn't resign himself to allowing her to deal with a constant emotional drain. Nothing had ever wrenched at him like the sight of her pale, shocked face or pain-filled eyes.

He should have known that anyone with as open a heart as Shane's could be hurt just as deeply as she could be made happy. And how, he wondered, could anyone who had dealt with that kind of pain since childhood be so generous and full of joy? The trial of a careless mother, the embarrassment and hurt of a broken engagement, the loss of the one constant family member she had known—none of it had broken her spirit, or her simple kindness.

But tonight she needed an arm around her. It would be his tonight—and whenever she needed him. Unconsciously he drew her closer as if to shield her from anything and everything that could hurt.

"Vance."

He thought she spoke his name in sleep and brushed a light kiss over her hair.

"Vance," Shane said again, so that he looked down to see the glint of her eyes against the darkness. "Make love with me."

It was a quiet, simple request that asked for comfort rather than passion. The love he already thought infinite tripled. So did his concern that he might not be gentle enough. Very softly, cupping the shape of her face in one hand, he touched his lips to hers.

Shane let herself float. She was too physically and emotionally drained to feel stinging desire, but he seemed to know what she asked for. Never had she felt such tenderness from him. His mouth was warm, and softer than she had thought possible. Minute after minute, he kissed her—and only kissed her. His fingers stroked soothingly over her face, then moved to the base of her neck as if he knew the dull, throbbing ache that centered there. Lovingly, patiently, he drew the quiet response from her, never asking for more than she could give. She relaxed and let him guide her.

With slow care, he roamed her face with kisses, touching his lips lightly to her closed lids as he shifted the gentle massage to her shoulders. There was a concentrated sweetness in his touch that was more kind than loverlike. When his mouth came back to hers, he used only the softest pressure, taking the kiss deep without fire or fury. With a sigh, she answered it, letting her needs pour out.

Passively, she let him undress her. His hands were deft and slow and undemanding. With a sensitivity neither of them had been aware he possessed, he made no attempt to arouse. Even when they were naked, he did nothing more than kiss her and hold her close. She knew she was taking without giving anything in return, and murmuring, reached for him.

"Shh." He kissed her palm before turning her gently onto her stomach. With his fingertips only at first, he stroked and soothed, running them down her back, over her shoulders. She hadn't known love could be so compassionate or unselfish. With a sigh, she closed her eyes again and let her mind empty.

He was drawing out the pain, bringing back the warmth. As she lay quietly, Shane felt herself settle and balance. There was no need to think, and no need to feel anything but Vance's strong, sure hands. All of her trust was his. Knowing this, he took even more care not to abuse it.

The old bed swayed slightly as he bent to kiss the back of her neck. Shane felt the first stir of desire. It was mild and wonderfully easy. Content, she remained still to allow herself the full enjoyment of being treasured. He was treating her like something fragile and precious. She wallowed in the new experience as he ranged soft kisses down her spine. Tension and tears were a world away from the Jenny Lind bed with a sagging mattress and worn linen sheets. The only reality now was Vance's sweet loving and the growing response of her pampered body.

He heard the subtle change in her breathing, the faint quickening, which meant relaxation was becoming desire. Still, he kept his hands easy, not wanting to rush her. The clock in the sitting room struck the hour again with low, ponderous bongs. Creakily the house settled around them with moans and groans. Vance heard little but Shane's deepening breathing.

The moonlight shivered over her skin, seeming to chase after his roaming hands. It only made him see more clearly how slender her back was, how slight the flare of her hips. Pressing his lips to her shoulder, he could smell the familiar lemon tang of her hair mixed with the lavender sachet lingering on the sheets. The room was washed in shadows.

Her cheek rested on the pillow, giving him a clear view of her profile. She might have been sleeping had it not been for the breath hurrying between her lips and the subtle movements her body was beginning to make. Still gentle, he turned her onto her back to press his mouth to hers.

Shane moaned, so lost in him she noticed no sound, no scent that didn't come from him. But his pace never altered, remaining slow and unhurried. He wanted her, God, yes, but felt no fierce, consuming drive. Love, much more than desire, pulled him to her. When he lowered his mouth to her breast, it was with such infinite tenderness that she felt a warmth, half glow, half ache, pour into her. His tongue began to turn the warmth into heat. She rose up, but seemed to take the journey on a cloud.

With the same infinite care, he took his lips and hands over her. Her skin hummed at his touch, but softly. There was no sweet pain in the passion he brought her, but such pleasure, such comfort, she desired him all the more. Her thoughts became wholly centered on her own body and the quiet delights he had awakened.

Though his lips might stray from hers to taste her neck or her cheek, they returned again and again. Her mindless answer, the husky breath that trembled into his mouth, had the fires roaring inside him. But he banked them. Tonight, she was porcelain. She was as fragile as the moonlight. He wouldn't allow his own passion and needs to overtake him, then find he had treated her roughly. Tonight he would forget her energy and strength and only think of her frailty.

And when he took her, the tenderness made her weep.

Twelve

In a thick, steady curtain, the snow fell. Already the road surface was slick. Trees had been quickly transformed from dark and stark to glittery. Vance's windshield wipers swept back and forth with the monotonous swish of rubber on glass. The snow brought him neither annoyance nor pleasure. He barely noticed it.

With a few phone calls and casual inquiries, he had learned enough about Anne Abbott—or Anna Cross, as she called herself professionally—to make his anger of the night before intensify. Shane's description had been too kind.

Anne had been through three turbulent marriages. Each had been a contact in the film industry. She had coolly bled each husband for as much as she could get before jumping into the next relationship. Her latest, Leslie Stuart, had proven a bit too clever for her—or his attorney had. She'd come out of her last marriage with nothing more than she had going into it. And, as she had a penchant for the finer things, she was already badly in debt.

She worked sporadically—bit parts, walk-ons, an occasional commercial. Her talent was nominal, but her face had earned her a few lines in a couple of legitimate films. It might have earned her more had her temper and self-importance not interfered. She was tolerated more than liked by Hollywood society. Even the tolerance, it seemed, was due more to her various husbands and intermittent lovers than to herself. Vance's contacts had painted a picture of a beautiful, scheming woman with a streak of viciousness. He felt he already knew her.

As he drove through the rapidly falling snow, his thoughts centered on Shane. He'd held her through the night, soothing her when she became restless, listening when she needed to talk. The shattered expression in her eyes would remain with him for a long time to come. Even that morning, though she had tried to be cheerful, there'd been an underlying listlessness. And he sensed her unspoken fear that Anne would come back and put her through another emotional storm. Vance couldn't change what had happened, but he could take steps to protect her in the future. That was precisely what he intended to do.

Vance turned into the lot of the roadside motel and parked. For a moment, he only sat, watching the snow accumulate on the windshield. He had considered telling Shane he intended to see her mother, then had rejected the idea. She'd been so pale that morning. In any case, he didn't doubt she would have been against it—even violently opposed to it. She was a woman who insisted on solving her own problems. Vance respected that, even admired it, but in this instance he was going to ignore it.

Stepping out of the car, he walked across the slippery parking lot to find the office and the information he needed. Ten minutes later, he knocked on Anne Abbott's door.

The crease of annoyance between her brows altered into an expression of consideration when she saw Vance. He was certainly a very pleasant surprise. Vance eyed her coolly, discovering that Shane's description hadn't been exaggerated. She was lovely. Her face had a delicacy of bone and complexion complemented by the very deep blue eyes and mane of blond hair. Her body, clad in a clinging pink dressing gown, was ripe and rounded. Though her glittery fairness was the direct opposite of Amelia's sultry beauty, Vance knew instantly they were women of the same mold.

"Well, hello." Her voice was languid and sulky, her eyes amused and appraising. Though he looked for it, Vance found not the slightest resemblance to her daughter. Overcoming a wave of disgust, he smiled in return. He had to get in the door.

"Hello, Ms. Cross."

He saw instantly that the use of her stage name had been a wise move. She flashed him the full-power smile that was one of her best tools. "Do I know you?" She touched the pink tip of her tongue to her top lip. "There is something familiar about you, but I can't believe I'd forget your face."

"Vance Banning, Ms. Cross," he said, keeping his eyes on hers. "We have some mutual friends, the Hourbacks."

"Oh, Tod and Sheila!" Though she couldn't abide them, Anne infused her voice with rich pleasure. "Isn't that marvelous! Oh, but you must come in. It's freezing out there. Appalling Eastern weather." She closed the door behind him, then stood leaning back against it a moment. Perhaps, she mused, the hometown visit wouldn't be so boring after all. This was the best-looking thing to knock at her door for quite some time. And, if he knew the stuffy Hourbacks, chances were he'd have a few dollars as well. "Well, well, isn't it a small world," she murmured, gently tucking a strand of delicate blond hair behind her ear. "How are Tod and Sheila? I haven't seen them for an age."

"Fine when I last spoke to them." Well aware where her thoughts were traveling, Vance smiled again, this time with cold amusement. "They mentioned that you were in town. I couldn't resist looking you up, Ms. Cross."

"Oh, Anna, please," she said graciously. With a sigh, she gave the room a despairing glance. "I must apologize for my accommodations, but I have some business nearby, and…" She gave a tiny shrug. "I'm forced to make do. I can offer you a drink, however, if you'll take bourbon."

It was barely eleven, but Vance answered smoothly, "If it's not too much trouble."

"None at all." Anne glided to a small table. She felt particularly grateful that she had packed the silk dressing gown and hadn't yet drummed up the energy to change. It was, she knew, both becoming and alluring. A quick glance in the mirror as she poured assured her she looked perfect. Thank God she'd just finished putting on her makeup. "But tell me, Vance," she continued, "what in the world are you doing in this dull little place? You're not a hometown boy, are you?"

"Business," he said simply, nodding his thanks as she handed him a neat bourbon.

Anne's eyes narrowed a moment, then widened. "Oh, of course. How could I be so foolish!" She beamed at him as the wheels began to spin in her head. "I've heard Tod speak of you. Riverton Construction, right?"

"Right."

"My, my, I am impressed." Her tongue ran lightly over her teeth as she considered. "It's about the biggest in the country."

"So I'm told," he answered mildly, watching her eye him over the rim of her glass. Without much interest, he wondered how much bait she would toss out before she tried to reel him in. If it hadn't been for Shane, he might have enjoyed letting her make a fool of herself.

With her carefully languid grace, Anne sat on the edge of the bed. As she sipped again, she wondered how soon he would try to sleep with her and how much resistance she should feign before she obliged him. "Well, Vance, what can I do for you?"

Vance swirled the bourbon without drinking. He sent her a cool, direct stare. "Leave Shane alone."

The change in her expression might have been comical under any other circumstances. She forgot herself long enough to gape at him. "What are you talking about?"

"Shane," he repeated. "Your daughter."

"I know who Shane is," Anne said sharply. "What has she to do with you?"

"I'm going to marry her."

Shock covered her face, then dissolved with her burst of laughter. "Little Shane? Oh, that's too funny. Don't tell me my cute little daughter caught herself a live one! I've underestimated her." Tossing her head, she sent Vance a shrewd glance. "Or I overestimated you."

Though his fingers tightened on the glass, he controlled

his temper. When he spoke, his voice was dangerously mild. "Be careful, Anne."

The look in his eye checked her laughter. "Well," she continued with an unconcerned shrug, "so you want to marry Shane. What's that to me?"

"Not a damn thing."

Masking both apprehension and irritation, Anne rose gracefully. "I suppose I should go congratulate my little girl on her luck."

Vance took her arm. Though he applied no pressure, the meaning was very clear. "You'll do nothing of the kind. What you're going to do is pack your bags and get out."

Enraged, Anne jerked away from him. "Who the hell do you think you are? You can't order me to leave."

"Advise," Vance corrected. "You'd be wise to take the suggestion."

"I don't like the tone of your suggestion," she retorted. "I intend to see my daughter—"

"Why?" Vance stopped her cold without raising his voice. "You won't get another dime, I promise you."

"I haven't any idea what you're talking about," Anne claimed with frigid dignity. "I don't know what nonsense Shane's been telling you, but—"

"You'd be wise to think carefully before you say any more," Vance warned quietly. "I saw Shane shortly after you left her last night. She had to tell me very little before I got the picture." He gave her a long, hard look. "I know you, Anne, every bit as well as you know yourself. There'll be no more money," he continued when Anne fell silent. "You'd be smarter to cut your losses and go back to California. It would be a simple matter to stop payment on the check she's already given you."

That annoyed her. Anne cursed herself for not getting up early and cashing the check before Shane thought better of it. "I have every intention of seeing my daughter." She gave him a glittering smile. "And when I do, I'll have a few words to say to her about her choice of lovers."

His eyes neither heated nor chilled, but became faintly bored. Nothing could have infuriated her more. "You won't see Shane again," he corrected.

Under the silk, her lovely bust heaved. "You can't keep me from seeing my own daughter."

"I can," Vance countered, "and I will. If you contact her, if you try to wheedle another dollar out of her or hurt her in any way, I'll deal with you myself."

Anne felt the first prickle of physical fear. Warily, she stepped back from him. "You wouldn't dare touch me."

Vance gave a mirthless laugh. "Don't be too sure. I don't think it'll come to that though." Casually, he set down the glass of liquor. "I have a number of contacts in the movie industry, Anne. Old friends, business associates, clients. A few words in the right ears, and what little career you have is out the window."

"How dare you threaten me," she began, both furious and afraid.

"Not a threat," he assured her. "A promise. Hurt Shane again and you'll pay for it. You're getting the best of the deal, Anne," he added. "She doesn't have anything you want."

Smoldering, she took a step toward him. "I have a right to my share. Whatever my grandmother had should be split fifty-fifty between Shane and me."

He lifted a brow in speculation. "Fifty-fifty," he said thoughtfully. "You must be desperate if you're willing to settle for that." Without pity, he shrugged off her problems. "I won't waste my time arguing legalities with you, much less morals or ethics. Just accept that what Shane gave you yesterday is all you'll ever get." With this he turned toward the door. In a last-ditch effort, Anne sank down on the bed and began to weep.

"Oh, Vance, you can't be so cruel." She lifted an already tear-drenched face to his. "You can't mean to keep me from seeing my own daughter, my only child."

He studied the beautiful tragic face, then gave a slight nod of approval. "Very good," he commented. "You're a better actress than they give you credit for." As he pulled the door to behind him, he heard the sound of smashing glass on the wood.

Springing up, Anne grabbed the second glass, then hurled it as well. No one, *no one,* she determined, was going to threaten her. Or mock her, she fumed, remembering the cool amusement in his eyes. She'd see he paid for it. Sitting back on the bed, she clenched her fists until she could bring her temper to order. She had to think. There had to be a way to get to Vance Banning. *Riverton Construction,* she reflected, closing her eyes as she concentrated. Had there been any scandal connected with the firm? Frustrated, she hurled her pillow across the room. She could think of nothing. What did she know about a stupid firm that built shopping centers and hospitals? It was all so boring, she thought furiously.

Grabbing the second pillow, she started to toss it as well when a sudden glimmer of memory arrested her. Scandal, she repeated. But not about the firm. There had been some-thing…something a few years back. Just a few whispers at a party or two. *Damn!* she swore silently when her recollection took her no further. Sheila Hourback, Anne thought, tightening her lips. Maybe the stuffy old bird could be useful. Scrambling over the unmade bed, Anne reached for the phone.

Shane was busy detailing a skirmish of the Battle of Antietam for three eager boys when Vance walked in. She smiled at him, and he heard enthusiasm in her voice as she spoke, but she was still pale. That alone brushed away any doubts that he had done the right thing. She'd bounce back, he told himself as he wandered into the antique shop, because it was her nature to do so. But even someone as intrinsically strong as Shane could take only so much. Spotting Pat dusting glassware, he went over to her.

"Hi, Vance." She sent him a quick, friendly grin. "How're you doing?"

"I'm fine." He cast a look over his shoulder to be certain Shane was still occupied. "Listen, Pat, I wanted to talk to you about that dining-room set."

"Oh yeah. There was some mix-up about that. I still haven't gotten it straight. Shane said—"

"I'm going to buy it."

"*You?*" Her initial surprise turned into embarrassment. Vance grinned at her, however, and her cheeks cooled.

"For Shane," he explained. "For Christmas."

"Oh, that's so sweet!" The romance of it appealed to her immediately. "It was her grandmother's, you know. She just loves it."

"I know, and she's determined to sell it." Idly, he picked up a china demitasse cup. "I'm just as determined to buy it for her. She won't let me." He gave Pat a conspirator's wink. "But she can hardly turn down a Christmas present, can she?"

"No." Appreciating his cleverness, Pat beamed at him. So the rumors were true, she thought, pleased and interested. There was something going on between them. "She sure couldn't. It'll mean so much to her, Vance. It just about kills her to have to sell some of these things, but that's the hardest. It's...ah, it's awfully expensive though."

"That's all right. I'm going to give you a check for it today." It occurred to him that it would soon be all over town that he had a great deal of money to spend. He would have to talk to Shane very soon. "Put a Sold sign on it." He glanced back again, seeing Shane's three visitors were preparing to leave. "Just don't say anything to her unless she asks."

"I won't," Pat promised, pleased to be in on the surprise. "And if she does, I'll just say the person who bought it wants it held until Christmas."

"Clever girl," he complimented. "Thanks."

"Vance." She lowered her voice to a whisper. "She looks kind of down today. Maybe you could take her out for a while and cheer her up. Oh, Shane," she continued quickly in a normal tone, "how did you manage to keep those little monsters quiet for twenty minutes? Those are Clint Drummond's boys," she explained to Vance with a shudder. "I nearly ran out the back door when they came in."

"They were thrilled that school was called off because of the snow." Instinctively, she reached for Vance's hand as she came in. "What they wanted was to work out the fine details of a few engagements so they could have their own Battle of Antietam with snowballs."

"Get your coat," Vance told her, planting a kiss on her brow.

"What?"

"And a hat. It's cold outside."

Laughing, Shane gave his hand a squeeze. "I know it's cold outside, fool. There's already six inches of snow."

"Then we'd better get started." He gave her a friendly swat on the seat. "You'll need boots too, I suppose. Just don't take all day."

"Vance, it's the middle of the day. I can't leave."

"It's business," he told her gravely. "You have to get your Christmas tree."

"Christmas tree?" With a chuckle, she picked up the duster Pat had set down. "It's too early in the season."

"Early?" Vance sent Pat a grin. "You've got just over two weeks until Christmas, and no tree. Most self-respecting stores are decked out by Thanksgiving."

"Well, I know, but—"

"But nothing," he interrupted, taking the duster from her and handing it back to Pat. "Where's your holiday spirit? Not to mention your sales strategy. According to the most recent poll, people spend an additional twelve and a half percent in a store decorated for the holidays."

Shane gave him a narrow glance. "What poll?"

"The Retail Sale and Seasonal Atmosphere Survey," he said glibly.

The first genuine laugh in nearly twenty-four hours burst from her. "That's a terrible lie."

"Certainly not," he disagreed. "It's a very good one. Now go get your coat."

"But, Vance—"

"Oh, don't be silly, Shane," Pat interrupted, giving her a push toward the stairs. "I can handle the shop. We're not likely to have customers pouring in with all this snow. Besides," she added, shrewd enough to know her employer, "I'd really love a tree. I'll make a place for it right in front of this window." Without waiting for a reply, Pat began to rearrange furniture.

"Gloves too," Vance added as Shane hesitated.

"All right," she said, surrendering. "I'll be back in a minute."

In little more than ten, she was sitting beside Vance in the cab of his small pickup. "Oh, it's beautiful out here!" she exclaimed, trying to look everywhere at once. "I love the first snow. Look, there're the Drummond boys."

Vance glanced in the direction she indicated and saw three boys pelting each other violently with snow.

"The battle's under way," he murmured.

"General Burnside's having his problems," Shane observed, then turned back to Vance. "By the way, what did you and Pat have your heads together about when I went upstairs to get my things?"

Vance lifted a brow. "Oh," he said complacently, "I was trying to make a date with her. She's cute."

"Really?" Shane drew out the word as she eyed him. "It would be a shame for her to be fired this close to Christmas."

"I was only trying to develop good employee relations," he explained, pulling up at a stop sign. Taking her by surprise, he pulled her into his arms and kissed her thoroughly. "I love that little choking sound you make when you try not to laugh. Do it again."

Breathless, she pulled away from him. "Firing a trusted employee is no laughing matter," she told him primly, and adjusted her ski hat. "Turn right here." Instead of obeying, he kissed her again. The rude blast of a horn had her struggling out of his arms a second time. "Now you've done it." She ruined the severity of the lecture with a smothered chuckle. "The sheriff's going to arrest you for obstructing traffic."

"One disgruntled man in a Buick isn't traffic," Vance disagreed as he made a right turn. "Do you know where you're going?"

"Certainly. There's a place a few miles down where you can dig your own tree."

"Dig?" Vance repeated, shooting her a look. Shane met it placidly.

"Dig," she repeated. "According to the latest conservation poll—"

"Dig," he agreed, cutting her off.

Laughing, Shane leaned over to kiss his shoulder. "I love you, Vance."

By the time they arrived at the tree farm, the snow had slowed to a gentle mist. Shane dragged him from tree to tree, examining each one minutely before rejecting it. Though he knew the color in her face was a result of the cold, the spark was back. Even if he sensed some of the energy was a product of nerves, he was satisfied that she was bouncing back. The simple pleasure of choosing a Christmas tree was enough to put the laughter back in her eyes.

"This one!" Shane exclaimed, stopping in front of a short-needle pine. "It's exactly right."

"It doesn't look much different from the other five hundred trees we've looked at," Vance grumbled, slicing the point of his shovel into the snow.

"That's because you don't have a connoisseur's eye," she said condescendingly. He scooped up a handful of snow and rubbed it into her face. "Be that as it may," Shane continued with remarkable aplomb, "this is the one. Dig," she instructed, and stepping back, folded her arms.

"Yes, ma'am," he said meekly, bending to the task. "You know," he said a few moments later, "it suddenly occurs to me that you're going to expect me to dig a hole to put this thing in after Chris tmas."

Shane sent him a guileless smile. "What a good idea. I know just the place too. You'll probably need a pick though. There are an awful lot of rocks." Ignoring Vance's rude rejoinder, she waved over an attendant. With the roots carefully wrapped in burlap and the tree itself paid for—by Shane over Vance's objection—they headed home.

"Damn it, Shane," he said in exasperation. "I wanted to buy the tree for you." The truck rumbled over the narrow wooden bridge.

"The tree's for the shop," she pointed out logically as they pulled in front of the house. "So the shop bought the tree. Just as it buys the stock and pays the electric bill." Noting that he was annoyed, Shane walked around the truck to kiss him. "You're sweet, Vance, and I do appreciate it. Buy me something else."

He gave her a long, considering look. "What?"

"Oh, I don't know. I've always had a fancy for something frivolous and extravagant...like chinchilla earmuffs."

With difficulty, he maintained his gravity. "It would serve you right if I did buy you some. Then you'd have to wear them."

She rose on her toes, inviting another kiss. As he bent down, Shane slipped the handful of snow she'd been holding down his back. When he swore pungently, she made a dash for safety. Shane fully expected the snowball that bashed into the back of her head, but she didn't expect to be agilely tackled so that she landed facedown in the snow.

"Oh! You really aren't a gentleman," she muttered, hampered by a mouthful of snow. Vance sat back, roaring with laughter while she struggled to sit up, wiping at her face.

"Snow looks even better on you than mud," he told her.

Shane lunged at him, catching him off balance so that he toppled onto his back. She landed with a soft thud on his chest. Before she could deposit the snow she held in his face, he rolled her over and pinned her. Resigned, she closed her eyes and waited. Instead of the cold shock of snow, she felt his lips crush down on hers. In immediate response, she pulled him closer, answering hungrily.

"Give?" he demanded.

"No," she said firmly, and dragged him back again.

The urgency of her response made him forget they were lying in the snow in the middle of the afternoon. He no longer felt the wet flakes that drifted down the back of his neck, though he could taste others on her skin. He fretted against the bulky clothes that kept the shape of her from him, against the gloves that prevented him from feeling the softness of her skin. But he could taste, and he did so greedily.

"God, I want you," he murmured, savaging her small, avid mouth again and again. "Right here, right now." Lifting his head, he looked down on her, but whatever he would have said was cut off by the sound of an approaching car. "If I'd had any sense I'd have taken you to my house," he mumbled, then helped her to her feet.

Hugging him, she whispered in his ear, "I close in two hours."

While Shane dealt with a straggle of customers who touched

everything and bought nothing, Vance made himself useful by setting up the tree. Pat's lighthearted chatter helped cool the blood Shane had so quickly heated. Following Shane's instructions, he found the boxes of ornaments in the dusty attic.

Dusk was falling before they were alone again. Because she was still looking pale, Vance bullied her into a quick meal before they began to sort through the ornaments. They made do with cold meat from the rib roast neither of them had touched the night before.

But as well as alleviating her hunger, the meal reminded her forcibly of her mother's visit. She struggled to push away the depression, or at least to conceal it. Her chatter was bright and mindless and entirely too strained.

Vance caught her hand, stopping her in midsentence. "Not with me, Shane," he said quietly.

Not bothering to pretend she didn't understand, Shane squeezed his hand. "I'm not dwelling on it, Vance. It just sneaks up on me sometimes."

"And when it does, I'm here. Lean on me, Shane, when you need to." He lifted her hand to his lips. "God knows, I'll lean on you."

"Now," she said shakily. "Just hold me a minute."

He drew her into his arms, pressing her head to his heart. "As long as you want."

She sighed, relaxing again. "I hate being a fool," she murmured. "I suppose I hate that worse than anything."

"You're not being a fool," he said, then drew her away as he came to a decision. "Shane, I went to see your mother this morning."

"What?" The word came out in a whisper.

"You can be angry if you like, but I won't stand by and

watch you be hurt again. I made it very clear that if she both-ered you again, she'd have me to deal with."

Shaken, she turned away from him. "You shouldn't—"

"Don't tell me what I shouldn't have done," he interrupted angrily. "I love you, damn it. You can't expect me to do nothing while she puts you through the wringer."

"I can deal with it, Vance."

"No." Taking her shoulders, he turned her around. "With an amazing number of things, yes, but not with this. She turns you inside out." His grip lightened to a caress. "Shane, if it had been me hurting, what would you have done?"

She opened her mouth to speak, but only released a pent-up breath. Taking his face in her hands, she pulled it down to hers. "I hope I'd have done the same thing. Thank you," she said, kissing him gently. "I don't want to know what was said," she added with more firmness. "No more problems tonight, Vance."

He shook his head, acknowledging another delay in mak-ing everything known to her. "All right, no more problems."

"We'll trim the tree," she stated decisively. "Then you're going to make love to me under it."

He grinned. "I suppose I could do that." He allowed her to pull him down the stairs. "What if I make love to you under it, then we trim it?"

"There's nothing festive in that," she said gravely as she began unpacking ornaments.

"Wanna bet?"

She laughed, but shook her head. "Absolutely not. There's an order to these things, you know. Lights first," she an-nounced, pulling out a neatly coiled string.

It took well over an hour as Shane shared her memories

about nearly every ornament she unpacked. As she took out a red felt star, she recalled the year she had made it for her grandmother. It brought both a sting and a warmth. She'd been dreading Christmas. It hadn't seemed possible to celebrate the holiday in that house without the woman who had always shared it with her. Gran would have reminded her that there was a cycle, but Shane knew she would have found a tree and tinsel unbearable had she been alone.

She watched Vance carefully arranging a garland. How Gran would have loved him, she thought with a smile. And he her. Somehow she found it didn't matter that the two people she loved most in the world had never met. She knew both of them, and the link was formed. Shane was ready to give herself to him completely.

If he doesn't ask me to marry him soon, she mused, I'll just have to ask him. When he glanced over, she sent him a saucy smile.

"What are you thinking?" he demanded.

"Oh, nothing," she said innocently, stepping back to view the results. "It's perfect, just as I knew it would be." She gave a satisfied nod before taking out the old silver star that would adorn the top.

Vance accepted it from her, then eyed the top branch. "I'm not going to be able to get this on there without knocking half of everything else off. We need a ladder."

"Oh no, that's okay. Let me up on your shoulders."

"There's a stepladder upstairs," he began.

"Oh, don't be so fussy." Shane jumped nimbly onto his back, hooking her legs around his waist for balance. "I'll be able to reach it without any trouble," she assured him, then began scooting up to his shoulders. Vance felt every line of her body as if he'd run his hands over it. "There," she said, settled. "Hand it to me and I'll stick it on."

He obliged, then gripped her knees as she leaned forward. "Damn it, Shane, not so far; you're going to fall into the tree."

"Don't be silly," she said lightly as she secured the star. "I have terrific balance. There!" Putting her hands on her hips, she surveyed the results. "Step back a bit so I can see the whole thing." When he had, Shane gave a long sigh, then kissed the top of his head. "It's beautiful, isn't it? Just smell the pine." Carelessly, she linked her ankles against his chest.

"It'll look better with the overhead lights off." Still carrying her, he moved to flick the wall switch. In the dark, the colored lights on the tree seemed to jump into life. They shimmered against garland and tinsel, glowed warmly against pine.

"Oh yes," Shane breathed. "Just perfect."

"Not quite yet," Vance disagreed.

With a deft move, he pulled her around into his arms as she slid down from his shoulders. "This," he told her as he laid her on the rug, "is perfect."

The lights danced on her face as she smiled up at him. "It certainly is."

His hands weren't patient tonight, but neither were hers. They undressed each other quickly, laughing and swearing a bit at buttons or snaps. But when they were naked, the urgency only intensified. Their hands sought to touch, their mouths hurried to taste—everywhere. She marveled again at his taut, corded muscles. He filled himself again on the flavor and fragrance of her skin. They paid no more notice to the warmth of the lights or the tang of pine than they had to the chill of the snow. They were alone. They were together.

Thirteen

It wasn't easy for Shane to keep her mind on her work the next day. Though she made several sales, among them the tilt-top table she had so painstakingly refinished, she was distracted throughout the morning. Distracted enough that she never noticed the discreet Sold sign Pat had attached to the Hepplewhite set in lieu of a price tag. She could think of little else but Vance. Once or twice during the morning, she caught herself glancing at the Christmas tree and remembering. In all of her dreams, in all of her wishes, she had never imagined it could be this way. Each time they made love it was different, a new adventure. Yet somehow it was as though they had been together for years.

Every time she touched him it was like making a fresh discovery, and still Shane felt she had known him for a lifetime rather than a matter of three short months. When he kissed her, it was just as thrilling and novel as the first time.

The recognition she had felt the instant she had seen him had deepened into something much more abiding. Faith.

Without doubt, she was certain that the excitement and the learning would go on time after time over the comfortable core of honest love. There was no need to romanticize what was real. She had only to look at him to know what they shared was special and enduring. With another glance at the tree, she realized she'd never been happier in her life.

"Miss!" The customer considering the newly caned ladder-back chair called impatiently for Shane's attention.

"Yes, ma'am, I'm sorry." If the smile Shane gave her was a bit dreamy, the woman didn't seem to notice. "It's a lovely piece, isn't it? The seat's just been redone." Calling herself to order, Shane turned the chair over to show off the workmanship.

"Yes, I'm interested." The woman poked at the caning a moment. "But the price…"

Recognizing the tone, Shane settled down to bargain.

It was just past noon when things began to quiet down. The morning's profits weren't extraordinary, but solid enough to help Shane stop worrying over the large chunk of her capital that she had given to her mother. The wolf wasn't at the door yet, she told herself optimistically. And with luck—and the Christmas rush—she could hold him off for quite some time. Two or three good sales would keep her books from dipping too deeply into the red. Professionally, she wanted little more at the moment than to calmly tread water. Personally, she knew precisely what she wanted, and she had every intention of seeing to it quickly.

She was going to marry Vance, and it was time she told him so. If he was too proud to ask her because he didn't yet have a steady job, she would simply have to persuade him to see things differently. Shane had made up her mind to take a firm stand that very day. There was an excitement bubbling inside her, a sense of purpose. Today, she thought, almost giddy from it, nothing could hurt her. She was going to propose to the man she loved. And she wasn't going to take no for an answer.

"Pat, can you handle things if I go out for an hour?"

"Sure, it's slow now anyway." Pat glanced up from the table she was polishing. "Are you going to another auction?"

"No," Shane told her blithely. "I'm going on a picnic."

Leaving Pat staring behind her, Shane raced upstairs.

It took her less than ten minutes to fill the wicker basket. There was a cold bottle of Chablis inside it, which she had splurged on madly. It might be a bit rich for the peanut butter sandwiches, but Shane's mind wasn't on proprieties. As she raced out the back door, she was already picturing spreading the checked tablecloth in front of Vance's living-room fire.

Wet, slushy snow sloshed over her boots as she stepped off the porch onto the lawn. The perfect day for a picnic, she decided, letting the hamper swing. The air was absolutely still. Melted snow dripped from the roof with a musical patter. The fast water in the creek broke through thin sheets of ice with an excited hissing and bubbling. Shane paused to listen a moment, enjoying the mixture of sounds. The feeling of euphoria built. She found it the most exquisite of days, with the sky coldly blue, the snow-laced mountains rising and the naked trees slick with wet.

Then the low purr of an engine intruded. She looked back, then stopped as she recognized Anne pulling up in the drive. All of her joy in the afternoon slipped quietly away.

She hardly noticed the fingers of tension that crept up to the base of her neck.

With her faultless grace, Anne picked her way over the melting snow in calfskin boots. She wore a trim fox-fur hat now to match her coat, and a small, smug smile. There were ruby studs, or clever imitations, glinting at her ears. Though her daughter stood rigid as a stone, she glided up to greet her with the customary brush of cheeks. Without speaking, Shane set the hamper down on the bottom step of the porch.

"Darling, I had to drop by before I left." Anne beamed at her with a cold gleam in her eye.

"Going back to California?" Shane asked flatly.

"Yes, of course, I have the most marvelous script. Of course, I'll probably be weeks on location, but…" She gave a gay shrug. "But that's not why I dropped by."

Shane studied her, marveling. It was as though the ugly scene between them had never taken place. She has no feelings, she realized abruptly. It meant less than nothing to her. "Why did you come by, Anne?"

"Why, to congratulate you, of course!"

"Congratulate me?" Shane lifted a brow. It was easier somehow knowing that the woman in front of her was simply a stranger. A few shared genes didn't make a bond. It was love that did that, or affection. Or at the very least, respect.

"I admit I didn't think you had it in you, Shane, but I'm pleasantly surprised."

Shane then surprised both of them by giving an impatient sigh. "Will you get to the point, Anne? I was on my way out."

"Oh, now, don't be cross," she said placatingly. "I'm really thrilled for you, catching yourself a man like that."

Shane's eyes chilled. "I beg your pardon?"

"Vance Banning, darling." She gave a slow, appreciative smile. "What a catch!"

"Strange, I never thought about it quite that way." Bending, Shane prepared to pick up the hamper again.

"The president of Riverton Construction isn't just a mild triumph, sweetheart, it's a downright *coup*."

Shane's fingers froze on the handle. Straightening, she looked Anne dead in the eye. "What are you talking about?"

"Only your fantastic luck, Shane. After all, the man's *rolling* in it. I imagine you'll be able to turn this little shop of yours into an antique palace if you want a hobby." She gave a quick, brittle laugh. "Leave it to cute little Shane to land herself a millionaire the first time around. If I had a bit more time, darling, I'd insist on hearing the details of how you managed it."

"I don't know what you're talking about." Cold panic was beginning to rush through her. She wanted to turn and run away, but her legs were stiff and unyielding.

"God knows why he decided to dump himself in this town," Anne went on mildly. "But it's your good fortune he did, and right next door too. I suppose he means to keep it for a little hideaway once the two of you move to D.C." *A fabulous house,* she thought on a flash of envy. *Servants, parties.* Carefully, she kept her tone gay. "I can't tell you how thrilled I was to learn you'd hooked up with the man who owns virtually the biggest construction firm in the country."

"Riverton," Shane repeated numbly.

"Very prestigious, darling Shane. It does give me cause to wonder how you'll fit in, but..." She shrugged this off and aimed her coup de grâce. "It's a shame about that nasty scandal though." Shane merely shook her head and stared at Anne blankly. "His first wife, you know. A terrible tangle."

"Wife?" Shane repeated faintly. She felt the nausea rising in her stomach. "Vance's wife?"

"Oh, Shane, don't tell me he didn't mention it!" It was exactly what she'd hoped for. Anne shook her head and sighed. "That's disgraceful of him, really. Isn't it just like a man to expect some wide-eyed girl to take everything on face value." She clucked her tongue in disapproval, thinking with inner appreciation that Vance Banning was going to take his knocks on this one. She didn't think of Shane at all.

"Well, the very least he might have done was tell you he was married before," she continued primly. "Even if he didn't go into the nasty business."

"I don't…" Shane managed to swallow the sickness and continue. "I don't understand."

"A spicy little scandal," Anne told her. "His wife was a raving beauty, you know. Perhaps too much so." Anne paused delicately. "One of her lovers put a bullet in her heart. At least that's what the Bannings would have everyone believe." The shock in Shane's eyes gave Anne another surge of gratification. Oh yes, she thought grimly, Vance Banning was going to get back some of his now. "Hushed it up rather quickly too," she added, then brushed the matter away with the back of an elegantly gloved hand. "An odd business. Well, I must run, don't want to miss my plane. *Ciao,* darling, and don't let that handsome gold mine slip away from you. There are plenty of women just dying to catch him." Pausing, she touched Shane's cap of curls with a finger. "For God's sake, Shane, find a decent hairdresser. I suppose he thinks you're… refreshing. Get the ring on your finger before he gets bored." She brushed Shane's cold cheek with hers, then dashed off, satisfied she'd paid Vance back for his threats.

Shane stood perfectly still, staring after her. But she didn't see her. She saw nothing. Trapped in the ice of shock, the pain was dormant. That would have surprised Anne had she given it any thought. As a woman who knew nothing of emotional pain, she would assume Shane would feel only fury. But the fury was surrounded by pain, and the pain lay waiting to spring out.

The sun bounced glaringly off the melting snow. A breeze, chill and sharp, whipped through her carelessly unbuttoned coat. In a flash of scarlet, a cardinal swooped over the ground to roost comfortably on a low branch. Shane stood absolutely still, noticing nothing. Sluggishly, her mind began to work.

It wasn't true, she told herself. Anne had made it up for some unexplainable purpose of her own. *President of Riverton?* No, he said he was a carpenter. He *was,* she thought desperately. She'd seen his work herself… He'd…he'd worked for her. Taken the job she had offered. Why would he—how could he—if he was everything Anne had said? *His first wife.*

Shane felt the first stab of pain. No, it couldn't be, he would have told her. Vance loved her. He wouldn't lie or pretend. He wouldn't make a fool of her by letting her think he was out of work when he was the head of one of the biggest construction firms in the country. He wouldn't have said he loved her without telling her who he really was. *His first wife.* Shane heard a soft, despairing moan without realizing it was hers.

When she saw him coming down the path, she stared blankly. As she watched him, her whirling thoughts came to a sudden halt. She knew then she'd been a fool.

Spotting her, Vance smiled in greeting and increased his pace. He was still several yards away when he recognized the expression on her face. It was the same stricken look he'd seen in the moonlight only a few nights before.

"Shane?" He came to her quickly, reaching for her. Shane stepped back.

"Liar," she said in a broken whisper. "All lies." Her eyes both accused and pleaded. "Everything you said."

"Shane—"

"No, don't!" The panic in her voice was enough to halt the hand he held out to her. He knew that somehow she had learned everything before he could tell her himself.

"Shane, let me explain."

"Explain?" She dragged shaking fingers through her hair. "Explain? How? How can you explain why you let me think you were something you're not? How can you explain why you didn't bother to tell me you were president of Riverton, that you—that you'd been married before? I *trusted* you," she whispered. "God, how could I have been such a fool!"

Anger he could have met and handled. Vance faced despair without any notion of how to cope with it. Impotently he thrust his hands into his pockets to keep from touching her. "I would have told you, Shane. I intended—"

"Would have?" She gave a quick, shaky laugh. "When? After you'd gotten bored with the joke?"

"There was never any joke," he said furiously, then clamped down on his panic. "I wanted to tell you, but every time—"

"No joke?" Her eyes glittered now with the beginnings of anger, the beginnings of tears. "You let me give you a job. You let me pay you six dollars an hour, and you don't think that's funny?"

"I didn't want your money, Shane. I tried to tell you. You wouldn't listen." Frustrated, he turned away until he had himself under control. "I banked the checks in an account under your name."

"How dare you!" Wild with pain, she shouted at him, blind and deaf to everything but the sense of betrayal. "How dare you play games with me! *I believed you.* I believed everything. I thought—I thought I was helping you, and all the time you were laughing at me."

"Damn it, Shane, I never laughed at you." Pushed beyond endurance, he grabbed her shoulders. "You know I never laughed at you."

"I wonder how you managed not to laugh in my face. God, you're clever, Vance." She choked on a sob, then swallowed it.

"Shane, if you'd try to understand why I came, why I didn't want to be connected with the company for a little while…" None of the words he needed would come to him. "It had nothing to do with you," he told her fiercely. "I didn't expect to get involved."

"Did it keep you from being bored?" she demanded, struggling against his hold. "Amusing yourself with a stupid little country girl who was so gullible she'd believe anything you said? You could play the poor working man and be entertained."

"It was never like that." Enraged by the words, he shook her. "You don't really believe that."

The tears gushed out passionately, strangling her voice. "And I was so willing to fall into bed with you. You knew it!" She sobbed, pushing desperately at him. "Right from the first I had no secrets from you."

"I had them," he admitted in a tight voice. "I had reasons for them."

"You knew how much I loved you, how much I wanted

you. You *used* me!" On a moan, she covered her face with her hands. "Oh God, I left myself wide open."

She wept with the same honest abandon he'd seen when she laughed. Unable to do otherwise, he crushed her against him. He thought if he could only calm her down, he could make her understand. "Shane, please, you have to listen to me."

"No, no, I don't." She pulled in breath after jerky breath as she struggled for release. "I'll never forgive you. I'll never believe anything you say again. Damn you, let me go."

"Not until you stop this and hear what I have to say."

"No! I won't listen to any more lies. I won't let you make a fool of me again. All this time, all this time when I was giving you everything, you were lying and laughing at me. I was just something to keep the nights from being dull while you were on vacation."

He jerked her back, his face rigid with fury. "Damn it, Shane, you know better than that."

Her struggles ceased abruptly. As he watched, the tears seemed to turn to ice. Without expression, she stared up at him. Nothing she had said so far had struck him to the core like that one cool look.

"I don't know you," she said quietly.

"Shane—"

"Take your hands off me." The command was devoid of passion. Vance felt his stiff fingers loosen. Freed, Shane stepped back until they were no longer touching. "I want you to go away and leave me alone. Stay away from me," she added flatly, still looking directly into his eyes. "I don't want to see you again."

Turning, she walked up the steps and to the door. After its final click came absolute silence.

★ ★ ★

Far beneath the window, the streets were packed with traffic. The steady fall of snow increased the confusion. Beneath the overhang of the department store across the street, a red-cheeked Santa rang his bell, ho-hoing when someone dropped a coin into his bucket. The scene below was played in pantomime. The thick glass of the window and well-constructed walls allowed no street sounds to intrude. Vance kept his back to his plush, spacious office and continued to watch.

He'd made his obligatory appearance at the company Christmas party. It was still going on, with enthusiasm, in a large conference room on the third floor. When it broke up, everyone would go home to spend Christmas Eve with their families or friends. He'd refused more than a dozen invitations for the evening since his return to Washington. It was one thing to do his duty as the head of the company, and another to put himself through hours of small talk and celebrating. *She wouldn't be there,* he thought, staring down at the snowy sidewalk.

Two weeks. In two weeks, Vance had managed to straighten out a few annoying contractual tangles, plot out a bid for a new wing to a hospital in Virginia and head a heated board meeting. He'd dealt with paperwork, and some minor corporate intrigue he might have found amusing if he'd been sleeping properly. But he wasn't sleeping properly any more than he was forgetting. Work wasn't an elixir this time. As she had from the very first moment, Shane haunted him.

Turning from the window, Vance took his place behind the massive oak desk. It was clear of papers. In a fury of frustrated energy, he'd taken care of every letter, memo and contract, putting his secretary and assistants through an orgy of work over the last two weeks. Now, he had nothing but an empty desk and a clear calendar. He considered the possibility of flying to Des Moines to supervise the progress of a condominium development. That would throw the Iowa branch into a panic, he thought with a quick laugh. Hardly fair to upset their applecart because he was restless. He brooded at the far wall, wondering what Shane was doing.

He hadn't left in anger. It would have been easier for Vance if that had been the case. He had left because Shane had wanted it. He didn't blame her, and that too made it impossibly frustrating. Why should she listen to him, or understand? There had been enough truth in what she had flung at him to make the rest difficult to overturn. He had lied, or at the very least, he hadn't been honest. To Shane, one was the same as the other.

He'd hurt her. He had put that look of helpless despair on her face. That was unforgivable. Vance pushed away from the desk to pace over the thick stone-colored carpet. But damn it, if she'd just listened to him! If she'd only given him a moment. Going to the window again, he scowled out. Laughed at her? Made fun of her? No, he thought with the first true fury he'd felt in two weeks. No, by God, he'd be damned if he'd stand quietly aside while she turned the most important thing in his life into a joke.

She'd had her say, Vance told himself as he headed for the door. Now he was going to have his.

"Shane, don't be stubborn." Donna followed her through the doorway from the museum into the shop.

"I'm not being stubborn, Donna, I really have a lot to do." To prove her point, Shane leafed through a catalog to price and date her latest stock. "With the Christmas rush, I've really fallen behind on the paperwork. I've got invoices to file, and if I don't get the books caught up before the quarter, I'm going to be in a jam."

"Baloney," Donna said precisely, flipping the catalog closed.

"Donna, please."

"No, I don't please." She stuck her hands on her hips. "And it's two against one," she added, indicating Pat with a jerk of her head. "We're not having you spend Christmas Eve alone in this house, and that's all there is to it."

"Come on, Shane." Pat joined ranks with her sister-in-law. "You should see Donna and Dave chase after Benji when he heads for the tree. And as Donna's putting on a little weight," she added, grinning at the expectant mother, "she isn't as fast as she used to be."

Shane laughed, but shook her head. "I promise I'll come by tomorrow. I've got a very noisy present for Benji. You'll probably never speak to me again."

"Shane." Firmly, Donna took her by the shoulders. "Pat's told me how you've been moping around. And," she continued, ignoring the annoyed glance Shane shot over her shoulder at the informant, "anyone can take one look at you and see you're worn-out and miserable."

"I'm not worn-out," Shane corrected.

"Just miserable?"

"I didn't say—"

Donna gave her a quick affectionate shake. "Look, I don't know what happened between you and Vance—"

"Donna…"

"And I'm not asking," she added. "But you can't expect

me to stand by while my best friend is unhappy. How much fun can I have, thinking about you here all alone?"

"Donna." Shane gave her a fierce hug then drew away. "I appreciate it, really I do, but I'm lousy company now."

"I know," Donna agreed mercilessly.

That made Shane laugh and hug her again. "Please, take Pat and go back to your family."

"So speaks the martyr."

"I'm not—" Shane began furiously, then broke off, seeing the gleam in Donna's eyes. "That won't work," she told her. "If you think you can make me mad so I'll come just to prove you wrong—"

"All right." Donna settled herself in a rocker. "Then I'll just sit here. Of course, poor Dave will spend Christmas Eve without me, and my little boy won't understand where his mother could be, but..." She sighed and folded her hands.

"Oh, Donna, really." Shane dragged her hand through her hair, caught between laughter and tears. "Talk about martyrs."

"I'm not complaining for myself," she said in a long-suffering tone. "Pat, run along and tell Dave I won't be home. Dry little Benji's tears for me."

Pat gave a snort of laughter, but Shane rolled her eyes. "I'll be sick in a minute," she promised. "Donna, go home!" she insisted. "I'm closing the shop."

"Good, go get your coat. I'll drive."

"Donna, I'm not..." She trailed off as the shop door opened. Seeing her friend pale, Donna turned her head to watch Vance walk in.

"Well, we have to run," she stated, springing quickly to her feet. "Come on, Pat, Dave's probably at his wit's end keeping Benji from pulling over the tree. Merry Christmas, Shane." She gave Shane a quick kiss before grabbing her coat.

"Donna, wait…"

"No, we just can't stay," she claimed, making the reversal without blinking an eye. "I've got a million things to do. Hi, Vance, nice to see you. Let's go, Pat." They were out the door before Shane could fit in another word.

Vance lifted a brow at the hasty exit but made no comment. Instead, he studied Shane as the silence grew long and thick. The anger that had driven him there melted. "Shane," he murmured.

"I—I'm closing."

"Fine." Vance turned and flicked the lock on the door. "Then we won't be disturbed."

"I'm busy, Vance. I have…" She searched desperately for something important. "Things to do," she finished lamely. When he neither spoke nor moved, she sent him a look of entreaty. "Please go away."

Vance shook his head. "I tried that, Shane. I can't." He slipped off his coat and dropped it on the chair Donna had vacated. Shane stared at him, thrown off balance by his appearance in a trimly tailored suit and silk tie. It brought it home to her again that she didn't know him. And, God help her, she loved him anyway. Turning, she began to fiddle with an arrangement of cut glass.

"I'm sorry, Vance, but I have a few things to finish up here before I leave. I'm supposed to go to Donna's tonight."

"She didn't seem to expect you," he commented as he walked to her. Gently, he laid his hands on her shoulders. "Shane—"

She stiffened immediately. "Don't!"

Very slowly, he took his hands from her, then dropped

them to his sides. "All right, damn it, I won't touch you." The words came out savagely as he whirled away.

"Vance, I told you I'm busy."

"You said that you loved me."

Shane spun around, white with anger. "How can you throw that in my face?"

"Was it a lie?" he demanded.

She opened her mouth, but closed it again before any impetuous words could be spoken. Lifting her chin, she looked at him steadily. "I loved the man you pretended to be."

He winced, but he didn't back away. "Direct hit, Shane," he said quietly. "You surprise me."

"Why, because I'm not as stupid as you thought I was?"

Anger flashed into his eyes, then dulled. "Don't."

Shaken by the pain in the single word, she turned away. "I'm sorry, Vance. I don't want to say spiteful things. It would be better for both of us if you just went away."

"The hell it would, if you've been half as miserable as I've been. Have you been able to sleep, Shane? I haven't."

"Please," she whispered.

He took a deep breath as his hands clenched into fists. He'd come prepared to fight with her, to bully her, to plead with her. Now, it seemed he could do nothing but try to fumble through an explanation. "All right, I'll go, but only if you listen to me first."

"Vance," she said wearily, "what difference will it make?"

The finality of her tone had fear twisting in his stomach. With a strong effort, he kept his voice calm. "If that's true, it won't hurt you to listen."

"All right." Shane turned back to face him. "All right, I'll listen."

He was quiet for a moment, then began to pace as though whatever ran through him wouldn't allow him to keep still. "I came here because I had to get away, maybe even hide. I'm not sure anymore. I was still very young when I took over the company. It wasn't what I wanted." He stopped for a moment to send her a direct look. "I'm a carpenter, Shane, that was the truth. I'm president of Riverton because I have to be. *Why* doesn't really matter at this point, but a title, a position, doesn't change who I am." When she said nothing, he began to pace again.

"I was married to a woman you'd recognize very quickly. She was beautiful, charming and pure plastic. She was totally self-consumed, emotionless, even vicious." Shane's brows drew together as she thought of Anne. "Unfortunately, I didn't recognize the last of those qualities until it was too late." He stopped because the next words were difficult. "I married the woman she pretended to be." Because his back was to her, Vance didn't see the sudden change in Shane's expression. Pain rushed into her eyes, but it wasn't for herself. It was all for him.

"For all intents and purposes, the marriage was over very soon after it had begun. I couldn't make a legal break at first because too many things were involved. So, we lived together in mutual distaste for several years. I involved myself in the company to the point of obsession, while she began to take lovers. I wanted her out of my life more than I wanted anything. Then, when she was dead, I had to live with the knowledge that I'd wished her dead countless times."

"Oh, Vance," Shane murmured.

"That was over two years ago," he continued. "I buried myself in work…and bitterness. I'd come to a point where I didn't even recognize myself anymore. That's why I bought the house and took a leave of absence. I needed to separate myself from what I'd become, try to find out if that was all there was to me." He dragged an agitated hand through his hair. "I brought the bitterness with me, so that when you popped up and started haunting my mind, I wanted nothing more than to be rid of you. I looked… I searched," he corrected, turning to her again, "for flaws in you. I was afraid to believe you could really be so…generous. The truth was, I didn't want you to be because I'd never be able to resist the woman you are." His eyes were suddenly very dark, and very direct on hers. "I didn't want you, Shane, and I wanted you so badly I ached. I loved you, I think, from the very first minute."

On a long breath, he moved away again to stare at the flickering lights of the tree. "I could have told you—should have—but at first I had a need for you to love me without knowing. Unforgivably selfish."

She remembered the secrets she had seen in his eyes. Remembered too, telling herself they were his until he shared them with her. Still, she felt the hurt of not being trusted. "Did you really think any of it would have mattered to me?"

Vance shook his head. "No."

"Then why did you hide it all from me?" Confused, she lifted her hands palms up.

"I never intended to. Circumstances—" He broke off, no longer sure he could make her understand. "The first night we were together, I was going to tell you, but I didn't want any past that night. I told myself it wasn't too much to ask, and that I'd explain things to you the next day. God, Shane, I swear to you I would have." He took a step toward her, then stopped himself. "You were so lost, so vulnerable after

Anne had left, I couldn't. How could I have dumped all this on you when you already had that to deal with?"

She remained silent, but he knew she listened very carefully. He didn't know she was remembering very clearly the things he had said to her their first night together, the tension in him, the hints of things yet to be told. And she remembered too his compassion the next evening.

"You needed my support that night, not my problems," Vance went on. "From the very first, you gave everything to me. You brought me back, Shane, and I knew that I took much more than I gave. Until that night, you'd never asked me for anything."

She gave him a puzzled look. "I never gave you anything."

"Nothing?" he countered with a baffled shake of his head. "Trust, understanding. You made me laugh at myself again. Maybe you don't see just how important that is because you've never lost it. If I could give you nothing else, I thought that for a few days I could give you some peace of mind. I tried to tell you again when we argued about that damned dining-room set." Pausing, he sent her a narrowed look. "I bought it anyway."

"You—"

"There's not a thing you can do about it," he stated, cutting off her astonished exclamation. "It's done."

She met the angry challenge in his eyes. "I see."

"Do you?" He let out a quick, rough laugh. "Do you really? The only thing you see when you lift your chin up like that is your own pride." He watched her mouth open, then close again. "It's just as well," he murmured. "It would be difficult if you were perfect." He moved to her then but was careful not to touch her. "I never set out to deceive you, but I deceived you nonetheless. And now I have to ask you to forgive me, even if you can't accept who and what I am."

Shane lowered her eyes to her hands a moment. "It's not accepting so much as understanding," she said quietly. "I don't know anything about the president of Riverton. I knew the man who bought the old Farley place, you see." She lifted her eyes again. "He was rude, and nasty, with a streak of kindness he did his best to overcome. I loved him."

"God knows why," Vance replied, thinking over her description. "If that's who you want, I can promise I'm still rude and nasty."

With a small laugh, she turned away. "Vance, it's all hit me, you see. Maybe if I had time to get used to it, to think it through... I don't know. When I thought you were just..." She made an uncharacteristically helpless gesture with her hands. "It all seemed so easy."

"Did you only love me because you thought I was out of work?"

"No!" Frustrated, she tried to explain herself. "I haven't changed though," she added thoughtfully. "I'm still exactly what I seem. What would the president of Riverton do with me? I can't even drink martinis."

"Don't be absurd."

"It's not absurd," she corrected. "Be honest. I don't fit in. I'd never be elegant if I had years to practice."

"What the hell's wrong with you?" Suddenly angry, he spun her around. "*Elegant!* In the name of God, Shane, what kind of nonsense is that? I had my share of elegance the way you mean. I'll be damned if you're going to put me off because you've got some twisted view of the life I lead. If you can't accept it, fine. I'll resign."

"W-what?"

"I said I'll resign."

She studied him with wide, astonished eyes. "You mean it," she said wonderingly. "You really do."

He gave her an impatient shake. "Yes, I mean it. Can you really believe the company means more to me than you do? God, you're an idiot!" Furious, he gave her an unloverlike shove and strode away. "You don't yell at me for anything I've done. You don't demand to hear all the filthy details of my first marriage. You don't make me crawl as I was damn well ready to do. You start spouting nonsense about martinis and elegance." After swearing rudely, he stared out the window.

Shane swallowed a sudden urge to laugh. "Vance, I—"

"Shut up," he ordered. "You drive me crazy." With a quick jerk, he pulled his coat from the chair. Shane opened her mouth, afraid he was about to storm out, but he only pulled an envelope out of the pocket before he flung the coat down again. "Here." He stuck it out to her.

"Vance," she tried again, but he took her hand and slapped the envelope into her palm.

"Open it."

Deciding a temporary retreat was advisable, Shane obeyed. She stared in silent astonishment at two round-trip tickets to Fiji.

"Someone told me it was a good place for a honeymoon," Vance stated with a bit more control. "I thought she might still think so."

Shane looked up at him with her heart in her eyes. Vance needed nothing more to pull her into his arms, crushing the envelope and its contents between them as he found her mouth.

Shane's answer was wild and unrestricted. She clung to him even as she demanded, yielded even as she aroused. She couldn't get enough of him, so that the desperate kisses incited only more urgent needs. "Oh, I've missed you," she murmured. "Make love to me, Vance. Come upstairs and make love to me."

He buried his face against her neck. "Uh-uh. You haven't said you're taking me to Fiji yet." But his hands were already searching under her sweater. As his fingers skimmed over her warm, soft skin, he groaned, pulling her to the floor.

"Oh, Vance, your suit!" Laughing breathlessly, Shane struggled against him. "Wait until we go upstairs."

"Shut up," he suggested, then assured himself of her obedience by crushing his mouth on hers. It only took a moment to realize her trembling came from laughter, not from passion. Lifting his head, Vance studied her amused eyes. "Damn you, Shane," he said in exasperation. "I'm trying to make love to you."

"Well, then at least take off that tie," she suggested, then buried her face against his shoulder and laughed helplessly. "I'm sorry, Vance, but it just seems so funny. I mean, there you are asking if I'll take you to Fiji before I've even gotten around to asking you to marry me, and—"

"*You* asking *me?*" he demanded, eyeing her closely.

"Yes," she continued blithely. "I've been meaning to, though I thought I'd have to overcome some silly ego thing. You know, I thought you were out of work."

"Ego thing," he repeated.

"Yes, and of course, now that I know you're such an important person... Oh, this tie is *silk!*" she exclaimed after she had begun to struggle with the knot.

"Yes." He allowed her to finger it curiously. "And now that you know I'm such an important person?" he prompted.

"I'd better snap you up quick."

"Snap me up?" He bit her ear painfully.

Shane only giggled and linked her arms around his neck. "And even if I refuse to drink martinis or be elegant, I'll make an extremely good wife for a…" She paused a moment, lifting a brow. "What are you?"

"Insane."

"A corporate president," Shane decided with a nod. "No, I don't suppose you could do any better. You're making a pretty good deal now that I think about it." She gave him a noisy kiss. "When do we leave for Fiji?"

"Day after tomorrow," he informed her before he rose and dumped her over his shoulder.

"Vance, what are you doing?"

"I'm taking you upstairs to make love with you."

"Vance," she began with a half laugh. "I told you before I won't be carted around this way. This is no way for the fiancée of the president of Riverton to be treated."

"You haven't seen anything yet," he promised her.

Exasperated, Shane gave him a hearty thump on the back. "Vance, I mean it, put me down!"

"Am I fired?"

He heard the telltale choke of laughter. "Yes!"

"Good." He tucked his arm firmly around her knees and carried her up the stairs.

★ ★ ★ ★ ★